The Good One

Kathryn Merrifield

Happy Birthday,
Melissa! ☺
Love, Kathryn

DEDICATION

To my grandmothers, Nanette and Jean.

CONTENTS

The Good One

ACKNOWLEDGMENTS

It takes a village to make a book.
Thank you to everyone who helped me:
Dina Miliken for the copyedit, Jeremy D'Arcy for the
cover design, Christine Del Negro for the editorial help,
Michael Goldstein for the corrections, Ian Kaiser for the
encouragement, Jennifer Osborne-Prescott for the
publishing help, and mostly, Luke Venna Rose, and Leo
for helping me understand my heart a bit better so I can be
a better me and a better mother to you. Thank you to
everyone in my village who helps me take care of them,
especially their dad.

ONE | Equipment - *June 1987*

Neil Berry stood on the uneven shingles atop the slanted roof, hesitant only because he was drunk. He'd been to the Stone's house countless times before, climbed up there to drink beers with Jeff while his mom worked the night shift at the hospital. They lived in a little ranch style house on Blossom Street in Alpharetta, Georgia. It was the summer of nineteen eighty-seven. The house was full with mostly uninvited high school juniors and seniors who had nothing else to do that night but crash Jeff's eighteenth birthday party. Friends invited friends and friends of friends. Beer cushioned the voices below him; laughter, hoots and hollers integrated into one pulsating din within music. It blared from inside, muffled so it was reduced to heavy bass that vibrated through the walls and roof.

Peter Gabriel's song, "Shock the Monkey," played loud and distorted from inside where he knew the drunk girls danced, arms around each other which neither held them up or pushed them down. Two had cried through a private made public drama and hair stuck to their faces where the snot and drool had dried. The boys ribbed and hassled each other, told old stories and pretended not to watch those girls though they did watch them. There were movie lines reenacted and repeated. There was laughter.

One girl had already left to vomit and returned to pass out on the sofa. Neil saw puke stuck in her hair as he walked past her through the living room where she lay on the sofa, her skirt hiked up so anyone could see more than they were supposed to see. He made his way toward the stairs just next to the occupied bathroom. A couple of girls waited there too. They leaned on the wall to keep themselves standing. No one talked in the line to the bathroom and no one seemed to notice his ascent upstairs. He was invisible.

He stayed up on that roof for a long time listening and drinking from one of the Budweiser cans stuffed into the pockets of a black hoodie he used for storage not warmth. His own body heat hung around him like a vice and perspiration only gently calmed its hold on him. The overflow from the septic tank reeked but it was familiar and did not make him queasy.

No one had gone to look for him. Drunk kids lost track of each other in the swirl of their own spinning minds. The roof overhang was enough to conceal him and allow for an aerial view of deviance. He normally would have thought nothing of it. It was a good party, a good time. Everything had changed and became twisted within him. Inside, stupid girls prepared for a morning walk of shame and boys got more stupid and drunk to talk about whatever meaningless bullshit struck them. Girls called each other radical and awesome. Boys were gnarly and ugly girls, "beat." Interior lights gave off a soft glow through the sliding glass door and windows like a halo to the periphery of the house. Someone had the brilliant idea to cloak the party in darkness so none of the outdoor lights were turned on.

A camera flash revealed the backyard. Neil leaned back, hidden from the revelation and those voices. Some girl snapped a shot of Neil's football friends with a couple of cheerleaders that hung all over them and also howled and laughed. He felt apathy and was glad the beer distanced him from the truth; made him numb.

He had to get out of that house, out of the center of things. They milled around the keg. Drank. Hugged some more. Some did beer bongs and took bong hits and others smoked joints outside. Glass Bartles and James wine cooler bottles caught what light there was as girls with high teased hair tilted them back to empty. Those were the girls who had followed their friends outside to chatter where there was quiet enough to do so. They talked about the girl on the sofa but the boys were already looking at her for the hiked skirt and the possibility of that.

Two girls huddled together as they sat on the low wall. One girl held her hair back as the other puked into the rose bushes then cried as the girl helping returned to the house to fetch a towel. She left the puking girl to struggle against the gravity of alcohol poisoning as she walked through thorns and didn't know it until those little pricks to the skin registered, piercing through the armor of drunk anesthesia. She sat back down on the wall, and Neil felt a little sad for the girl because she had never been someone. Anyone.

He got distinct views from the invincible distance of the roof and liked it. It was a temporary freedom from the straight jacket of not telling, not coming clean with the truth. There was power in that distance that allowed the perspective to look in from the outside. Neil was an insider, a player not a spectator. He was always in on the joke. Always in until it all came down. It all changed. It was not the first time he'd been up there but the first time he had seen all of the bullshit of his posturing adolescence for what it was. The bullshit of people for what they were.

Jeff was genuine and probably the only one who would discover him missing. He wondered when Jeff would come looking for him and find him because he was the only other one who knew of the lookout. Jeff had his hands full as he kept tabs on the house. Responsible as he tended to be, the party was out of hand, but even Jeff was a bit too drunk to reason that one out. If there was anyone reasonable it was him.

Neil started to charge admission once the first keg ran low and the uninvited started to show up. It was Neil's idea and Jeff was too busy to stop him and a party that had suddenly gotten out of control.

Above the roofline, Neil identified his friends by their flipped up collars, feathered hair, wide brim trucker hats, Led Zeppelin, Iron Maiden and Ozzy Osborne baseball shirts with the white front and back with black sleeves hemmed at their skinny forearms. By their muscle t-shirts and black parachute pants. Friends seemed lesser friends with something to hide. He was hidden.

Neil watched and drank for a long time or what seemed long to him before Annene's black head appeared out from under the edge of the roof. Little Claire with her dirty blond head of hair and skinny shoulders followed. They sat on the low brick wall for a few minutes and he watched as they quietly talked. Neil wondered if they would see him but realized that no one thought to look up.

Jeff's parents were out of town and the kids partied with impunity. Rich kids without consequences. No rules to the senior lounge. Neil felt like an old man as he reflected amid the pit of drunk internal silence and surrounding muffled noise. The sky was clear every day so there was nothing to notice except the reliable heat and a crescent moon that kept the sky mostly dark above the dim light below him and street lights in view beyond the surrounding homes.

The moon wavered and wandered as his head spun more. He drank from another of the beer cans stuffed inside the hoodie pockets. He finished the can and set it down carefully at his back. He waited to make sure it remained there, afraid it would fall to the ground and reveal his secret.

Then he couldn't remember why they were all there. It was a party, obviously, but the reason was absent and he tried to make his way back to the path of facts, dark as the night that surrounded him. It was Jeff's birthday and now everyone from their little high school was there, all so painfully loud, drunk and stoned into joy.

"Red Rain" played from inside and Neil wept, helpless to a future that was blocked by the consequences of his past. It was a cliché, and he was a kid everyone pretended to know.

She was the only one who knew him. She told him this and he believed it. Neil repeated it to himself though it made him slip into morbid despair.

His friends joked through the night as they tried to get a rise out of him. He responded with quiet apathy. Not the usual Neil who was up for the usual alpha male banter. A popular kid. A leader who trusted himself. He was vain like most boys his age. It was all about the hair and football and all of the genetic attractions to get a girl.

Or, in Neil's case, a woman.

Jeff claimed that we were all puppets to our DNA's need to procreate. He was right. And wrong.

Neil pushed up his sleeves and took the last beer from his pocket. He was wasted now but didn't care. Gently, he pulled open the tab to the can and drank then spit as a painful wail rose inside him pushing snot out his nose, and he cried and held up his head and the can with bent knees pulled into his chest. He wiped his nose on the sweatshirt sleeve bunched over his bicep and cried more and took in more of the beer and the loud silent pain when the can slipped from his damp hands.

He reached for it and stumbled and slid across those roof shingles and off that roof.

Within that dimmed halo of light to the side of the house he lay on the concrete ground as the voices moved further away and his heart slowed and stopped.

It was not so far up. Only two stories.

But the noise faded completely and there he was finally alone but closer to something. Closer than he had ever been.

TWO | Fragrance – *December 1986*

Claire stood in front of the white wicker vanity in her
bedroom as she looked into the round mirror. She wore
an oversized navy blue sweatshirt with a wide collar that
exposed one bony shoulder and left the other concealed
but still sharp as it poked through the fabric. White cotton
underwear with a blue paisley print peeked below the loose
elastic waistline of the shirt. She tilted her head down to
look at her legs and placed her feet together, side by side
checking to make sure the fleshy part of her upper thighs
did not touch. She was eating again but would not let her
legs rub against each other to create a friction not unlike
sandpaper rubbing together when she walked or stood just
like she stood in front of that mirror unmoving. The
thought gave her chills, made her skin pucker and brought
forth a surge of self hate. There were some rules she
needed to keep as part of the prohibitive structure to
Claire's powerful existence. Part of the standards she
needed to survive, keep in control and intact. She was not
satisfied and made a commitment to herself to ward off
temptation for that day. She sipped a Diet Coke from the
vanity. Breakfast.

Brushing her yellow-brown hair that fell to the middle

of her back, she held handfuls of it at mid-point of its length then combed out the tangled ends. She repeated this process several times until the brush was easily pulled through. It was thick yet healthy enough to warrant compliments that never registered. She never felt it. There was always room to be better and none of it was good. She was not. How could she be?

She put the brush down on the bureau, cluttered with lipsticks, bottles of Sea Breeze, Jean Nate body splash with the black ball cap and Love's Baby Soft perfume, a curling iron, hair dryer, two combs, and a round brush. Stray hairs the color of straw were left on the brush and the sleeve. Claire pulled a fist full of hair out of the brush bristles and pinched them off the sweatshirt, denying the connection of hair loss to what the professionals told her happened as a result of malnutrition. She was fine. She knew their comments were true but would not let it inside.

Her nose almost touching the mirror, eyes narrowed to focus, she felt the surface of a raised red splotch on her chin, a pimple, with her index finger.

She rolled her eyes and mumbled, "Why do I always get these stupid things? My face looks like chicken skin." It was the only one and her round smooth face was still tinted from the summer sun already gone. It never really disappeared in Georgia, just faded with the seasons.

She reached into the right hand drawer of the bureau and pulled out a white tube, unscrewed the top and squeezed a dab of the contents onto her finger. She rubbed the clear gel on the pimple, screwed the cap back on and tossed the tube back into the drawer with the makeup brushes, compacts of blush and powder and sticks of eyeliner in shades from blue to black.

She stared into the mirror, pulled up the sweatshirt and turned to the side where she rubbed her hand from the lowest rib of her waist to her hip. Between her index finger and thumb she pinched her side where she gathered a small amount of flesh between her fingers. She gave a disgusted look into the mirror then pinched again. This time she held onto her stomach and then her inner thighs that barely touched each other except for the topmost flesh of her legs. Fixated on the mirror she stood pinching her skin over and over again, her eyebrows arched toward more concern and verging anger.

The hatred was immense and progressed suddenly from the disgust of her body, the way she felt when her legs brushed together, the small protrusion of her empty belly and the soft curves that were forming at the sides of those vertical lines of narrow hips. She had no waist. Maggie had always called her a tomboy. Maggie Hinkley, curvy with brightly blond, though dyed, hair was always beautiful and comfortable as the object of attention and as the one everyone wanted. Honey to bees, she was. Claire found herself unable to live up to that forced sweetness. There was fear that she ducked from and could never live up to. Claire was Maggie's daughter. Always in name but never quite capable of the implications.

Maggie was gone. Claire was used to her being gone though. She was gone long before she disappeared.

Claire tried to abstain from the thought of her mother because she missed her, and the effect of that emotion felt caved in and hollow even though caved in and hollow could also be empty and clean like her tummy that morning. A new start. The mother she had when she was young was different, so Claire thought, never too young to understand that what she remembered could be subject to a daughter's desire to be loved for the shy, sensitive, lanky girl with the small breasts and no hips. Maggie loved perfection and took such care in her appearance so that it overshadowed everything else about a quiet girl afraid of loud voices. Maggie was confident, constant chatter and Claire was silent.

It was that way for Claire, but she still wanted, even needed, her mother there to help her choose a dress for the winter formal. If nothing else, Maggie had impeccable taste in clothes that far exceeded the modest budget of a lawyer who worked in a small town on small cases. Claire's father, Ernest, tried to confront Maggie with the monetary effects of her high-end style. Maggie could spend money, and Ernest never had enough of it for her. That was only one of the reasons she left, Claire knew - dissatisfaction and whatever else that made her stray from a small town in Georgia to somewhere else or dead. Claire knew dead was not the reason. Her mother's instinct toward self-preservation was too strong to die. She disappeared because she left and that was that.

Claire knew her parents were fighting by their silence and silence was contagious. Whatever Maggie did was that way. It spread. She smiled and her smile prompted others to smile. She laughed and others laughed. Social, she could guide the mood in a room to the place she needed it to go. Unless she did not need it.

Claire actually preferred the fighting to the silence. Now all her dad could do was sit in it, let it surround him like it was insulation. Only her grandmother, Bernice, broke through all of that. Claire went from living with a mother who barely noticed her to living with a father who could not adapt to the confusion and schedules of life alone with a teenage daughter still deprived of the higher woman knowledge he could not transmit. Claire went from being invisible to being cared for by a grandmother who knew too much about being a mother. She never left Claire alone, and Claire had no idea how to deal with it. She bristled against her grandmother's love until she finally accepted it. That acceptance hurt. Oddly, she knew that with the acceptance of it was the acceptance that her mother did not love her enough to stay.

Grandma Bernie was always there for her. Always available. She was there long before Maggie left. She was there when Claire was admitted to the hospital at ninety-five pounds when she passed out at school and hit her head on the lockers outside of Social Studies. Bernie had been trying to feed her and connect with her since then, recently diverting the focus from food to crafts, to make eating less stressful. Claire tried, but eating disgusted her by what it did to her body, and no matter how she tried to tell herself that curves were good she did not believe it. She needed to stay strong and the food made her weak and ugly even when the boys whispered that she had a flat chest and was the anorexic girl. Being too skinny got her more attention than she wanted, so she turned the corner with it. Maggie being gone also took the pressure off the perfection thing. Bernice had taught her to make dinner for herself but she mostly made it for her dad while she took bites of cereal. At least it was something, and it was not bloody or dead just mashed up into a form unlike its original self. Eating it hurt nothing.

She took a banana clip from the drawer to the left that held hair clips and bands and snapped it in place at the base of her neck then powdered her face starting with her forehead. The phone rang just as she muted the shine. The compact still in her left hand, she picked up the receiver and answered, "Hello?"

It was Bernie's voice. "Hi honey."

"Hi Grandma. How are you?"

She was really always there for her.

"Fine. You're up early. Did I wake you up? I could call you back if I woke you up."

"No, I've been awake for a while. Getting ready to go shopping. What time do you want to leave? I have to be back at three o'clock to make Dad dinner, but he said he'd pay the rest of what you give me for a dress. I convinced Annene to come with us if that's okay. Grandma Estelle doesn't feel well but she'll come if we keep it short."

Claire propped the phone between her shoulder and cheek then closed the compact and tried not to look at herself in the mirror.

"Annene said she's probably going to get one too. A dress. She may wear the purple one she's working on. She may get shoes. I don't know."

Annene, despite her reputation and hair and awkwardness, was Claire's friend now. The bond between their grandmothers brought them together which made the women happy. Pleased. Boys at school called her a lesbian because of the way she dressed in Doc Martins and snug black jeans. There was a lot of black and in Georgia that did not fit in with anything.

Bernie's voice lowered and with a twinge of disappointment she said, "Oh, that's right. Why did I think it was next month?"

"It's a winter formal. We just got out of school a couple of days early. Then we have the dance. Then the official break."

"I'm sorry dear, when I was in school, we went to class. We didn't get days off to get ready." It was a genuine apology. She remembered nothing anymore.

"They treat seniors differently though. We get privileges."

"Oh. I wonder if there are any dresses on sale before Christmas? We can go to Penny's instead if you want," Bernice said.

"Oh," Claire stammered, "I thought we could go to the other shops. When we were there last weekend we..."

"Who did you go with last weekend?"

"Annene," Claire replied.

Annene liked to shop and despite her affinity with the color black, she was addicted to fashion. Claire did not much like to do anything but welcomed the chance to be dragged along. It kept her mind off the two things she never wanted to think about: food and her mother.

"Who drove you?" Bernie asked.

"Her mom drove us and I looked around but didn't find anything. I told you all of this. Don't you remember?"

Bernie went from never forgetting a thing to a few things slipping. She forgot little things like her keys. She never forgot details of a story Claire told her so this was a change.

Claire looked at herself in the mirror with shame in her eyes. She scolded herself for saying it. Maybe she had not said a word. Maybe there was never a real thing to say anymore.

"Is that boy taking you to the dance?" Bernie asked, intentionally redirecting Claire from the lapse in her memory. They were getting more obvious and she had forgotten his name.

"Yep. Neil's taking me. Anenne and Jeff are going together though Annene said she'd still be fine with a cardboard cut out. Yeah, we're going together, but we're all going in a big group and getting a limo..."

"A limousine?" Bernie asked, her voice louder, incredulous.

"Yeah, Grandma. Let's just leave early, okay?"

Claire tried to sound firm and strong. But, she had stepped on the scale again to find that it lied no matter what the digital display read – it was wrong if it was right and it was right if it was wrong.

"Okay, honey. Boy, when I was your age I never went in a limousine anywhere."

"Did they have limousines then?" Claire asked. She strained a laugh to relieve her grandmother. When Bernie did not reply, she thought she may have hurt her feelings.

"Grandma. I was just kidding, you know." She really felt badly about it. Bernie was loving and warm and up for a bit of banter and teasing but Claire knew she worried. Claire had given her something to worry about and so had Maggie, the hinge to it all. She had left them and Bernie had glued Claire to her side because neither one of them could ever get to Maggie, gone or not. In Georgia or anywhere.

Claire still hoped. Maybe if she changed more?

After a short pause, Bernie said, "I'll be there at nine thirty."

"Oh, you're driving?" Claire asked with a bit of surprise that cut off her thoughts.

"Grandpa has to go to the hardware store so he'll drop me off."

He was always at the hardware store and now Claire's father was always with Frank.

"What's at the hardware store? Isn't he doing any Christmas shopping?" Claire asked.

"I don't know. I thought when he retired he would play golf with his friends. Now he's just in the garage a lot. I don't know what he does in there. It's like a big secret."

"Uh, huh," Claire said.

She looked down at the carpet and slid the toes of her right foot under a pair of jeans that lay in a heap. Bending her knee, she lifted them off the floor to her free hand and opened the closet door to the left of the vanity.

Maggie had put so many mirrors in the room, on the four panels of the two tall closet doors and the vanity. She liked mirrors. Claire would have believed that she installed them all to make the rooms look bigger if her mother did not spend so much time looking at herself. A glance in the mirror of every room, sometimes a few opportunities to inspect herself, and she made no claim to conceal them because there was nothing wrong with this.

"Okay Grandma, I'll see you at nine. Annene's coming, okay?"

"Of course, honey. You told me." Her voice was kind.

"Okay, I'm gonna get ready. Bye," she said, and made a kissing sound over the phone.

Grandma Bernie kissed back.

Claire kept the receiver propped in the same position, pushed the button to hang up the phone and dialed Annene's phone number. After the fifth ring a slightly hoarse and tired voice answered, "Hello."

"Hi Annene. Did I wake you up?"

"Yes. What time is it?"

"It's early. I wanted to call and tell you that my grandma is coming to pick us up at nine thirty. So, can you get here by then or do you want us to come get you?"

"Just come pick me up. Can you call me before you come too? I'm going back to sleep, okay?"

"Okay, go back to sleep."

Annene slept late but Claire knew she would get up to go shopping with them. She would be ready on time. She would show up most likely in a bad mood but there.

"What are you doing up this early up anyway? It's winter vacation," Annene mumbled, half into the pillow and half into the phone.

"I don't know. Go back to sleep," Claire replied.

"I'm so tired. We were up last night celebrating our festival of lights. Judy gave me some money to spend. How much are you going to spend on a dress?" she asked.

"I have no idea. Go back to sleep. I'll see you later."

She knew but she would not say. Everything that cost something worried Annene and so she became resourceful. Judy worked constantly and slept during the day because of it so she could not come. Annene was alone too in her own way. But, she was tough.

"Okay, bye." Annene said, and hung up the phone, her face still on the pillow where she stayed for some time before she moved another inch.

Annene Berry finished with the liquid black eyeliner and removed a pink and green container from a clear makeup bag. She brushed over her lashes several times each and screwed the mascara shut. She picked up a magazine and flipped through the pages then put it down and looked at herself in the mirror again.

"Whatever," she said, and tossed the magazine on the bed.

It was a twin bed with a child's canopy frame and a plain black comforter. Annene spent hours at times lying on her bed as she listened to records on the turntable before she moved on to compact disks when her father bought her a stereo for her sixteenth birthday. The compact disk collection grew from Rick Springfield to Joan Jett, Blondie and Pat Benatar. Music, teenage angst and black hair, brought to mind things that scared her mother who had no remaining energy or resources to deal with it.

"My daughter. You were such an angel until you were fourteen. Then you turned into a monster," Judy told her.

"Mom, it's called independent thought," Annene replied. "You should try it sometime."

"You just like to argue with me," her mother insisted. Judy Berry was a shorter and more robust version of her daughter. Gravity's effects showed under her eyes as shadows and lines.

"Mom, it's the generation gap. What do you expect?"

"Never mind," Judy replied. The conversation was a typical part of the morning ritual, as common as Annene's breakfast of toast or Twinkies and a Diet Coke. It was as predictable as each day that Annene overslept for school and Judy tormented her into wakefulness as each took turns turning on and off the overhead lights.

Judy turned on the light. Annene got up and turned off the light. Judy returned to the room where she again found her sleeping. She switched the light on again and went to her daughter's bedside.

"Wake up," she said. "Time to go to school," she said those days.

But, it was vacation, so she stayed in bed and tried to push the thought of breakfast from her mind. A party dress was the next step, that and wishing for a flat stomach. It could happen with a women's magazine one-day fast. Reality told her that she wouldn't have the energy to stay awake for the bad cover band if she fasted. It was an illusion but every girl seemed only to think about appearances. And Claire. She had that history of starving herself by her own will and sickness. Any of the normal girls and boys were cruel about it. Girls her age were vacant and mean. Annene could face that. Could face being called a lesbian because she was smart and wore black and never had a real boyfriend. Because she was smart and wore black, a way to mute the color that swirled around in her mind. It calmed her down.

They would never get The Untouchables to come back to the small auditorium to perform for their prom because, unlike the year before, their winter formal committee had no imagination. It would be a wedding band or DJ. Boring stuff. Georgia stuff and a lot of dresses with fluffy sleeves. They were behind trends, always.

Annene would wear the deep purple dress, the one that her grandmother, Estelle, saved for her. Estelle could barely get a hold of the past, but it was not because she failed mentally. Estelle did not want to disclose something about herself, and it was obvious. Perhaps with some coaxing, Annene could find out why her grandmother never wore it. Why she let it hang in her closet for forty-two years. It was not fashionable when Judy was in high school, so Judy refused. Annene knew Judy, her mother, had a stubborn streak. It was a family gene. They all had it, but Annene and her grandmother did not clash. Annene and Estelle had a generation to buffer them. That Annene knew.

The dress was simple and hung by its spaghetti straps in the closet: the satin scarf of variant violet hues wrapped around a hook like it was the too thin neck of a silver screen actress. It was simple enough to stay in style.

"Some things take time. Estelle told her granddaughter. "I bought it and never wore it. I almost did," she always began then stopped herself before the words got out. Annene was different. The girl wore black and dyed her hair every six weeks with Clairol hair dye she bought at the pharmacy. Claire assisted when she was available but Annene had mastered application techniques and could do it alone to the same effect. She fit her hands into the plastic gloves and separated the chunks of hair. She painted on the dark goo and rubbed it through the dull brown roots. Reddish stains would persist around the hairline for a couple of days but it would fade quickly. Usually, by the end of the weekend.

She was lucky enough to have finally grown back her eyebrows after she accidentally burned them off while building a fire on a school camping trip with Claire. It was September, just after school started. An overnight trip that required little more than Annene's presence. But when Annene chose to participate, to stoke the campfire flames, they shot up and singed off her eyebrows. Mrs. Clement, the chaperone of the school trip, relinquished blame to the girl's lack of common sense.

When the EMT's asked what happened, she explained that the flammability of the little hairs was amplified by the ammonia content to the hair dye. She applied dye to the area the night before to match her hair and may not have removed it all. The residue lingered and so went Annene's eyebrows. Torched.

"It's like pouring lighter fluid on your hair. Washing your hair with lighter fluid then lighting a match. The fluid acts like a magnet."

The man in the white uniform looked at her like she was an odd worm which was fine since Annene felt awkward as a standard and even more so without eyebrows and a normal, even hairline. She was thankful that Judy allowed her the time to stay home until at least partial growth appeared. Annene was grateful for her mother's act of mercy. The hair grew back just slightly and Annene returned to school after a couple of weeks healed and skilled at drawing in eyebrows with a pencil. A black pencil.

"Kids that age can be terrible," Judy explained to Estelle. "It's already difficult enough with Annene."

Estelle cringed. Her granddaughter was anything but

awkward in her own mind. "The most inspired are those who have the mind to not always do what's normal. What is normal anyway, Annene? Nothing. Average is normal. And, you. You are anything but average. Remarkable child of God..."

"Okay Grandma." Annene cut her off at the mention of God. Too much God talk amongst atheist parents caused tension. But at the time, Annene prayed to God that her eyebrows would grow back and when they did, Estelle's mention of God did not bother her so much as it had in the past. By winter break, they had almost fully returned.

Estelle told her that it would be a fine time for her to wear the dress. That it had been in the closet for so long that she should just go ahead and wear it.

"But you said I should wait."

"Only because that dress is awful good luck."

With that, the conversation closed. Annene knew she would not hear anymore about the dress, but she would go ahead and wear it and her fully-grown eyebrows would be plucked and shaped in a terse arch.

Of all the adults in Annene's world, Estelle got her attention. Estelle knew her granddaughter like she knew her own bones, where she was most prone to aches and where she harnessed strength.

Annene would still go with her friend and spend time with Bernie. Bernie did not mind that Annene always wore black, and understood that Claire needed her friend the same way Bernie needed Estelle. The explanation would come.

What else would a girl do but sleep through a few more hours of a winter morning? Dark as it was, maybe a shower or a bath with the new bath gel before shopping and some Nag Champa incense just to prod her mother's suspicious mind.

Judy labeled other goth kids as pot smokers and druggies. But, Annene just liked the scent for what it was and not its capacity to mask weed fumes.

When Judy passed the room, Annene told her, "I'm meditating."

The thought of it got her out of bed and she walked to her small dresser where she opened the metal latch to a cherry wood box with a brass half moon and star on the top. She removed the blue, white and red box of incense, opened the side of the carton with her right hand and pinched the wooden end of the stick which she slipped out of the long rectangular carton. Then, from the incense holder that held more sticks of a different brand of incense she removed a yellow lighter and lit the stick of Nag Champa with an already lit, cheep devotional candlewick. It was covered with a picture of the thin Indian Buddha on the side, which Annene did not prefer at all, given that a thin Buddha seemed much less happy than a fat one. A fat one could help her achieve what she wanted as she crammed the AP reading list and reviewed outlines at the kitchen table where she ate Fritos with Heinz Chili Sauce or Ritz crackers with Skippy Super Chunk and Smuckers Strawberry Preserves. Between bites, the fat Buddha could skim J.D. Salinger, anticipate multiple choice questions and decide whether or not a purple tint to her hair would repel her winter formal date. The red tint would clash with the purple and a change would probably be in her best interest. A Buddha would do with purple if he had any hair at all.

"I like you just the way you are," Jeff said.

She claimed to see right through him. She yelled at Neil, her older brother for sicking Jeff on her to begin with. Neil told her that it was not his idea but Jeff's. Jeff asked her to the dance on his own free will and really liked her. It was so truly insane and adolescent, the thought. Annene had no idea how much Jeff felt for her, how deep those adolescent emotions that had barely peaked at eighteen ran through his body.

It was at a party where they met, really met, outside of

the flirtations that Annene passed off as absurdity. Boys Jeff's age were just mean little fuckers convinced that mild forms of cruelty preceded a date. Annene knew about such things. Her grandmother was a gossip columnist and informed her of the primitive courting gestures of young men.

"What's that thing in your nose?" Jeff had asked. He appeared through the kitchen side door behind Neil as he arrived home after school. Books sprawled across the kitchen table, Annene hovered over them already, peanut butter, jelly and crackers at the side and her eyebrows full and perfectly arched. Those brows furrowed at the interruption to her steady concentration.

"It's a nose ring," Annene replied. "What does it look like?" she asked. It was obvious she was not looking for an answer.

She was dressed in black from a turtleneck to Doc Martins stitched with yellow thread. Jeff wore a black T-shirt with The Specials album art on the front.

"Oh," he said, and looked at her too long for her comfort. Like he was studying her.

"It looks like a nail in a tire. You know when you run over a nail, Jeff, and it sticks in it and the only way you can get it out is to pull it out? But, then you have to patch the tire because all of the air comes out."

Jeff just looked at her blankly and tried to resist a smile.

Annene glared at her brother, rolled her eyes, then lowered her head to her studies.

Annene sat in front of the altar she created and stared at family photographs of her parents and grandparents, Estelle and Jack, lit by two candles that flanked the tabernacle that held the scroll written in Korean that not one of the other Buddhists would translate. The whole practice was getting weirder but it still made her feel better about things that had mostly gotten away from all love to strange and alone. Her father was dead and Estelle was not well. Jack was mentally gone. Her guru told her to chant for them, for what she wished for them and this all worked to the extent that it made her feel like she had a choice in something larger. She was beginning to think she had no choice no matter how long she sat there in the near dark room with those little bits of fire, of light.

Light came through the bedroom door. She heard her mother's voice just moments before the bright fissure hit her eyes.

"Annene," she called. Her head appeared behind the door.

Annene looked over her shoulder and squinted. "God, it's so bright."

"What are you doing here?" Judy asked. She held the knob of the open door.

"Sitting."

Judy held her tongue without success.

"Now who are you trying to be? A monk? Claire is here with her grandma."

"Who's driving?" Annene asked, and raised herself one leg at a time from the floor.

"Claire," her mother answered.

"Good. Grandma told me she'd stay home but I convinced her to go. She won't drive with Claire's grandma."

Judy waved the air. "That stuff smells awful."

"It's giving me some clarity of mind, Judy. Relax. You're way too tense."

"Please stop calling me Judy," her mother said. "I don't understand why you call me that. What happened to the times when you would just call me 'Mommy'?"

"You don't listen when I call you Mom so I call you by your God-given name."

Annene was convinced that the practice would remove her anxiety. A television documentary and her older artist friends from the art shop job told her so. Tools for meditation helped: two candles placed on either side of a small cabinet, incense and a stool that raised her just above her heals and took the pressure off her knees. Her mind went undisturbed during these times of meditation aside from the nose ring that she would intermittently spin in its place as the little hole healed.

Leaning over, she blew out the candle and let the incense burn in its steady stream of smoke that faded just above her head to nothing but a scent so clear and tranquil even Annene thought herself happy.

Claire's head peered above the Cadillac steering wheel. Bernie let her drive the car because she didn't trust herself driving with the girls.

Annene shifted in the back seat.

"I don't know why I'm even going. I have a dress. Grandma said I can wear the purple early. She said it's good luck. I'm sure though that she's just afraid I'll get stood up by Bozo and doesn't want me to spend the money."

"Who's Bozo?" Bernie asked, and turned around from the front seat of the car to Annene seated behind her. Estelle sat behind the passenger's seat.

"It's Jeff. He invited me to the dance the day before yesterday."

Bernie's eyes lit up. "That's great," as she gave in to her Pennsylvania accent that makes a period into a bookmark. "In my day a boy was supposed to give you some notice, but..."

"Things are different now." Estelle said. Her voice hushed and gravelly, she coughed repeatedly into the back of her hand. She smoked since she was fourteen years old.

"Yeah, it fits me. Of course I feel brilliant knowing I can fit into a woman's dress who is over forty years older than me. I'm dying my hair too, by the way," Annene added.

"Annene," Bernie said, looking at Estelle through the rearview mirror. Speaking for her. "You'll look fine. Why do you want to do that? It's going to ruin your hair if you dye it over and over again."

Annene ignored her. "Judy thinks I'm a freak."

"So that's what's going on? You had another fight?"

"No, I just hate everyone. I told her if she didn't send me to a shrink I'd start praying or something. I don't think she had meditation in mind. Definitely not chanting to a mantra." Annene laughed.

Bernie spoke up, "Maybe honey, if you didn't call her by her first name. Maybe she'd feel..."

"Like a mom?" Annene interjected, finishing Bernie's thought for her. "I told you, she doesn't listen to me. I call, 'Mom' and she doesn't answer. So, I call her 'Judy.'"

Claire looked over her shoulder. Her thin arms hung from the sides of the steering wheel as though they were accordion hinges on a vanity mirror affixed to a wall but with only one bend in the arm. Twisted at the back of her head, Claire's hair was almost the exact shade of Bernie's but lighter and without the faintest hint of gray roots visible on the old woman's head. Claire's pale blue eyes were concealed with tortoise shell Ray-Ban sunglasses. Wayfarers. She reached for the dial and turned up the volume with her delicate fingers. Bernie asked her to turn it down.

"You know your grandfather lost his hearing from loud noises, honey."

"Those were fighter planes in the war, Gram," Claire said.

"Oh, will..." Annene blurted excitedly. She gripped the backrest of the front seat, jutting her head forward. "Turn it up. Turn it up."

Claire let go of the steering wheel with her right hand and moved it toward the dial. Bernie pushed away her hand. "Wait, you drive." She said and pointed at the road ahead. "I'll turn it up. So worked up about a song."

"It's The Clash, Grammy," Claire said, bobbing her head to the rhythm.

"Oh," Bernie said, again with a look toward Estelle who cleared her throat.

Annene closed her eyes and sang, "You didn't stand by me, no not at all...,"

"Just give it a chance," Claire almost shouted from the front seat. "You only have to go out once. He likes you, Annene."

"Tell me about this boy. Who is he?" Bernie asked, intrigued.

"He's Neil's friend."

"Oh, that's nice," she said, her approval rang through in her voice.

It was obvious by her smile that Annene's older brother attracted the type of boy Bernie would approve of. Neil Berry was Annene's sole source of torture and disdain since birth. Annene was born into the world fighting him until she entered high school when things calmed down between them, and he left her alone to be herself with her fringy friends. Claire made the most difference though. She moved back from Atlanta after her mom left and started going with Neil.

Claire turned the radio dial and spoke at the segue, a moment of unclouded airspace within the leather Cadillac interior.

"Alright, you can turn it down now. The treble is much more subdued," Annene shouted from the back then apologized for the sound that still rang in her ears. "Sorry, I didn't realize I was being so loud."

She slouched back into the maroon leather interior then slid to the right, off the hump in the center and into the indentation that cradled her body.

"Tell Grammy how you met Jeff," Claire said.

"She knows how I met him."

"No, how you really met him," she objected, and turned to Estelle. "They met at the party the weekend before last. Jeff walked up to her while she was insulting another girl's shoes then moved onto the fact that the guy standing next to her smelled like Irish Spring and that she would rather gag on a glassful of raw sewage than have to talk to someone who smelled like mint."

Bernie listened intently, her eyes on Claire's too thin profile, then looked toward Annene who sat in the back seat intentionally ducked well out of Bernie's sight in the rearview mirror. Bernie tried to get her in frame and craned her neck and shoulders to her left to make eye contact with the girl.

"You're not serious. You didn't really do that, did you? We at least had to be polite in my day," Bernie said.

"Well, apparently being rude works because Annene's got a date," Claire said.

"Those shoes were awful. I told Jeff that if he smelled like Irish Spring the night of the dance that all bets were off," Annene said. "Gladiator shoes. Who wears gladiator shoes in the Eighties? I don't care if it's a trend. It's stupid."

"Your father used to use that soap. He used that and Old Spice. It made him smell fresh," Bernie said, happy that she and Estelle's oddly configured granddaughter found some common ground.

"He smelled like a breath mint, right?" Annene said, and pulled herself even closer and up against the back of the seat.

"This guy smelled like one of those strong licorice mints which is fine if it's in a person's mouth but not so fine if it's all over their body. You're not supposed to smell soap. Not on a man."

Bernie listened from the front seat, her mind full speed as she thought about the past. It tripped her up into the present.

"You know they make soap from fat?" Claire said. "Fat and something else. Grammy's been reading about it," she told Annene.

"But vegetable oil too. It depends on who's making it. The alchemy," Bernie said.

"Tell her what you told me. Grammy's been working on her Christmas crafts. She's making bars of soap."

"That's interesting, a little creepy, but interesting." Annene stopped herself from adding, *Don't people your age usually give up on everything besides golf, soap operas and talk shows?* But, she refrained. Claire was right when she said she should try to be nicer. Even though she thought it was pointless, she tried despite her anger at things to be kind. Things like Estelle smoking herself into emphysema, her father being dead. For being a dead creep.

"You're not knitting with that group of ladies anymore? Grandma stopped going. She said it was because of her arthritis and those women needed deadlines. It got weird."

"Things have changed a lot. Soap making is interesting," Bernie said, mostly like it was an apology. "I got the idea from Frank of all people. He kept complaining about waste and refused to throw out the soap chips. I had a whole bag of them. Then I had a dream about it, which, to me, means that I've been thinking about it a lot. It was on my mind."

It was not entirely the truth. She wanted to get Claire in the kitchen with her, doing something that took the pressure off eating. She needed to keep Claire close. Even so, sitting next to her in the front seat of the Cadillac, Claire was still wasting away. She got better after Maggie left but she still had to watch her granddaughter closely.

"Tell her the story that you told me," Claire said, her voice louder than usual. She let go of the wheel and placed her hand on her grandmother's knee, urging her on.

"Tell her what you told me," she said again. This time she turned to Bernie and with a single motion, swerved the car slightly to the right where a woman walked her dog at the side of the road. A trimmed white poodle with a red leather and rhinestone collar trotted alongside the woman.

"Claire, you have to keep your eyes on the road. You almost hit that woman." Her voice raised in alarm.

"Yeah, you almost took out the dog, Claire. Someone

would consider that a civil service, Grandma Bernie."
Annene laughed.

"It's not the dog's fault," Claire said. She steered the
car away from the roadside. As she drove away she peered
into the rearview mirror to look at Mrs. Clement behind
her. Annene turned around to see what the woman would
do having nearly escaped being flattened by a seventeen
year-old behind the wheel of a Cadillac.

"She just gave you the finger," Annene reported, then
turned back around toward the front seat where she clung
to the backrest and fought for the view in the mirror.

"I can't see, Annene," Claire snapped, both amused and
startled by her error.

"Did she really give me the finger?" Claire asked, half
smiling.

"I can't believe she gave you the finger," Annene
repeated, her eyes wide and smiling. "Mrs. Clement, the
team spirit camper, yogi, gym teacher gave you the finger?"

"Honey, you have to keep your eyes on the road. You
get too easily distracted," Bernie said.

"Yeah, I know," Claire said, shaken.

"She's just learning, Bernice. Lighten up," Estelle said
from the back seat, her voice muted.

Bernie instantly regretted the criticism. The girl was
already all balled up in it like a potato bug with little legs as
knives that closed in on itself.

"You're awfully quiet today," Bernie said, her back to
Estelle. There was too much to worry about.

"That Mrs. Clement is not exactly in the right giving
you the bird." She patted her knee then flipped down the
mirror to view Estelle in the back seat. They made eye
contact and just to be sure Bernie understood, Estelle
cleared her throat and rolled out few coughs. It was
common, the background noise of rattled air from infected
lungs, that it gave a sense of normalcy to the situation that
jolted all of them.

"Just ignore me and keep your eyes on the road,

honey."

Bernie's tone was patient but understanding and Claire was allowed to drive even though the girl did not have much experience behind the wheel aside from the times she borrowed the car - not nearly as entertaining as stealing the car in the middle of the night. Annene, always after a fight with her mom, called Claire and whispered into the receiver. "I've got the keys." Always she sounded like she was about to carry out a military exercise.

They cruised along Peachtree Drive past the millionaire's house, "Mr. Covart, the one who left his wife for a twenty year-old," Estelle said. She was always abreast of the town gossip.

"Abreast" made both the girls laugh quietly and Estelle knew it.

"Everyone knows he owns every inch of land from here to the Atlantic Ocean." She was a filter for happenstance but not a very good one as her tendency to exaggerate was profound. The millionaire invented the pink rust remover that both Annene and Claire once used on their bikes to make them shiny again. Otherwise, he was a lonely man who spent time in his lab, a shed at the back of his house. Estelle never made up stories but listened to the ones others told about him. And though she wrote about a lot of things, Estelle kept clear of his life. He was one of those that was not so lucky though it seemed like he was. She could see through the seams of any story tied together, exaggerated or not. She knew what was the truth and was not anything close to it.

Annene began stealing Judy's car in the middle of the night when she was fourteen and only five feet tall. As fate would have it, three years later, she was still the same height, only it was easier to see over the wheel since she no longer had to duck at the few cars that passed her on the road at two o-clock in the morning. She went to elaborate means in her attempt to cover her ass. Driving was Annene's freedom from Judy though Claire did not understand the need for it. Judy was overbearing but she didn't go anywhere aside from work. She had to take care of her father who lived with them. She never smiled.

Claire did not so much miss Maggie as much as she missed the woman who she remembered as a little girl. That woman vanished long ago and both Ernest and Claire shared in a brief glimpse of what she could have been had she held on to each of them. If they held on to each other.

Though Ernest remained, he was not so much the emblem of perseverance. He was always alone.

Nothing was easy for anyone. Not anymore.

Claire looked ahead to the entrance, a mural of multi-colored tulips along the foundation above the hedges and pansies of yellow, blue and orange in the foreground of the flowerbed.

Having almost run over the gym teacher and cheerleading coach, Claire was glad to arrive at the Lenox Square Mall store where they had to pass every mother and daughter shopping team on the way to the other side of the complex to get to Contempo Casuals, a small store with less expensive and trendier clothes. They would find shoes at Dillard's where they dye satin shoes to match a dress. Claire tried to stay focused on the task at hand as they walked through the ground floor of the mall. The second level hovered above them, blocked by the Plexiglas guardrails that revealed just the bottom half, from the waist to the ankles, of shoppers who shuffled past the edges of her eyes, moving so slow and relaxed they appeared to have nowhere to go. Nowhere to rush. Claire wanted to rush in and out and get it done. The teenage girls who travelled in packs with big, gold hoop earrings and color, still showed their bare legs as it was not yet too cold to wear a miniskirt or shorts. December in Georgia was reliable that way. Claire heard Annene and Bernie's voices in the background as she took in the details and slipped inside herself at the vision of those packs of girls with their mothers who joined them to help and talk nonstop about whatever was at the ends of their mouths at the moment. Whatever was on their lips. Even if it was her. Even if it was Maggie. Those clear, Plexiglas bannisters at each level above created an empty funnel that ascended high, obstructed only by advertisements for jewelry and stores pictured on static flags that hung from the vaulted ceiling from strings attached to the beams above. Through that ceiling was the clear sky and light that was wrong and glowed fluorescent, light bouncing off of everywhere to shine and show the little nuances of self Claire would rather hide. There was nowhere to hide there. No one to hide in or behind. Nothing to conceal her mostly from herself. Every one of those girls was a reflection of Claire's shortcomings. Every one. Even the girls who were normal-sized and geeky.

Then there were the mirrors that made her look fat and horrid. More fat and horrid than ever. Her stomach growled as the fragrant vapors from the food court located at the northernmost cavern of the mall, reached into the back of her throat and into her stomach, contracting her hollow insides into a low growl.

Inside and deep within the mall structure gave a strange, hollow tone to their voices as they spoke with distraction to the store windows they passed by. Bernie, Estelle, and Annene, with their rubber-soled feet in white Reikas, wide toe-ruched loafers, Doc Martins, and jellies made no extra noise as they stepped with focus and haste across the white linoleum tiles. Claire wore hot pink plastic jellies, equally mute, a pleated turquoise mini skirt and black t-shirt with ruffled sleeves. Annene was in uniform black jeans and black t-shirt. Bernie wore a turquoise velour lounge outfit and Estelle, a cream blouse and black slacks. Members Only jackets, acid-washed jeans, and parachute pants fitted the male mannequins behind glass storefronts. The stiff, blank-faced females wore bright colors, just like Claire. Just like her hair, their wigs were teased high.

Claire thought herself fat in comparison to them and hated the softness to her own body. She wished it was hard like those stiff, faceless, plain, inanimate figures. It was closer to her empty insides that she tried to ignore as her stomach cinched in response to the acute smells from the food court. She told herself not to care that she was hungry, but instantly diverted her attention to the inevitable stares of the pack of girls who talked low and pointed at her as they passed. Bernie took her by the elbow and pulled her in close to her side, like a bird under wing. A broken little bird. Claire did not have a moment to wonder that maybe she was just being paranoid to think they were talking about her. They could have pointed to the glass storefront just beyond her. It could have been Annene's appearance. But, no, it was Claire. The girl whose mother disappeared. The girl who was sent to the hospital for starving herself. Those events combined managed to slip her several notches down the rungs of Alpharetta High School Society.

Bernie told her that it would stop when people found something else to focus on. It was the first rule of gossip, and Estelle would know as much. But, this was Alpharetta, Georgia and there wasn't much else to talk about. It was almost a full year before that happened, and Claire discovered that new residents to Alpharetta were almost as close to being as interesting as those who disappeared. "New to Georgia" struck up conversation and intrigue, and focus on The Hinkley Family dimmed.

Jeff Stone was another target of the Alpharetta Mafia gossip, and she felt for him, having been there herself. Claire was comforted by the thought as she returned her grandmother's gesture with a pull that brought them closer, their arms hooked into each other. She silently relished in the dysfunction of their group; the oddity of two best friends and their hip grandmothers who knew how to love them like no one else seemed to be able to figure out.

Three hours later, the women appeared from inside the building with several handled shopping bags. Pleased, Claire, Annene, Bernice and Estelle turned the corner where Mrs. Clement, a thin woman with skin too tanned and with curly, brassy, brown hair brushed into a static bush, stood just off to the right smoking a cigarette. She held a leash - the white toy poodle stood at the end of it. Startled, she threw the cigarette on the ground and stepped on it. Waving her hand at the air to clear the smoke, Mrs. Clement pulled down her white sweat suit jacket and tugged the matching velour pants up an inch from her hips to her waistline. She lingered in that cloud of smoke for a few seconds before she recognized them as the drivers and passengers of the car that almost ran her over. They exchanged wide-eyed looks.

The moment they were within earshot, she spoke with a stern and loud voice to Bernie.

"You shouldn't let your granddaughter drive that car barreling down the street like that."

Without pause, Bernice responded evenly. "I'm sorry. Mrs. Clement, it is, right? I'm too old to drive the car and my husband, Frank, couldn't come with us on this shopping trip," she lied. "Men just don't like to do this kind of thing."

Large, round sunglasses covered the gym teacher's eyes. The skin on her face was tanned but leathery and her hands were the same, but also freckled. Her hair was shoulder length, a dull brown and frizzy. Annene always forgot her gym clothes and Mrs. Clement did not like her. She liked the cheerleaders that she coached and the girls who played sports. Annene did neither.

Placed on the ground next to Mrs. Cement, was a portable dog suitcase with handles and vents. She set the poodle down on the concrete and the dog immediately sniffed around the pansies that bordered the walk while Mrs. Clement listened with a look of disgust on her face.

"My driving is really awful, you see. It was my fault

Claire got distracted. Perhaps you should carry your dog in the tote bag if you feel like going for a stroll along the highway." Bernie nodded her head continuously.

"Neither of us should be behind the wheel." Estelle confirmed.

Annene smiled. Mrs. Clement said nothing but packed her scruffy dog in the carry bag and trudged across the pedestrian crosswalk to the elevator that led up to the second floor of the parking structure.

"I hate that dog," Annene said, when her gym teacher was too far away to hear. She waited until the parking structure elevator doors closed behind her to say it. "I hate poodles. Who needs a hypoallergenic dog in Georgia?"

Claire laughed and Bernie inhaled deeply, shocked as she tried for calm.

"It's a defenseless animal, Annene," Bernie said, patient.

"It's ugly," Annene replied, "I don't care. You know what I think about little dogs, right?"

"Yes," Estelle said. "We know."

Annene punt kicked an invisible ball into the air. "We kick them into the street."

Bernie shook her head. "I stood up for you, though. That I don't support. You can't blame animals for their people."

Annene nodded. "You're right."

"Thank you, Grandma," Claire said.

"Can you believe she smokes? Who knew that Mrs. Clement smoked? She's the gym teacher. Gym teachers aren't supposed to smoke."

"I used to smoke," Bernie said. "Way back when it was fashionable and I was a layout designer for *Vogue*. "That was before anyone knew it was bad for you."

"Oh, come on. We knew it was bad. We just liked it too much," Estelle said.

Annene made no attempt to stifle her reaction to what

felt like a mental sling shot, completely out of the blue.

"You worked for *Vogue* Magazine?" she asked, her disbelief blatant. No effort to conceal any of it. "*I* don't even read that magazine."

"No one reads it," Claire said.

"Yes, when I lived in New York."

"And you moved to Alpharetta, Georgia? Are you crazy?"

"Yes," Bernie replied, grinning. "I used to be. Not being able to drive slows you down a bit, dear."

"Then she became a nurse," Claire continued.

"Frank, Claire's grandpa moved here for a job and I came here after a while. We tried to break it off but we were too in love. Too lonely without each other. He had a great job in advertising but he got transferred to Atlanta. I had to decide what was more important to me."

"You gave up a job at *Vogue* so you could be with him and become a nurse? I don't know if people do that anymore," Annene said.

"Annene," Claire said, cutting her off. Protective.

"No, I don't mean that it's bad. I just see you as working at this high fashion magazine and you moved here so you could decorate houses."

"Actually, that was my third career. I dropped out of nursing school before that because I got pregnant and just didn't have much of a knack for science, as hard as I tried. It's interesting but I wasn't any good at it."

"To Alpharetta though? I don't see how anyone would actually choose to live here."

"Alpharetta is beautiful. You don't know what a good thing you've got. It was a good place to raise Claire's dad."

"I know," Annene said, pained. "Judy tells me all the time. She sneered and changed her voice to the pedantic and shrill tone her mother used with her. 'Not everyone lives the way we do, Annene. Someday you'll be grateful and understand why I'm telling you all of this.' It's always the same speech. Like I don't appreciate it. Come on."

The three ladies arrived at the side of the Cadillac. Claire remained quiet as she opened the trunk and loaded the handled Dillard's bags and plastic garment bag that held her dress. She laid the dress out across the shoe bags and closed the trunk. She liked it. It was not too much of anything. A lot of the girls would be wearing black dresses and she could fade into the mirage of them in the moments when Annene, in her purple glory, was occupied elsewhere.

Annene broke the silence with her words that cut through the well-placed fabrications of Alpharetta. She told the truth and that, Claire knew from the start, was the reason she loved her friend so dearly. No lies. The reality of her words, even in their most brutal sense, made Claire laugh or gave her comfort, except when she was mean, because when she was mean, she could be cruel. Annene's angst-ridden state that chewed out Mrs. Clement and the poodle could offend anyone, but it was honest. It made Claire grateful that she had a white mutt, Hildy, a mix of Husky and German Sheppard, who greeted Claire with not only a wagging tail but also a circular motion to that swing that distinguished Hildy as one of the happiest dogs Claire had ever known.

Hildy was always there when Claire got home.

She felt sorry for Mrs. Clement's dog getting the bad rap it did. Animals aren't their owners. Bernie was right. So right that she held onto the thought for a long while.

Claire had always been shy, but the past months left her more withdrawn since her mother, Maggie, disappeared. Disappeared, as in, "left." Claire tried not to speak. Tried not to appear, but to vanish like her mother. Only Claire's vanishing was haunted and withered, slight and gone. Transparent and surrounded by a self she would rather vanish from. A self that felt surrounded by barbed wire that cut into her with the slightest movement, the faintest spoken words, too many eyes on her. Food in her small belly. At the same time, Annene refused to leave her alone.

Annene spoke her anger when she felt it. She was always herself and seemingly unafraid to be so. Annene was the only girl who did not gossip about Claire and her family, focusing in on the lack, the second version of the new girl who came back to Alpharetta from Atlanta when her father could not hack it alone without a wife and mother to his daughter. It could have been easy for Annene because that kind of vicious gossip was in her blood. Her grandmother, Estelle Berry, was a gossip columnist, but they shared more than they did not.

Estelle and Bernie had been friends for years, since their boys were in school. Claire and Annene came together as part accident, part fate and all need.

Psychologists at the eating disorder treatment center told Ernest Hinkley that Claire had a problem connecting with people. Overheard by one of the kids, the information spread and the girl had difficulty making friends as soon as she returned from Atlanta to Alpharetta. Claire and Ernest, her father, moved back from Atlanta to Alpharetta to be closer to Bernice. They'd only lived in the city two years before Maggie left, and when she did the only choice for Ernest and Claire was to return home. It was Maggie's idea to live in Atlanta in the first place.

Claustrophobic, the place choked out her talent and gave her nothing to be but a mother among southern women who found peace in places Maggie could not find. They had all hoped that the move would lift her spirits, that she would stop blaming her husband and daughter for her gloom, the way she left the room hunched over and lurked in the corners of the house submerged in days of sadness. She could not escape from it, no matter what Claire or Ernest did to cheer her.

Annene had never been her friend at that school before she left for Atlanta. Claire never needed her. Life was normal. Claire was normal and even popular for a girl who never fit in anywhere, but everywhere. Annene was not normal. Now, not normal was normal for Claire.

Two years changed Claire's everything.

She was always by herself, but rode a Vespa and needed a friend. So, there was Annene, picking her out of the fringe and sifting through Claire's excuses to stay alone.

Bernie conceded to let Annene drive with a bit of convincing, "I promise I'll swerve out of Mrs. Clement's way this time."

Estelle inhaled with a long wheeze. "You know as well as I do that she's driving home. She only had to walk the dog to go tinkle."

"Maybe if she squeezed it really hard it could go in the flower bed in front of the mall," Annene replied.

Claire took her seat at the back of the car and looked out the window to a view of a concrete wall.

"Let her, Gram. She's a good driver. Really," Claire said as she faced Annene and Bernie who stood between the open driver's side door and the frame of the Cadillac.

"Come on, let me drive Bernice. Please. Grandma Bernie."

"Fine. Promise not to call me Bernice," she said, signaling to Claire to give Annene the keys. "It makes me feel like an old fart."

"Yes," Annene said. She shot her arms up, triumphant.

"You tell your mother about this and you know what she'll do."

"I know, I know. Grandma always lets me drive. I'm an excellent driver. You have my word. I won't breathe any of it."

Annene took the wheel while Claire watched, knowing from their secret outings in the Pacer that Annene was a good driver. Bernie entered the front seat, passenger side. She modeled perfect etiquette, bent at the waist, made contact with the leather interior as she sat, then swiveled around to face the windshield all the while keeping her knees together until her feet reached the floor boards when she crossed her ankles, hidden by the long drape at the hems of the velour fabric. Bernie was of a different time where manners were practiced and her body was polite. But none of that respectful front ever receded behind a heavy layer of warmth that remained in the forefront of all she said and did. Not easy to do. Annene put the key with the black plastic logo on the head into the ignition and turned it on. She waited for a few moments while the engine hummed then pulled the automatic gearshift from the steering column and pushed it over to the left.

"Reverse is my best gear," she said. She looked over her shoulder.

Claire and Bernie remained silent with Annene at the wheel until Bernie realized Annene touched the pedals with just the tips of her toes.

"Adjust the seat, Annene," she said, and reached across.

Annene slid forward at an angle and tapped the brakes until she got a firm hold. Once stopped, Bernie reached further across her lap and pushed one of the sliding silver buttons on the door armrest. Humming, the seat moved forward so both of Annene's feet, not only her toes, rested on the pedals, easily.

"I got it," she told Bernie, who pushed herself back to the passenger side with some effort.

"Okay," Annene said, and shifted the car to reverse and swept her arm over the backrest. "When are we being picked up?"

"I called. The car is picking us up at six o'clock," Claire said.

"You called? Didn't the boys call?" Bernice asked.

"No. Dad said he would pay for the limo so I called."

"I don't know, ladies. It's just that in my day things were different. There were rules."

"There aren't rules anymore, Grandma Bernie. Women are emancipated," Annene said. She smiled and turned to Bernice who pointed to the windshield.

"I'm not exactly from the dark ages, you know," Bernie chirped.

"We're completely from the dark ages, Bernice," Estelle corrected.

"Gram worked. She had a job," Claire said from the back seat.

"We both had jobs. We were progressive because we had to be," Estelle said. "But, we had families and there's only so much you can do."

"I don't mean to offend you. It's just that we don't have to wait for a guy to call. You just have to be rude," Annene said.

"Rude is the new normal, Bernice," Estelle said, coughing.

"What do you mean, you have to be rude? We were polite in my day. My father would never let me call."

"Judy doesn't like it either but she doesn't forbid it. I think she probably thinks it's the only way I could get a date in the first place."

"Annene," Bernie said, as though trying to cover the truth.

"Jeff asked you to the dance though," Claire said.

"Yeah, but I was rude, right?"

"This is what I mean by rules, honey," Bernie began, then added, "Keep your eyes on the road."

Annene returned her eyes to the road.

"There were two of them that I listened to and those are: No calling him and don't call back until he calls twice."

"Isn't that lying?" Annene asked. "It's a game."

"No."

"I think it's lying because you're playing games," Annene insisted.

"I know. That's what I thought too long before I had the capacity to think for myself," Estelle said. "You have to know what you want."

Annene focused on driving. She passed the

millionaire's house on the highway, quieted by the drone of the engine and her position behind the steering wheel.

"I don't think that would work for me," Annene said. "Judy was surprised that I had a date in the first place. It seems so complicated. Claire, on the other hand. Claire could do that."

"No, I couldn't," Claire argued, and pulled herself up to the seat less urgently than Annene, her wide eyes reflecting in the rearview mirror appeared to be on the verge of explosion if she kept her mouth shut too long. She opened and closed her mouth as though she was going to speak then didn't.

"I mean, it's just that the four of us thought it would be fun to go together to the dance. Jeff and I are friends, anyway. I think that's the best way, to be friends."

Claire kept her eyes fixed on the road ahead and to the side as it curved along the hillsides of the expertly cut front lawns and a series of houses that Bernie referred to as "McMansions."

"Your Grandpa Frank and I were friends even when things first began," Bernie said, her words trailed off as she stared out the window at the scenery that passed. Southern mansions and perfectly trimmed lawns blurred into a trail of color as though a rainbow tried to catch up with falling drops from the sky. She stared out the window for a few moments before Claire spoke.

"I think Mom would like my dress. I think she would like the scarf that tied around the neck."

Bernie looked into the rear view mirror at Claire still focused out the window. Bernie had to keep her thoughts to herself because, while she claimed not to hate Maggie, and tried not to show it, Claire and her grandmother had that common ground: their mutual incapacity to connect with Maggie Hinkley. It made Bernice angry and pained to watch Claire drown in that as every day all of them tried to save Claire from wasting away in the emptiness that gave her strength.

Bernie shook off the thought as she tried to recall the pleasant images of her life, blurred in the periphery of those strong emotions. Images from her history sped through her mind in flashes without order or a single pause as they drove along the highway until they came to the yellow, diamond-shaped caution road signs that warned of the curvy road ahead.

Annene tapped the brakes, expertly. "I think," she began before Bernice interrupted.

"I think she would too. What's most important is that *you* like it. *You* have to wear it."

"Yeah, at least Grandma Bernie didn't force it on you," Annene said.

"You love that dress. What?" Estelle said, too loud and coughed then cleared her throat before she continued. "You don't like the dress I saved just for you? You've talked about that dress since you were a little girl. At least that's what you told me. You said you couldn't wait until you were a senior to wear it to prom," Estelle said.

"I thought I was wearing it to prom, not the winter dance."

"You don't have to wear it," Claire said.

"I know," Annene replied.

"Then don't. Your grandma saved it for you," Claire said.

"Dear Lord, no. Estelle saved it because she never thought she was suited for it," Bernie said. "She loved it but it looked awful on her."

"She's right," Estelle said.

"And, it suits me?" Annene asked, miffed. "It clashes with my hair."

"Yes. You look great in it. It's vintage. You like that style and you're giving it a personal touch with your fantastic fashion sense and skills."

"No, I don't. I don't like it," Annene said.

"Then wear something else," Claire said.

"No."

"Why?"

"Because I'm afraid I won't have another chance to wear it. It's not like I've had a lot of dates, you know. Jeff's Neil's friend, anyway. Neil probably bribed him to go out with me."

"Oh, come on now, honey. You're young," Estelle said.

"What does that have to do with it?" Annene said, her eyes shifting to the reflection of her grandmother.

"If I could remove anything from my youth, I'd take out the insecurity." Bernice said.

Estelle interrupted. "Your eyebrows just grew back in, Annene. Things will change."

"They will? I don't really know if I want them to change."

"Of course they will, honey. Nothing ever stays the same," Estelle replied. She cleared her throat and sat up straight then looked quickly at the rearview mirror where she watched Annene trace her eyebrows with her index finger, one hand on the wheel. Estelle pointed ahead toward the windshield then reached forward from the rear passenger seat and placed her hand on Annene's back. She patted gently.

Annene looked ahead. Estelle made it all alright.

THREE | Measures

Annene stood in the kitchen behind Bernie and watched her stir a mixture of sodium hydroxide solution into a pot of melted fat. The mixture was thick and a white coating stuck to the wooden spoon.

"These things take time," Bernie said, transfixed.

"So, you put the lye in that goop?"

"Yes."

"It's fat, right? Lipids or something?"

"Fat. This one is fat but we'll make glycerin soap later. We use vegetable oil for that."

"Glycerin soap is that funky clear stuff," Annene said, pointing into the pot with the cracked black handles.

"It looks like amber," Claire said. The friends stood next to each other.

"It looks like a complexion soap I used a long time ago," Bernie said.

"Yeah, but it's body soap. It's non-toxic. We can make it different colors and I have some oils to scent it."

"How long have you been doing this?" Annene asked.

"Not that long," Bernie said.

"*Why* did you start doing this?" Annene said. She rolled her eyes and shook her head.

44

"She got bored of stitching. Us old bags are boring," Estelle said from the living room sofa, her voice barely audible as it wavered while she tried to stifle a cough - to hold it between the base of her neck and the empty scars of her tonsils would make it impossible to breath. It squeezed itself between the trachea and pharynx.

"Oh, come on, Grandma. It's not that you're boring. It's that a person can only have so many knitted products." Annene argued. She splayed her hands on the kitchen table covered with crocheted and knitted placemats and a runner all in the same color sage green.

"Estelle just doesn't like it because you have to keep your mouth shut to do it," Bernie said.

"Yours is open. How can you say that?" Estelle continued knitting and pearling with small needles held close to her face. She kept the movement small and precise. Despite her large knuckles she worked evenly and without haste.

"Never mind. Keep looping," Bernie replied. "Annene, this is called soponification, when the acid, the lye, and the base mix with one another and react."

"How do you know so much about this?" Estelle asked, looking up from her fast moving hands to find Claire reading from a paperback book kept open by the weight of the oversized pages.

"It's in my recipe book," Bernie replied. "She's reading it."

Claire pointed to the typed words in the book, and looked at Bernie. "It says that the fat is an acid." She shrugged.

"I don't understand how all that fat can clean your pores," Estelle said. She'd trudged over to the pot and looked inside. She held in her right hand the set of Susan Bates number four knitting needles and ball of yarn in the other hand. The corner of her mouth was turned up in a Lucille Ball cringe.

"It stinks," she added.

"It says here that soap molecules have heads that attract water and tails that repel it. It is sort of like a magnet."

"It sounds like a sex ed class," Annene said.

"Annene," Estelle, corrected her.

"What?" Annene said, mock defensive. "Little heads and little tails sound either like pollywogs or sperm."

"How do you know about that?"

"Grandma, I may not have any dates but we did learn about sex in school, you know?"

"You did?"

"Yeah."

"When?" Bernie asked, intrigued.

"In junior high school. They have you look at slides. Everyone got embarrassed and laughed. It was so weird," she said, and scrunched up her round face. "Did you have the same thing, Claire?"

"It was so embarrassing. I was mortified because this boy I liked was sitting right next to me during the whole thing. We never spoke after that."

"They would never have anything like that when I was young. It was thought improper. As a matter of fact, I would think that it was improper myself, now. We learned biology, but we were monitored very closely. My Aunt Ethel convinced me that anatomy was sinful."

"Oh, Bernie, stop being so goddamn old," Estelle teased, flopping her hands down in her lap. She had joined Claire at the kitchen table though the girl was not there in body. "Kids these days need to know about this stuff. Everyone just pretended to be so pure, but they weren't. When Bernie was a little girl, she said she would never wear a short skirt when all of the other girls were wearing the style."

"Then I started wearing those Lucile Ball house dresses that Diane von Furstenberg turned into the wrap dress, and Estelle wouldn't let me hear the end of it."

"Cool," Annene said.

"Grandma, that's not even very short."

Estelle corrected her. "It's short for Bernie. Bernice Hinkley wouldn't wear short dresses until she moved to the city and started working for that fashion magazine. Then she thought she was hot as..."

"Estelle, stop that now. I was just shy." She nudged Annene, nodding. "Your grandmother was one of the first flappers, you know."

"Hank didn't think you were shy. Hank thought you were a real hot number. I remember. He and your Grandma, Claire. Hank McGuinnes took her out on the town to all of the fancier restaurants and even..."

"Estelle, can we stop with this right now? You're going to disrupt my concentration."

"What kind of attention span do you need to make soap?" Annene asked.

"It's the same type of attention you have to pay to making gravy, Annene," Bernie said.

"Or lighting campfires," Claire mumbled. Her eyes scanned the magazine pages without looking up. She wondered if they remembered her being there in the room with all of them, saying nothing, while they talked about melting fat. Her own voice sounded odd. Out of place. Tweaked.

Bernie continued, " You have to keep adding the broth from the giblets and flour. With this you have to add the lye to the fat or oil or it doesn't mix properly."

"Grandma, lye is acid, by the way, so it burns if you're not careful," Claire said.

"Oh, come on. Is anyone in this house any fun anymore? I was just telling you that you were very reserved at one time and you came out of your shell."

Estelle watched as Claire looked up from *Vogue*. The cover model was Twiggy thin and sullen like most of the Paris runway models. Claire ran her hand down her thigh to her calf as she looked at the model on the cover then returned her attention to the article. It was coming off if she managed to control it. The hips developing would shrink and her small tummy would flatten and that little barely conceivable belly would disappear to become concave. The scale read a loss of five pounds and her jeans, the skinny pair, were loose and that feeling of dark, ugly fuzz in the pit of her stomach welled up in her. Just looking at the picture of the woman, she wished she was a sculpture that could be cut in half. Empty though her belly was, she continued scanning the pages and turned back the top right corner with her lithe fingers. Anger brewed at the ugly bulge inside her. Something and nothing were the same in the nourishment of her famine.

"I can't believe you worked at this place. You seem so different now," Claire said from the kitchen table where she sat with Estelle, who had moved from the adjoining living room to the breakfast room.

"What?" Estelle said. "My hearing must be going."

"Look who's getting old," Bernie said.

"Be nice. I want to hear about you and that Hank guy."

"Estelle, you tell the story."

"You sure? I don't want you to wind up poisoning yourself," she said, sarcastically. "I mean, you could really wind up getting hurt."

"Oh, Estelle, get a job," Bernie said. She rested the spoon on the side of the pot and her hand on her hip.

"Grandma, don't stop stirring. It'll get all lumpy."

"Oh, how do you know about soponification, Claire." Annene shook her head.

"This is the dorkiest thing I've ever done. It's weird," Annene said. "If you want soap go buy some."

Estelle shot her a look that locked onto Annene's eyes then fixed on the top of Claire's head bowed as she turned the magazine pages.

"Well, you said it's like gravy. And, you can't stop stirring gravy because it gets all lumpy, right?"

"You're a smart girl, Claire. It runs in the family," Bernie said.

Claire just looked at her blankly before she lowered her head and smiled faintly.

"I'm hungry. Are you hungry, Claire?" Annene asked.

"No, I'm fine."

"You girls can run and get something to eat. I'd make you something here but, frankly, I'm concerned that the food will be affected."

"What? By the smell?" Estelle asked. "It'll be fine." She did not look up from the row of knitting almost finished. Toward the end of one of these rows, she never looked up.

"Will you mind your own business?" Bernie reprimanded gently.

"No, there's some lunch meat in the refrigerator and you girls can make the sandwiches here on the breakfast table."

"How do you know there's lunch meat in the refrigerator? What are you doing snooping through my love letters and my refrigerator?"

"Oh come on Bernie, you always have lunch meat in the refrigerator. And, you also always leave your love letters out for people to read."

"Oh no, here we go again," Bernie said.

"What does that mean?" Annene asked. She moved from the opened refrigerator with the turkey wrapped in white paper, the bottle of Hellman's Mayonnaise and French's mustard in hand.

"Just tell the story, will you Estelle? Fine. Tell it. Tell it all. I don't care anymore."

Estelle smiled wide. Bernie looked at her and shook her head.

"Where's the bread?" Annene asked. She moved away from the table. Claire stopped reading and waited. She felt her hands seize the pages more tightly and her jaw clench.

Before Bernie could answer, Estelle replied, "In the oven," then set the needles down and started in for a story.

She cleared her throat. "Frank and Bernie were dating for about a year. He was an ad man and she was this hotshot layout designer for that exact magazine."

"I was not a hotshot. I shuffled around copy and photographs and got yelled at by hotshots. Come on. You're a gossip columnist for crying out loud," Bernie blurted to Estelle.

"Do you want me to tell the story or are you going to keep interrupting me?"

Bernie raised her hands in the air in surrender.

"Grandma, keep stirring," Claire said.

"You hungry, Claire?" Annene asked. She separated the bread and placed them in the toaster oven.

"No, not really," she said. "Grandma Estelle. Tell the story," she said. She changed the subject and flipped once again through the magazine.

"So, Bernie started dating this man, Hank McGuinness. He worked in Frank's firm and took Bernice to a company dinner one night."

"It was a party, Estelle."

"Okay, a party. A dinner party. And, Frank was there. Hank left a couple of weeks after that on an extended business trip and Frank showed up the night of a blackout to ask if she needed any help and then they never stopped talking. One thing led to the other and Frank proposed to Bernice. By the time Hank got back, they were engaged."

"I've heard that story before."

"Did you know that she was engaged to Hank at the time?"

"No," Annene replied, cynical.

"And," Estelle continued, "That she was pregnant with Ernest when Frank proposed to her. They had a shotgun wedding and Bernie had to cancel everything with Hank. They had an engagement party and that's why I bought the dress."

"That's why you never wore it? You never wore it because you thought it was bad luck so you gave it to me?"

Annene rolled her head around with her eyes, her mouth turned up. "Seriously?"

"It's not bad luck if it skips a generation, Annene. Don't worry, honey."

Annene twisted the bread bag so it hugged the crust tight and replaced the twist tie. She closed the toaster oven. "I'm so hungry. This thing toasts fast doesn't it?" she asked.

Claire smiled at Annene then told Estelle, "Her blood sugar drops and she gets cranky." She said it in a way that was half amused and half envious that Annene could feed her hungry self.

"I don't get cranky, Claire. At least I eat. I don't starve myself."

Claire's smile faded. She had nothing to say.

"I can't believe you gave me that dress to wear knowing that it was bad luck."

"Annene, the point is it wasn't bad luck," Bernie interjected. "The point is it was good luck because I've been happily married for the last forty-three years. The point is," she continued, "If you would listen for a minute and breathe... You'll get your sandwich in a minute. The point is, if I married Hank, my life would have been much different."

"Yeah, you would have had a cottage in the Swiss Alps, a house in the Hollywood Hills, a chateau in the South of France, a London flat, and an apartment on Park Avenue. You would have had an assistant to help your assistant and you would have never had any time for the likes of me," Estelle added, breathless and self-satisfied. "Claire, your grandmother would have had more money than God."

"Was this Hank guy loaded or what?" Annene asked. Claire watched her friend bite into the sandwich without caring about the consequences. She would occasionally comment about jeans getting tighter, but she never cared like Claire. Two slices of bread at two hundred calories and the rest from all of what Bernie called "good fat." She felt her body stiffen against it to resist.

"Loaded isn't the word. He took over that advertising company and made millions. Frank left the company when Hank got back from that business trip. Frank almost killed him."

"No way!" Annene said, dragging out the words. She wondered why her friend sat there with little to say about the conversation. Claire's face looked blank. The bell went off on the toaster oven and Annene quickly removed the slices that had gone slightly black. She tapped her fingers on the sides to test the heat, then picked it up quickly and dropped it on the counter.

"Grandpa almost killed someone?"

"Well, not really. They got in a fight and Frank left the company" Bernie replied. "Hank was Frank's boss."

"When I told him I was pregnant he really went nuts," Bernie said, intently stirring the mixture in the pot. She did not look up.

Annene started to scrape the burned face off the toast into the sink but rested the knife on the lip of the sink as she processed the information. She held several pieces of turkey in her hand and turned around, "You were pregnant?"

"Yeah, we had to get married. Frank insisted. I knew he was an honorable man then."

"You went from not wearing a short skirt to sleeping with your fiancé's employee?"

"Transformed, she was, Annene. The truth is out. God, I hate keeping secrets."

"Why are you telling me this?" Claire asked.

"I'm telling you this because I'm not a saint. Not by any means. No one is, honey."

Claire flipped through the magazine pages without looking at them, one after the other, the same pages from cover to cover. She turned them too quickly. She laid her hand flat on the pages. "Can we talk about this later, please? It's making me uncomfortable."

"Why?" Estelle asked. "Your grandmother thinks there shouldn't be any secrets."

"I was perfectly happy not knowing," Claire said.

"The only reason Grandma didn't tell you was that your mother disapproved. She didn't want you to know."

"Yeah, and she's gone now, so you can spill the beans?"

"No, honey. I just don't think it's healthy to hide things," Bernie said, as she stirred the pot. "I'm sorry. We don't have to talk about this anymore. I just wanted you to know."

"Thank you. I *don't* want to talk about it now. You could have at least told me privately," Claire said. She closed the magazine in her lap.

"I'm not going to tell anyone, Claire. I'm your best friend and I want to talk about it," Annene said. "How did you get married, pregnant? Wasn't that like a huge taboo back then? I mean, it's not so great now, but it used to be really bad."

Bernie stirred the mixture in the pot and took up another spoon designated to scrape off the thickening liquid soap from the larger of the two as though it were vanilla cake batter.

"How do you know if it's ready?" Claire asked.

"How can you ask such a question? Don't you want to know how your father was conceived, for crying out loud?" Annene said.

"Not really," Claire mumbled. Embarrassed, she lowered her head to read the magazine she reopened without looking, laid out in front of her on her lap. Pushing back the chair with her knees against the table, she got up from the table and went to the counter, her mouth turned down in obvious distaste. "Where are the carrots?"

"You're gonna turn into one of those really skinny girls, Claire. Me, I don't have to worry about a thing. I eat to keep my energy up..." Annene said.

"Grandma, are there any carrots? I just want a carrot," Claire asked.

"They're in the refrigerator. There's dip too, if you want it."

"Don't you taste it to test if it's ready or not" Estelle said to Bernie from the table. She quickly stitched back and forth to form the one row of deep purple yarn tied in slip knots to form the beginning of another scarf.

"Who the heck wears a scarf in Georgia, anyway?" Bernie asked Estelle.

"Do you two ever stop?" Claire asked.

"No, she's used to it," Bernie said, defeated. She rested the wooden spoon on the inside of the pot and let her hands fall to her sides.

"I'm in your life to make sure you cough up the truth, Bernie."

"But, about my husband and son. You just don't have any tact?" Bernie replied.

"You two are getting way too crabby. When we get old, Claire, do you think we'll get that mean?"

"They're just kidding though," Claire said. "Grammy's making that stuff because it has a greater value than just soap. She told me that she and Grandpa Frank had to save their soap chips and mush them together. They were too poor in the Depression to afford new soap." The subject had changed but not for long.

"Let alone anything else. We made everything. We made something out of everything." Bernie stirred the pot and did not look up.

"Are you serious?" Annene asked.

"It was bad there for a while. When we were growing up things were different. It was long before Ernest was born though. He got the good end of things. You didn't throw things out just because it was broken or there wasn't enough of it. You made it into something else." She shrugged. "We got pretty creative. Kids these days have so many luxuries. Many don't even know anything about it."

"I know when the Depression was, Grandma."

"So do I," Annene said, and bit into her sandwich. The words were audible through a mouthful of food. "I probably wouldn't have lasted very long. Judy says I'm a bit of a princess."

"You are a princess, Annene," Estelle said.

"Me? Oh, come on. A princess doesn't accidentally burn off her eyebrows trying to light a campfire. They don't go camping." She was talking with her hands and eating, and to Claire, it was fine for her friend to do that. When Claire did it she was a pig. A big, fat, ugly pig who could not stand a single crumb at the side of her mouth. Maggie hated that kind of mess. The kind of mess that patches up the small little cracks between teeth with a residual spackle that only kids who lived in a house with too many mirrors could find.

"Yes, they do," Bernie said, and laughed to herself. She added flakes of lye to the mixture. "Stand back a bit. It's sodium hydroxide and it's pretty poisonous. I don't want you to end up eating any of it."

"What?" Annene asked, her words muffled. She swallowed. "What does that mean?" Still stuck on the camping comment that Claire made, she reached with her index and middle finger and rubbed the curve of her eyebrow.

"It means you're better at shopping," Estelle said.

Insulted, Annene tried to respond but waited while she chewed through another bite.

"I'm gonna go," Claire said. She folded the pages of the magazine together and rolled it into a tube that she held in both hands, tight enough to bend the thick stacked slick pages.

"Where are you going?" Annene asked. She had finished half of the sandwich. "I'm almost done. I'll go with you."

She ran her tongue over her teeth and her skin rose with the movement that stopped when she swallowed and poured herself a cup of tap water. She drank it quickly in two or three gulps and set it on the counter.

Claire shifted her weight between her feet that under the slight weight of her body did little to suppress the urge to flee and fly from the discomfort of just being among that normal time with the actual people who loved her. She felt none of it.

"No, I have to get back home. Dad's going to be there soon and I told him I'd make him dinner. I have to see what we have."

"Why doesn't he just come over?" Bernie asked. She was doing all of this for Claire, part knowing and part not knowing.

"I think he wants to stay at home. He gets really tired lately." She looked at the floor as she said this.

"Some men just aren't good at being alone," Estelle said. "Ernest seems like that type of man."

"Ernest is very independent," Bernie said.

Claire flushed, "I just want to walk, Annene. I need the exercise anyway."

"No, you don't. You need to eat something. Why are you so antsy all of a sudden?" Annene asked.

"Why do you think?" Claire said, irritated that the subject came around and she ushered it through like she would as a bouncer who let someone underage into a bar. All of it was just too much to take.

"I know he's independent, but he was always home by six thirty for dinner, right? You always say how dependable he is and dependable men usually need someone to depend on them."

Annene shot her grandmother a look. Claire stood looking at the floor for a few moments before she announced, "I'll call you in a little bit okay?" She shifted back and forth on her feet.

"Okay, honey. Take your time," Bernie said. She looked over her shoulder for just a moment, long enough to catch sight of her granddaughter's frail wrists and tendons that bulged like wires. Her thin legs were lanky even though they were covered in denim. Bernie stared back into the pot too much to the center then held her head back from the pungent smell and fumes but continued stirring. "What are you going to make, honey?"

"I don't know. Whatever is there. Probably chicken and rice. He's on a diet, he says, so I'm trying to be respectful. It doesn't matter anyway because he winds up going to Baskin Robbins afterwards when he takes Hildy for a walk and eats a pint of ice cream in front of the TV."

"That sort of defeats the purpose. At least I eat healthy. Tapioca pudding is rice, right?"

Annene tried too hard to get the message through to her friend and she knew it. She was never subtle in the way she conveyed she cared about a person. You care means you do not shut up about it.

"Right," Estelle said. "She loves my tapioca. It's comfort food."

"Maybe you should make some of that for Ernest. I bet he'd like it."

"Maybe," Estelle said.

Claire put her hand on her grandmother's shoulder and, Bernie's back turned, kissed her on the cheek. "Bye Grammy. I'll see you later."

"Call me later."

"Okay, I will," Claire said and took a bite of the carrot in her hand.

Annene took another bite of the other half of the sandwich set on the counter and waved as Claire walked out the door. Using the back of her hand, she wiped her mouth.

"Use a napkin, Annene. Please. Your mother would have my head if she knew I put up with that."

"Who are you, Miss Manners now?" Bernie said from the stove.

She turned the dial with one hand and removed the pot with the other while the flame dimmed and clicked until it extinguished. Turning around, she faced Annene who wiped down the counters with a sponge, pushing crumbs into the sink. The tin molds laid out and gathered on the counter to the right of the sink were each shaped like the outline of an upside-down loaf of bread.

"Annene, can you help me by holding the molds in place while I pour this in?

"Isn't that hot?"

"Yes, put the gloves on, quickly though before it solidifies."

"Alright."

Annene stood over the molds and watched as Bernie poured the mixture into them, the fluid flowing in one perfect stream from the rim of the pot and over the rose petals and herbs that lined the bottoms.

"Aren't the petals going to wilt in there?"

Bernie said nothing, her thoughts siphoned by worry. Bernie felt like a failure every time Claire ran away from her affection. She would feel that failure and continue trying.

"No. They shouldn't. The book said they shouldn't. They're fresh flowers and the herbs are dried so they should be fine. The soap should hold them intact once it hardens. It's like wax. Candle wax keeps butterflies intact and flowers alive in candles for years. You've seen those, right?"

"You've seen them, Annene. You just prefer those other ones," Estelle clarified.

"What other ones?" Bernie asked.

"The ones on her altar," Estelle answered, her hands back to knitting, the tips of the metal needles clicking like waiting nails tap to polished glass.

"Never mind."

"It's nothing to be ashamed of, honey. All of the celebrities these days are Buddhists."

"You're a Buddhist?" Bernie asked, tilting back the pot once the first mold reached the top. Another moment and the mixture would have spilled over.

"Watch out Grandma Bernie, you almost ruined that one."

"I thought you were Jewish," Bernie added, still holding the pot.

"Bernice, if you don't pour the next one that stuff is going to harden and you're going to have a plate-sized bar of soap and a ruined pot."

"Oh, keep your opinion to yourself, will you? I didn't know this. I thought she was Jewish."

Beads of sweat formed on her brow but she could not let go.

"No, Judy is Jewish. We don't discuss my practice. It gets her edgy."

"You do seem much calmer lately. Estelle, isn't Annene much calmer?"

Estelle looked up from her knitting.

Annene interrupted, "Can you please pour that because Grandma's right, if you don't hurry it's going to harden. Bernie looked at Annene, focused on the molds and the perfect stream of liquid soap flowing from the pot. Bernie, tipped and timed it perfectly so that each mold was filled to the rim, quickly. She breathed hard and her arms quivered though the weight was lifted as the pot emptied.

"Not bad for the first go around."

She took a kitchen towel from the counter and patted her face starting at the hairline then her flushed cheeks. "We should see how it worked in just a couple of hours," Bernie said. "Now I have to clean up."

Annene took that as her summons to leave and briskly wiped the crumbs from her black long-sleeved shirt. She shook the potholders she did not use, then tucked them back into the drawers where Bernice found them. Estelle watched her granddaughter who cautiously maneuvered around Bernie who took a long breath before she grasped the handles of the pot again and lowered it into the sink.

Annene walked over to the sofa where Estelle sat and kissed her grandmother on the forehead.

"What? Are you walking too?" Estelle said, looking up. "If you wait a minute I can drive you."

Annene had already kissed Bernice on the cheek and, walking quickly with her back to the grandmothers, replied, "I want to see if I can catch up with Claire. I'll see you later. Thanks for lunch."

She waved and turned with a fast, detached smile.

The water gushed out of the faucet into the pot. Bernice put her fingers under the tap to test the temperature as she passed her fingers under the water then swung the faucet so that it flowed into the tureen. Steam rose from the sink and Bernie watched as the pressure from the water crashed down, easing back the mixture until the force of the water pushed away the substance that had the density of Elmer's Glue. She waited there and watched the fragments of her blurred reflection in the silver bottom. The pot filled halfway with milky water before she spoke.

"I think this Christmas will be nice. This time, it will be a good one. The past," she began then stopped herself and shook her head. "I completely botched that one," Bernie said. "I was trying to show her that nothing in life is perfect and instead I violated her trust and made her feel worse. Being a grandparent is no easier than being a parent."

"Claire is having a hard time. What kind of woman would leave her child like that? I don't understand how she could do that," Estelle said.

"I don't understand either, and I've tried to. But you can never understand a person. You can't unless you are that person. And, Maggie. I tried. I really tried. I just can't." She paused a moment. "I wish you wouldn't bring it all up with Claire around. It's just too hard on her. It's difficult enough as it is."

"You can't expect just to toss it aside, Bernie. That's not like you. You have to be..." Estelle argued. Again she dropped her busy hands into her lap, frustrated. "Isn't that why this all began in the first place? Everyone is so quiet. I can't be. It's not healthy and it's not my nature. Someone has to talk to her and her father can't possibly read that girl's mind."

"I do talk to her, Estelle. We talk every day," Bernie countered. "But, I can't replace her mother, and I feel awkward even trying."

"You don't need to do that, Bernice. She just needs something. No one's asking you to be a mother. She just needs someone to show her the right way to live. Look how thin she's gotten in the past few months. She's getting worse, not better."

"I know. I will." Bernie turned the faucet knob to shut off the water and stared at the pot. "I wonder if all of this guck will come off?"

Estelle lifted her hands again, continuing the needlework.

"It'll come off. It's soap, Bernice. It's fine. It'll come off and the pot will be cleaner than it's ever been. You like things clean, Bernie. It'll be fine." Estelle coughed then lit a cigarette, inhaled on it deeply then set it in the tray, the stream of smoke rising.

"When are you going to stop that?" Bernie asked.

Estelle ignored her but not the cough.

"You're right," Bernie said. "It'll come off."

She looked into the milky water and nodded her head. Suds gathered all around the pot and caught the overhead light and reflected like a mirror the impressions of objects around Bernie's kitchen. She poked at the suds and popped them one by one with the knife Annene had left in the sink.

"You're right," she repeated. "It'll come off."

FOUR | Glycerin

Ernest Hinkley fumbled for the house key in his pocket, muttered a few words to himself, and found it. He turned it in the lock which stuck two or three times before it made the full rotation. A ring sounded for the third time from inside, seemingly louder than the two prior. The answering machine would pick up after five rings so he rushed clean through the living room with half spirited urgency. Another day had ended and to reach the phone would not prove his meaning in that day. Still, it could always be Maggie. The thought turned in on itself then, and any gratitude for the end of the day instead found sadness.

Ernest placed the beaten briefcase on his office desk. He released a long sigh and pulled at his necktie then unbuttoned the topmost button of his white and blue striped oxford shirt. Both hands on the edge of the desk, he glanced at the lit red light of the voice message machine beside the phone to the left of the desk and turned on the accountant light with the green glass shade. He unhooked the latches on the worn brown leather-bound case and opened it to the papers layered inside divided with manila envelopes. He withdrew one envelope and slid out the sheets of paper, unfolded them slowly, then held onto one and placed the others on the table. His eyes fixed back and forth to the words of the letter until he reached the last line.

Ernest Hinkley aged quickly that year. He was a man in stark contrast to his youth. Photos alone seemed to testify to this as his study was decorated with them. Family portraits hung on the wall that traced back to his youth of light brown hair, an indelible smile and athlete's physique. Good straight posture. There on his desk, was an Ernest who stood at the center of his high school team. They were dressed in soiled white and red uniforms and fell out of photographic formation as they rolled over each other, arms raised and mouths open for celebratory howls. He could hear them through that image. Behind the chair where he sat was a framed degree, the words etched out his credentials as esquire and books stuffed in every space of the bookshelf to the right of the entrance just ahead of him reflected that. He could still hear Maggie's voice when she announced dinner from the kitchen. The only words he had left of her were in those papers served earlier that day.

Ernest looked to the portrait on the wall, professional and retouched and framed in the meticulously carved gilded but not gaudy wooden frame, a tasteful match to the very formal portrait of the Hinkleys. Claire was just two years younger in the portrait and just in the course of the past year had also transformed. She had become thinner and more defined through the cheekbones while Ernest appeared ten years older with his graying hair thinner. It had gone from an attractive salt and pepper to old gray. The grooves under his eyes had changed from shadows to charcoal smudges. His waistline grew, as the rest of him atrophied.

Maggie wore white the day they sat for the portrait and Claire chose periwinkle blue at her mother's strong suggestion. Ernest wore pin stripes though Maggie warned him not to wear a pattern in the photo, for fear it would look too busy and detract from the precise composition she was after. She was right, and each glance at the photo served as that reminder.

He moved mostly photos and some furniture and left the Atlanta house to renters, resolved to make a small profit on what remained of their monthly mortgage. Alpharetta, with all of its flaws; the women's Mafia gossip group and the dull case load Ernest could expect gave him a certain comfort in returning to his roots. They had not been gone long and assembled their modest house scaled to Ernest's needs. Maggie wished for more while Claire was content with simplicity. She would never ask for more. For Maggie it was never enough.

He wondered what it was with women.

When the papers arrived, Ernest was not surprised by the enclosed letter, written in his wife's hand, but was saddened by her failure to mention Claire.

"I don't think she likes me," Maggie once told him. "I feel odd. It's a very strange feeling thinking your daughter doesn't like you. It's the worst kind of rejection."

"How can you say that? Claire loves you, Maggie."

"I don't know," she said, then corrected herself. "I do know. Remember the time I took her to the ladies' bridal shower? I remember it. I dressed her up in this beautiful pink dress with ruffled underwear. You know, those diaper covers toddlers wear? I did that and the second I walked into that room at the club, she started screaming. I mean, I've never heard anything like it. She was awful. I had to turn around and leave. She didn't calm down until I got her back to her room in our first house and turned on the mobile above her crib. It always calmed her down."

"That has nothing to do with you, Maggie. She was afraid of people. She wasn't used to seeing all of those women. If that happened to me," he began. "If I had to do that I'd probably respond the same way," Ernest laughed and he knew that his estranged wife hated him for it.

Ernest's humor, the small jokes that once made her forget her troubles could not wash it away. It made an impression so lasting, that look of concern over failure and loss and hanging on that her husband was afraid to look her in the eye. Maggie's mind was never quiet with the satisfaction of motherhood other women felt and enjoyed in peace. So, she left Claire alone most of the time.

"It's strange, Ernest. It's strange how you can place so much on a dream and then when you arrive, it's not exactly the way you imagine. You know? Like, I thought, when Claire was born. I thought that things would be so different. We would love the same things and do the same things and we would instantly understand each other. But, I don't understand her, how she stays in that small quiet world of hers and she does not lose her mind with all of that silence."

"Maggie, she's a child," Ernest objected. "Just a child with an imagination."

"No. It's not that she's a child. Some things you can't change. You can't change this. You just can't change."

Ernest remembered her every move.

Maggie kept her back to him then walked to the door that lead out of the living room to the base of the stairs. He had watched as she ascended the stairs to the bedroom, her shoulders slumped and the motion so slow he felt her defeat and failure because it was also his own.

Claire's face appeared behind the once closed door to her playroom, a room she outgrew years before but she still used as a reading room. Ernest invited her to sit.

She heard everything.

"Your mother, Claire. She loves you. You know that?

His voice was gentle but unconvincing, covered with layers of guilt that were not his own but in his possession.

His collateral damage.

Claire nodded her head. "Yeah. She wants me to be like her. Was she always like this?"

Her eyes were so wide with the bare need for the truth that he had no recourse to give her the child-buffered version of anything.

"No. She was different but people grow and when people grow they change."

"I don't want to grow," Claire had said.

"Too late for that. You're pretty tall for your age but if you don't you'll be a short young lady."

"Doesn't matter."

"What doesn't matter?"

"Doesn't matter. I want to always be the same even if Mom…" She stopped herself.

Claire cleared her throat, and shook her head to clear her eyes.

"Does she really think I don't like her?"

She rubbed her arms, then.

"I think your Mom just wishes she had more to talk to you about, Claire. That's all. You're perfect just the way you are."

Ernest sat in the chair, the book opened on his lap. His glasses hung from the collar of his shirt, unbuttoned twice with one hand. He still wore his work clothes after dinner, sleeves rolled to his elbows the way Maggie once liked for its endurance through long hours of work and late dinners or none. Sleeves revealed much about a man and his wife so Maggie would not allow short-sleeved, button-down shirts because that made him appear lazy.

Claire wore her white flannel nightgown with the flowers and eyelet collar and cuffs. Thick, white oversized socks covered her feet and were rolled down to the ankle. Her hair was pulled up in a hair band with two green balls intertwined, holding it together. Lying down on the sofa, she pulled one of the two stacked pillows out from under her head like she would sleep there.

"I just don't like the same things she does. I don't know why. I try to like those things she wants me to like but I can't. It feels weird."

Ernest put his glasses back onto his face and lowered his eyes to his book.

"Your mom just isn't herself these days. I think she's under pressure from her clients."

Ernest lifted his eyes up over the rims that rested low on his nose to look for a response.

Claire's breathing slowed, and as it did, her father watched the girl drift out of consciousness with the ease of a cloud that slipped across the sky.

It amazed him how quickly she could fall asleep.

Ernest had not heard from Maggie in one year and in one year his first contact with his wife was through divorce papers accompanied only by a letter written in large and loopy yet perfectly formed script.

Everything had been status quo. Nothing out of the ordinary. No shifts in mood. Only the similar detachment of cool Maggie just before she disappeared.

Each night he spent wondering whether the woman would write, or whether she would phone, or reappear, or be found dead. Maggie left the questions unanswered. Despite twenty years of marriage Ernest could not attest to knowing his wife. Maggie, in her cool repose mixed with Southern charm, left a dark channel of mystery between them. Ernest made it his work to uncover truth but he could never find hers. Never in a million years. It was the thing that drew him to her and what repelled her in the end.

Posted from Hollywood, California, the envelope was forwarded from the Hinkley's Atlanta address. His arm extended to get a clear view of the address label, Ernest examined the envelope then took out the case for his reading glasses from the briefcase. He eased the pliant, metal arms over his ears with one hand, one at a time, then leaned into the leather cushion and read the letter again from the beginning:

Dear Ernest,

I am so sorry to have to contact you this way but the past year I think I have found another way of life that feels right. I don't know exactly how to say this, but I think it's better for the both of us that we stay apart. I don't see any other solution. I know you deserve a good wife and Claire deserves a good mother. I spent years trying to be all of those things to you, and never felt any good at them.

I hope you know it has nothing to do with you, Ernest. You were my husband for twenty years and those years I tried so hard to do what was right. I need to do what is right for me. I'm in therapy and have set up business in California. I'm seeing a man - a Hollywood producer who I met at an audition. It's so strange the way things happen...

I'll leave it to you, how you would like to divide our things. You have always been fair.

Ernest set the letter on his desk and held his head in his hands. There he remained quiet for a long, very silent and very still moment, his breath slow and calm until it suddenly doubled up and jolted into immediate weeping. He tore the glasses from his face onto the floor to give the tears room to fall. He banged his fist on the letter smeared by his pain and self-pity and anger.

Only a few minutes passed before he pulled a handkerchief from his pocket and wiped his eyes and face then clenched it tight around his nose. The news was too new for much more sadness.

Maggie was happy. Maggie was fulfilled. Maggie had gotten what she wanted, and the woman that Ernest had built his life around was gone.

Claire yelled from the entrance, "Dad, I'm home," before she opened the door to his office. She knew better than to enter unannounced. He spent his nights in that room with the door closed since her mother left and she knew he needed to avoid her at times no matter how much it hurt her.

Ernest lifted his head and wiped his eyes, then ran his arm over the few drops on the wood surface rather than use the handkerchief. Quickly, he removed a file from the briefcase that he quickly shut and pushed aside then shielded his face with his arm that propped his head up over the materials he pretended to read. They covered the papers from Maggie. He always faked working. It was easier those nights that sadness was too much to face Claire. He needed to be strong for her. Crumbling was not an option. Life had already gone to pieces for his only daughter.

Claire knocked on the door. "I'm going to make dinner now. Anything you want?"

Clearing his throat he replied, "No, whatever you want to make is fine with me." Ernest's eyes were a shade pink from the tears and blocked with his hand so he could feign its use to focus.

When Claire left the room, he uncovered the folded papers, slid them back into the envelope and placed them inside the briefcase. He fastened it shut.

Claire walked into the kitchen and opened the pantry closet door to the shelves lined with Campbell's soup varieties, S&W canned corn, pasta wrapped in plastic, Uncle Ben's rice, Ritz crackers, and Cheerios. They were shelved separately according to category. Claire spent hours after the move, arranging them just as her mother had trained her to do. It was almost as if she was training her to take over the business of running a home. Like she knew she would leave. She had to have everything just so. The counters wiped clean after the dishes were washed immediately after dinner. A pantry of food categories. These habits stayed in place because Maggie had trained Claire. So, in this way it was as though she was entirely gone, and while both hated that about her, it was still present without any words to claim it.

Dinner was the most conspicuous. Claire and her father sat around the table in the same arrangement every night with that one empty chair. One hallow space in the configuration. Ernest insisted that the new house resemble the old Alpharetta home as much as possible, scaled down as it was.

Dinner would be ready at six thirty. Always.

It was five thirty. Claire walked out of the pantry to the vacuum-packed refrigerator and pulled hard on the door, which stuck to guarantee peak refrigeration. It took at least two hard tugs to get it open. She scanned the inside. She'd lied about the market to Bernice and had no intention of going since she already shopped the day before. She would make her father's favorite, chicken Parmesan with just enough bitter cheese to taste. He was on a diet to lower high cholesterol readings. She removed the package from the refrigerator and took out broccoli, parsley and onion from the vegetable bin then closed the door shut. Placing the contents on the kitchen counter, she turned once again to the pantry and took down the olive oil, garlic salt and box of Uncle Ben's rice. Under the sink she pushed open the swivel cabinet and removed the red pot and the Pyrex dish for baking then removed one lemon from the antique scale on the island in the center of the kitchen. The brass scale was dated from the 1800's and one of the many from Ernest's modest collection started by Maggie upon his graduation from law school. Fruit filled the hammered brass bin on one side and bread on the other. They could only get it to balance if they tried.

She went through the dinner preparations and washed the chicken, doused it with oil, chopped parsley, garlic salt, and parmesan, then garnished it with thin sliced lemon. The water boiled in the red pot and she dumped in one measuring cup full of rice.

While it cooked she finished her homework at the

kitchen table.

It was six thirty when Claire yelled, "Dinner," to her
father who had made his way into the living room easy
chair and sat under the brass floor lamp with the thatched
cover that lit the boiler plate contract he'd strained to read.
Ernest put it down, removed his glasses and placed them
at the side antique table. He rarely brought work home
from the office and preferred to use his time to work than
read the paper. It was his reassurance to Claire, to show
her that he could pass the time doing something normal
and calm. His proof that he could still keep a roof over
her head. No story but his own resonated in his mind
anymore. He hated himself for the pity of it. He loathed
the emotion, the internal truncation that blocked the real
and simple things, the activities he once enjoyed but was
too rigid to withstand as he held all of it together from the
outside. When he left the house, he felt the voices of
those who pretended to know him through the story that
his wife had left her own daughter. There was no other
story. That was the only story. It was the story of Maggie
and the sad life she left.

Placing his hands on his knees, he rubbed his thigh
back and forth, ironed out the creases in his slacks with his
hands over the loosened pressed pleat once down the
middle, and raised himself from the chair to shuffle slowly
into the kitchen. Claire was already at the table, picking
through a small green iceberg lettuce salad she had made
for herself.

"That chair just sucks me in. I don't think I got a lick
of work done. Good thing I have you to cook for me."

"Yeah, otherwise you'd be eating ice cream for dinner,"
Claire said.

He looked at the salad bowl in front of her. "Aren't
you going to have any of this, honey? It looks good."

He pointed to the dish set on the placemat at his seat to
the right of his daughter and her slight, sloped shoulders.

"No, I'm not very hungry. I ate earlier. You eat."

She offered a conciliatory smile.

"You're getting really thin, Claire. You have to eat."

"I *am* eating, see," she said, and lifted a bite of the salad, iceberg lettuce, beefsteak tomato, pealed and chopped carrot, to her mouth and chewed heartily. "You know I can't eat a lot, anyway. First everyone tells me how chubby I am, then I get thin and you talk about how skinny I am."

"That's not what I mean. I never told you, you were chubby. It was just baby fat. Your mother…"

"I know," Claire interrupted. "My stomach is bothering me. I'll eat later if I feel better. Okay?"

"Okay," he said, and cut into the chicken breast on his plate. It oozed bubbles of fat from the olive oil and parmesan and Claire tried her best not to wince but still turned her upper lip up.

He released a long sigh, speared the piece of what looked to Claire like compacted tendons, put it into his mouth and chewed, his eyebrows slanted. At the edge of his seat, he began to speak to her in a tone that told her it would be a long talk. Long for Ernest, her father, who was short on small talk.

"Now, I don't know how to tell you this but, I got a letter in the mail today. I'm only telling you because it's the right thing to do and not the thing that's going to make anyone feel good."

Ernest shoveled a fork full of rice into his mouth, chewed and nodded his approval then cleared his throat and continued. Juice from the chicken both masked the metal taste in his mouth and made it worse.

"It was a letter from your mother. She served divorce papers with it. Do you know what that means?"

Claire dropped her hand to the table so the fork clinked against the plate when it made contact. He spoke to her like she was a little girl. It was slow and gentle, but the slow and gentle of it made her angry.

"Where is she?"

"She said she wanted to find a place that was comfortable for her."

Claire swallowed the lettuce. Involuntarily, she extended her arm with her palm open.

"Where is she? I... I need to see the letter," Claire said, and shifted in her seat. Claire's eyebrows lowered as she concentrated on her father's words like to do so would pull the periphery around her tight so she could hold onto them and subdue what imploded and burst inside her.

Her father spoke words intended to soothe her, but she could not draw forth the details of that emotion. Words fell away as she clung to this first information, her mind speeding with questions. To realize her mother was not dead both excited and maimed her and she felt her back hunch forward as the cavity around her heart caved in on itself, exposed all hidden hurt though anyone who knew her understood that shield. It was not anger or confusion anymore. It was all Maggie.

All Maggie.

All Maggie.

No Claire. No reason for Maggie to stay. Barely a mention, she was sure, without reading the letter herself she got this much. But she had to read it.

Her eyes remained fixed on the kitchen table and she mirrored her father's composure. Shut herself off again. Clamped down.

"Aren't you going to eat your dinner?" she asked, and held the fork tighter. "It's going to get cold. Then you won't want to eat it."

"I can heat it up, Claire. I want to talk to you about this now. I know how hard this all has been for you. It's a difficult time and you can't expect to deal with it by just shutting it off. You haven't talked about it and I'm worried about you." He let out a long sigh. "Grandma's worried and we need to talk this through."

Claire ignored him. "Dad, I don't want to put it in the microwave. Just eat it, alright?"

Ernest looked for a long while into his daughter's eyes, a brown so dark it concealed her pupils. Or buried them.

Lowering his gaze he speared the piece of chicken and put it in his mouth. Claire pierced the lettuce again with her fork. She watched her father, satisfied.

"Can I see the letter?" Claire asked.

"Claire, all she told me was that she moved to California and is involved with a Hollywood producer and is living the life she always wanted. She's happy."

"Oh, she's happy and we're here in Alpharetta waiting for her to let us know if she's even alive. She's happy?"

"Claire, I don't know what to say. I'm as angry as you are."

He took a long breath and placed the fork and knife beside the plate and slid to rest his back on the support of the chair. Two fingers, his thumb and middle finger of his left hand, he rubbed his temples, his hand shielding his eyes that closed tight.

"Angry? Dad, I'm not angry. You know, I always tried to be that perfect little girl for her, going to tea and eating little biscuits at all of those functions for her business and she'd just stare at me with that blank expression like I was some sort of alien."

"Claire, your mom loves you..." Ernest began before Claire interrupted.

"Dad, she didn't love me. Do you know what she told me when I sang for her? I decided, I'm going to let Mom see something I think is so important, and you know what she did? She told me to get into the kitchen and make dinner and not waste my time. 'Do something productive,' she said."

"She just had a difficult time understanding you, Claire," his eyes opened. "Your mother. She had a hard time understanding me and I was married to her for twenty years. She never belonged in all this," he said, and gestured with open arms to their home shaking his head. "It's not your fault."

"Oh, I know it's not my fault. It's not my fault she is such a coward she can't even stick around. What was so wrong with this place?"

"Your mom always had big aspirations, Claire."

"Oh, so this wasn't good enough? You're telling me that she had to go to Hollywood to fulfill her dreams? It sounds like a bad movie. Made for TV movie."

Claire paused and put down her fork. Let go of it.

"Did she say anything about me in the letter? "

"She didn't address you, no," Ernest replied. Head lowered, he almost whispered.

"And, it's not my fault?" she asked, defiant.

"No, it's not your fault, honey."

Claire pushed the kitchen chair back with her knees and got up from the table. She took her plate to the sink then turned around and faced her father.

"It just seems that no matter how much I want her to accept me, she'll always try to stuff me in a pink fluffy dress and Mary Janes one size too big and will have to leave the ladies' luncheon because I started scream. She can't even stand the sound of my voice."

Claire shook her head and jut out her lower jaw.

"It's not you, Claire."

"I know. What, did she say she wasn't any good at being a mother? At least she's right about something," Claire said, and took in a long breath, her hand on her hip.

"She is your mother, Claire. Our problems, your mom's and mine, had nothing to do with you."

The phone rang from Claire's bedroom. "I have to get that."

"We need to talk more. It's the middle of dinner," Ernest said. His words reached for her but clenched only at the space between them.

"I'm done," Claire said, her hands set on the table and arms shaking just long enough for each of them to notice when their eyes attached for barely a second until she turned her back and walked into her bedroom with its pink walls and eyelet comforter, its whitewashed furniture and mirrored closet doors.

Claire snatched up the phone.

"Hey, can you come over? I have to get out of here."

She stifled a noxious bout of tears with a deep breath.

"How did you know it was me?" Annene asked, flat.

"You're the only person who calls me except Neil and he's out with Jeff."

"Are you okay?" Annene asked, though she knew the answer. Claire rarely asked for Annene. Annene moreso pushed herself on her friend.

Claire ignored her and sat on the pretty, flowered bedspread. "When can you be here?"

"In a half hour. I have to finish up dinner. I was going to come by but it was too late. I left right after you did and walked home. I'm never doing that again."

"Annene, I'm talking to my dad. Can we talk when you get here?"

"Sure. Are you okay?"

"Yeah, I'm fine. I'll tell you when you get here."

Curiosity would get Annene there faster. Concern too and Claire did not mind being vague though it made her feel wrongly manipulative. Claire sat down cross-legged on the queen sized bed and looked at herself in the mirror. What looked back was weird. They'd been waiting all of that time for the queen to arrive. They'd kept the house clean, silver polished, fridge stocked, pantry organized by cans and boxes and soup and cereal, only to find the queen herself had moved on and made another life.

Nothing moved from its spot, really, in Alpharetta, Georgia. Nothing moved or changed. Clothes still hung in Maggie's closet and Claire resisted the urge to walk in there just to be close to her as she had done countless times over the past year. Just to be close to her, she touched the silk dresses where they hung. Just to be close to her. That warm soapy scent that mothers have. It was her only comfort, being there. Even that photo of them together left her with a feeling of detachment. Of something false and gone. It was the scent.

Alone in her room with the door closed Claire muffled her sobbing into the white, cotton covered pillow. There was some room and space to cry just briefly.

Her father always knew when to leave her alone.

FIVE | Lye

The doorbell rang a half hour later and Claire raised her head when the knock came to her bedroom door.

"Claire," her father said in a tone too loud to be hushed. "Claire? Annene's here."

"Okay," Claire replied, rubbed her eyes that resisted as she tried to open them, her sight too narrow to squeeze through a tight space. The lids were puffy and sight, narrow. "Just a minute."

She raised her head off the pillow and propped herself up with arms so thin that they appeared longer than they were in proportion to her slight frame. After a moment or two, she pushed herself up from the bed and peeled away the down comforter. She'd slept for less than fifteen minutes. It felt like hours. Her mind was still in the groggy space of half sleep and her eyes were pink and swollen. Mascara smeared to gray underneath the lower lid of her left, sleeping side.

"Dad, tell her I'll be just a few, okay? I have to wash my face."

Pulling her hair back she tied it with a rubber band and shuffled into the bathroom, turned on the faucet and ran her hand under the water. She took a long look into the mirror, cupped her hands under the faucet and let it pool there before she splashed it on her face. She unscrewed the top of the Noxema jar and smeared it from her forehead to her cheeks then over her eyes and chin. Her eyes closed, she wet a washcloth and swept the gray foam from her face. She patted it dry with a small rose- colored towel.

Another knock came from the closed, white door, the bathroom this time.

"Hey, you ready?" Annene's voice was louder than her father's. "The car's running. Can I come in?" she asked, but did not wait for a response.

Claire turned around and removed the rubber band. She let her hair fall to her shoulders.

"Let's go," Annene said.

Claire averted her eyes and picked up a wide hairbrush that she pulled through her hair so it laid straight all around.

It was obvious to Annene that she was crying.

"You barely move when you sleep. I don't see how you end up with that kind of bedhead," Annene joked.

A corner of Claire's mouth turned up in a half smile. She blinked hard a few times.

She often appeared so peaceful to her friend. Annene said that the stem of a lily could slip between her fingers and the petals would be undisturbed in the morning.

"The bed head looked better," Annene joked. "You okay?"

"I'll tell you about it when we get in the car."

Claire picked up her purse on the bedroom vanity and walked into the living room. Annene followed her. Claire leaned over her father who sat in the wing chair under the brass floor lamp. A book was open in his lap, but Claire knew the page number from at least the day before or the one before that.

"I'll see you in a bit, Dad," she said, and kissed him on top of his head.

He looked up through the glasses. "Okay."

"I'll be home early."

"Be safe, okay," he replied.

"With me? Of course," Annene said, and shrugged her shoulders. "See you later, Mr. Hinkley."

Outside, Claire slammed the passenger side door and Annene shifted the car into drive. "I wish Judy had a stick," she said. "Neil taught me how to drive a stick and this thing bugs me. I wonder if Judy'll buy me a car."

"Doubt it. You're a girl and she won't do it." There was probably a better chance when your dad was alive.

Annene shook her head. Shook off the comment, mean though it was. "Neil is such a capitalist. He is so odd."

"He's not that odd. He invited me to the dance."

"Yeah, well. You don't have to live with him. You also don't have to share a bathroom with him. He smells, like all the time. The bathroom stinks. His bedroom stinks."

Claire laughed. "So does yours, Annene."

"No it doesn't."

"Yes it does. You just burn incense so the smell goes away."

"Boys are just dirty. He's a slob and Judy expects me to clean up his messes. It makes me mad." Annene pulled away from the curb. "It pisses me off. You. You're just throwing the mean comments my way today, aren't you?"

Claire ignored her and stared out the window to the ranch style homes with their thatched, tar roofs. Their pristine square front lawns and boxwoods at the base of those brick facades and siding.

"My dad got a letter from my mom today," she said, finally.

"What?" Annene said, looking back and forth from the road ahead to Claire.

"He got a letter," Claire repeated, flat.

"And?"

"She's alive," Claire offered, without emotion again,

despite herself and the feelings that ripped inside her.

"What a miracle that is. Figured that one out for myself. Where is she?"

"She's in Los Angeles with some Hollywood producer. Dad said she's happy. That's what the letter says."

"I'm sorry, Claire. I know how hard it is for you. That just sucks." The response sounded rehearsed even to her own ear.

"We just don't get each other. I can't believe she just fucking left. She just left!" Claire said, as her eyes welled up with tears. She blinked hard and cleared her throat.

"Yeah, Claire. But, she's not right doing what she did. You can't just leave your kid. Mothers don't do that."

Claire turned to Annene, "Maggie does. Maggie does whatever she wants. Maggie dyes her hair. Maggie was a homecoming princess. Maggie is a real estate agent. Maggie gets her house the way she wants her house. Claire wants to be with her dumbass boyfriend. He's the one she always talked about. He was the one who got so drunk and stoned before the homecoming dance that he couldn't even drive her home," Claire said.

Her voice was so saccharine, chipper and laced with surliness, that it distracted Annene. Claire never hated anyone. Never spoke about anyone the way she did about Maggie. She was a different person when she talked about her. Not even close.

Annene overshot the turn in the road and veered for a moment into the oncoming traffic lane.

"Jesus, Annene," Claire said, and gripped the passenger side seat of the AMC Pacer Judy would drive to work later but that Annene had for the meantime.

"What? I'm sorry." Annene held the steering wheel tight.

"Can I turn on the radio?" Claire asked. She reached for the volume dial.

"No, talk to me, Claire."

"I did. There's not much else to say. Can we just go?"

She turned the music up to Bruce Hornsby, "Mandolin Rain," as the solid and heavy piano notes carried the lyrics, "listen to my heart break, every time she runs away."

Annene turned it down.

"So that's it," Annene said, frustrated, focused on the road ahead, familiar and predictable. It was the same highway they had driven just days before when Mrs. Clement chewed them out in front of Dillard's. Cars shot past more frequently as theirs approached the intersection ahead.

"I like this song," Claire said, and turned the volume dial to the right. The speakers blared a Pat Benatar track, "Hit Me With Your Best Shot." Claire mouthed the words then sang at full volume.

"Fine," Annene screamed over Claire. This would always be the dynamic. Annene overwhelmed everyone with her intensity, and when compared to other girls her age, she could not seem to damp it down with cosmetics and weight loss. She could not ignore Claire's pain and would not let it go.

She spoke over her friend's off key voice. "You think *I'm* a freak. You're a freak, Claire." Annene turned the volume down. "You're in my car."

"It's not your car. It's Judy's car."

"Fine. Judy's car. Just turn it down. My grandma said Grandpa Berry is almost deaf from loud noises."

"I know, from the war. This is music though not gun fire." Claire said.

"What did your dad say?" Annene persisted.

Claire sighed in and out a breath deep for her. "The letter came today. It said where she was, that she didn't consider herself a good mother. I think he said that. Yeah. Then he said something about her being sorry she hadn't written before but she's in California. That's it."

Annene veered to the left again. "Did she say she wants to see you?"

"No," Claire said.

Claire started to cry without movement or drama. Just tears that rolled down her face like lonely drops of rain that joined each other there in streaks on her face to her chin.

"You have to talk about it, Claire. I know I'm always in your face but you have to. You can't just pretend everything's perfect. I just can't believe that. It's not you though," she said.

"My dad said the same thing."

"Hey, maybe she's a drug addict?" Annene said. "Oh, no. Porn. That's what it is. Maybe she totally went off the deep end and became a drug-addicted porn star. Now she's living with her porn star producer husband in porny Hollywood."

Claire forced air through her nose and laughed abruptly. It was an exhausted laugh. She wiped the snot and tears away again with the back of her hand.

"It's like a bad made-for-TV movie," Claire said. She cleared her throat and sniffled.

"Coming to Lifetime Television, a story of one woman's triumph over her southern upbringing and stale life as a suburban housewife who becomes the porn actress wife of a Hollywood porn producer."

"That's funny. How do you know so much about porn?" Claire asked. She was manic but calm and threw her hands out in front of her, disgusted at herself for the wet tears and mucous that covered them.

One hand on the steering wheel, Annene reached into the cluttered back seat of the Pacer for a box of Kleenex and handed it to Claire.

"I found my father's collection of porn before he and Judy got a divorce. Before he moved out. I think Neil still has some if it. It's a fairly disgusting thing to find if you're someone's daughter or sister. More than disgusting."

"Gross," Claire said. She cringed.

They shared a quiet moment of shared revulsion before Annene spoke.

"Hey, " she said.

"What?"

"Jeff's meeting Neil at my house. We're almost there. Why don't you just come over and we'll rent a movie?"

"Are they going to infiltrate the den?" Claire said, sniffling. "I really don't want to be around them today."

"No. It's my night. Come over. We have pizza for dinner. Did you eat?"

"No. I made chicken for my dad. I hate chicken. I'm just not hungry."

"You have to eat, Claire. You're too skinny."

"Yes ma'am. Who needs a mother with you around? You are such a Jewish American Princess."

"Judy's working tonight so we can party," Annene said. "I think Neil's got some weed. Maybe if you get the munchies you'll be able to eat."

"Interesting rationale, but I'm not going to. I got wigged out when we coated cloves with toothpaste and smoked them when we were sophomores."

"Yeah, but that's different. I think that causes brain damage. Marijuana does not cause brain damage. It's a social lubricant."

"I got dizzy and threw up."

"Neil says it's different. He's not the sharpest tool in the shed though. He's acting so weird lately. I don't get it. He's actually being kind of nice lately. Morose, but nice. Post-pubescent depression. Any thoughts?"

"Probably…" Claire said, but stopped herself.

Annene turned into the mini mall entrance, a one level development of stores that structurally appeared identical to each other aside from the store fronts which advertised a produce store, bagel shop, postage center, pet supply store, and the local video rental store called Alpharetta Video, a store only twenty by twenty feet in size packed so tight that two people could not fit side by side in an aisle.

Claire and Annene entered the store, front to back, and looked up at the tapes slotted like shelved books in wire racks that had been joined together and hung on the walls. A Chinese man - old, small and wearing a faded and worn Izod sweater - turned from the TV screen where Bruce Lee hurled chops and kicks. When he heard the cow bell ring and clang against the glass door, he bowed to the girls as they entered, keeping his eyes on Annene. She shrugged it off and headed for the classics section in the back and just to the right of the register where she lingered and browsed. Claire stayed in the front of the store where she scanned the New Releases section featured on the wall, then met Annene at the register. She held three tapes wedged between her arm and ribcage.

"It's my turn, you know," Claire said.

"I know," replied Annene. I'm just looking for next time."

The plastic cassette wheels rattled in the box as she placed them on the counter.

"Can you put these on hold, please?" Annene asked the stout Korean man behind the counter. His eyes were shifty up close and his words were sparse.

"For when?" he asked.

"For tomorrow," she replied.

"They'll be here tomorrow," he said, firm.

"I just want to make sure I can get them. So, can you put them on hold?"

"Fine," he said. He took the black video cases from the counter and placed them at the top of the wire rack on wheels behind him.

"Thank you," Annene told him, and lowered her eyes.

The man nodded and turned around. Annene didn't feel his eyes on her back this time like she usually did.

SIX | Protection

Jeff leaned over the side of his bed, pulled up the comforter and slid the copy of *Playboy* between the box springs and the mattress. He pulled the bedspread to the headrest, covered the gray pillows and smoothed the blue cotton fabric. His face was flushed, pink and hot. Sweat beaded on his brow that he wiped with the dry side of the towel.

The phone rang.

He cleared his throat then answered, "Hello."

"Are you coming over?" Neil asked.

"Yeah, I'll be there in a minute, dude."

"Dude, Claire is here." His tone was impatient.

"What?"

"Bad one, dude."

"What?"

"Bad one."

"You're stoned," Jeff said. He took the phone away from his ear, looked at it and shook his head.

"Yeah, dude," Neil said.

"I'll be over in a second. I have to take a shower and finish reading a chapter for bio."

"You still think you're going to be a doctor, dude?

Give it up."

Jeff hung up the Corvette phone. The receiver was shaped like the body of the car, from the hood to the top. Every time he used it he promised to get a new phone, one not so juvenile, but he forgot between each use.

Neil's words stung and Jeff sometimes could not tolerate him. But, he happened to be Annene's brother and it was the only way he could get close to her at that particular moment. Neil had become a committed stoner over the past months and preferred Jeff's company to the company of his jock friends who had gotten sick of him. Jocks never like it when someone makes them lose. He felt a little sorry for Neil because he was an outcast, like Jeff was and could be. Something profound had infected him, making numbness a better alternative to being alive.

Jeff shook it off, his focus lost to concern. There was something to discover but he would not know or be closer to Annene just standing there looking at the dumb Corvette phone.

The incentive made him rush, first to the other side of his unmade bed and past the Led Zeppelin poster on the bathroom door then quickly into the shower. He breathed deeply but could not get his breath.

Annene was an odd girl with high walls around her that made him curious and nervous. It was a familiar kind of panic to him. The panic that realized loss with each move he made closer to her despite everything that stood in the way between his fear and instincts that told him to keep going in the direction he was going.

He would finish the reading later.

Neil's eyes were bloodshot and his eyelids heavy when he opened the door to Jeff who arrived at the Berry house empty-handed.

"I got beers, dude," Neil said, proud and cocky but muted like he was moving under water.

"Where's the pizza?" Jeff asked.

"On the table. I had a piece. It's hot."

"How hot?"

"It burnt the top of my mouth. My tongue," Neil said, as he opened and closed it, feeling around the inside of his mouth with his tongue. He made a series of facial gestures that stretched his face in every direction. "It cooled off though."

Jeff shook his head. "It actually doesn't burn your tongue. It just makes your taste buds dull by burning the surface."

"Right, dude. Or, should I say, Dr. Dude." Neil laughed to himself.

"You're completely wasted already, dude. Where's your sister?"

"She'll be here in a minute. She's getting a movie."

"They picked it?"

"Chick night," Neil confirmed. "It's all good. They get all sentimental and you can put the moves on them," Neil said. He raised his eyebrows and nodded.

He was such a fucking idiot.

Jeff waved the comment aside as Annene appeared on the stoop where she met the two young men. Neil dragged on a joint then put it out on the brick wall. "Are you guys going to leave the porch or are you going to stay here all night?"

Annene smiled at Jeff, lowered her head and moved around him. She left a cushion of space between them that conveyed itself as vague distrust. Claire followed her friend and Jeff's eyes followed Annene like they were led on a line by his heart.

Neil nodded at Jeff then walked around the back of the sectional sofa and kissed Claire on the forehead.

SEVEN | High Notes

"Annene, you're so depressing lately. You should smoke," Neil said.

He turned to his sister who sat across the room. His glazed and pink eyes narrowed and he smiled so that his cheeks assumed comic book definition. Annene said he looked more like The Joker from Batman, but Claire was more forgiving.

"Cheshire cat," Claire joked.

"Whatever," Annene said. "I don't see it. The Cheshire cat is kind of cute."

Annene propped open the slim paperback between her thumb and pinky finger like she gave the hang ten sign to prop open the pages.

"Listen to this," Annene said. She spoke loud enough to overcome the volume of the television set. The woman on screen told her husband she was leaving him.

"Listen," she said again to make certain she had their attention.

Claire, Annene and Neil sat on the sectional. Jeff sat in a worn Lazy Boy chair opposite Neil. Claire sat on the other end of the sofa, away from Annene who, every now and then, would look at her brother and turn up the left side of her upper lip.

This hotel - the Amazon- was for women only, and they were mostly girls my age with wealthy parents who wanted to be sure their daughters would be living where men couldn't get at them and deceive them; and they were all going to posh secretarial schools like Katy Gibbs, where they had to wear hats and stockings and gloves to class, or they had just graduated from places like Katy Gibbs and were secretaries to executives and simply hanging around in New York waiting to get married to some career man or other.

Annene stopped and looked up. "Can you believe that?"

"What is that?" Claire asked, her eyes returned to the television screen where Diane Keaton cried as Liam Neeson begged her to accept his love and leave her husband and family.

"*The Bell Jar.* Sylvia Plath," Annene replied.

"That's the most depressing thing I've ever read," Claire said.

"Yeah, no wonder," Neil confirmed. He rested his eyes back to the screen after he looked away for a moment.

"Oh, shut up. You don't know anything," Annene fired back without a moment of hesitation. It was easy to take advantage of his slight mind. "You act like an idiot when you're stoned and you're a moron to begin with."

Neil let out a long, winded sigh.

"Where'd you get it?" Claire asked, straining her neck to take a look at the cover that faced away from her but toward Jeff.

"Estelle's bookshelf," Annene said. "She said I could read it. She said it was a huge influence to her early career days. "It trips me out that people actually lived like that."

"I've read that book twice. It's one of my favorites. You're right, it's depressing though," Claire said.

"Listen to this."

These girls looked awfully bored to me. I saw them on the sunroof, yawning and painting their nails and trying to keep up their Bermuda tans, and they seemed bored as hell. I talked with one of them, and she was bored with yachts and bored with flying around in airplanes and bored with skiing in Switzerland at Christmas and bored with the men in Brazil. Girls like that make me sick. I'm so jealous I can't speak.

"Did you like the part about Doreen, the southern girl?" Claire asked.

"No, I'm southern and I'm not like that," Annene replied. "I did not relate."

"That's because Judy couldn't afford to polish you," Claire said, cold.

Annene blinked her eyes a few times as she looked at Claire. It amazed her that Claire could go from silence to lightening that lit up a dark sky but scorched the tallest of the trees. Letting it out made it real, though. It stung.

"No, it's because I refused to be *polished*. You're polished though." Annene gave a smarmy smile. To anyone else she could have responded cruelly. If not for Claire's tears and the circumstance and just knowing her friend, she would have defended herself with a remark more caustic than she knew Claire was capable of.

"It was my mom's job. She loved that whole debutante thing. The only part I enjoyed about that was helping the kids at that home."

"What home?" Jeff asked, his eyes on the television then to Claire's legs and lap before he met her eyes.

He was listening. "The one for battered wives and their kids," Claire replied.

"You like the most depressing stuff, Claire," Annene said.

Neil stared at his sister. "Look who's talking." He gestured toward the book.

Jeff was quiet and chose words he did not speak. He wore a black T-shirt with Rush Live 1986 written in white and red on the front. His hair was parted conspicuously even and straight, combed rather than swept through with splayed fingers.

Neil sustained what remained of a stoned smile, the

diminutive smirk of arrogant youth and perfect teeth. Normally, he could disarm with his effortless, neutral smile. Even a straight face. He patted the blue and white upholstered sofa seat with his right hand and Claire's leg with his left. Their hips touched, but he was numb and distant and Claire could feel it but doubted herself.

She got up anyway when Neil tried to grab her hand, a reflex to get away from him. Too slow and too stoned, it left no impression. Disingenuous, but Claire could not define it entirely as that. She walked toward the adjoining kitchen. Every house in Alpharetta where they lived was a model home with the same floor plan. Claire didn't have to think to find her way. Even so, she spent almost every weekend at Annene's house since Maggie left, so she could have found any object inside their house, blind.

"You going to eat the pizza or not?" Claire asked.

Jeff looked away from the screen to Annene who ignored her but watched as she carried the box from the kitchen to the coffee table closer to them.

"The way she talks about New York. It's so exciting and the people seem so smart. Do you think it's really like that?"

"Sylvia Plath didn't like it," Claire replied.

"Sylvia Plath didn't like anything, Claire. It's not a true story anyway."

"She killed herself, you know," Jeff said. "I think it was New York that killed her. She wrote that just before she died."

Annene returned Jeff's attentive eyes. Unlike Neil's that flitted around the room without any sign of focus or cognitive activity, Jeff had a solidity or purposefulness that manifested itself in his voice that, by comparison (unfair as it was), made Neil's sound hollow and insincere. Where Neil managed to be coercive, even suave when sober, Jeff's manner was simple and spare; a bit misanthropic at times, but he managed neutrality. He was not arrogant but listened and observed. Jeff was a rock. He was silent to the recklessness around him. Home was difficult. It was akin to playing possum and it was a survival skill.

"To be a poet of any substance you have to kill yourself. That's why I decided to be a doctor. People take notice of you when you're alive because you help other people live. You don't have to die to be appreciated."

Annene laughed and her eyes lit up with wonder. Jeff was smart.

Neil waved Claire over to him. Claire changed her mind and lingered for a moment, her mouth nearly gushing with hunger, before she half closed the box to the pizza and returned empty-handed to the sofa next to Neil. She had to stay strong. To keep it together, she gritted her teeth.

"No you don't," Claire objected. "You don't have to die. She shifted under the weight of Neil's arm.

"Jeff, sshhh. Watch the movie," Neil said, too slowly. His eyes were heavy and, though seated, he swayed.

"Shut up, Neil. You don't even know what it's about."

Neil shrugged and Claire stared blankly at the screen. "What is this anyway?" he asked after a few moments.

Annene shook her head and continued to glance between the pages of the paperback book and television screen.

Neil leaned forward and took the pizza by the crust end, then held it in front of her face to tempt her. It was sloppy.

Melted gooey cheese and tomatoes drifted to her nose. She shook her head. "It's called, *The Good Mother*," Claire said, flat. Neil turned toward Annene then to Jeff who raised his eyebrows in acknowledgement. Annene's eyes rose above the pages of the book so that her friend was back in her range of vision.

"She won't eat, Neil. Don't bother. She's on some kind of hunger strike or something," Annene said, lifting her head but not her eyes.

"I'm not hungry," Claire said. "I'm not on a hunger

strike. God, why is everyone so concerned? I just don't feel like eating."

Annene lifted the book up so her eyes disappeared behind the covers.

"You're too skinny, that's why. I've seen you not so skinny and you're too skinny now." Claire ignored Neil and Annene managed an empathetic smile to Jeff who did not return the gesture. Jeff watched Claire without movement, his eyes darting back and forth from the edges of his peripheral vision where she sat stiff on the sectional to the television screen. He pretended to watch the movie. The woman on screen had just left her husband and was struck with the sudden and paralyzing realization that she was in love with her lover, not the man to whom she was married years before.

Annene interrupted again, to recite a few more lines. "Oh my God, this is so good. Listen. It sounds like Grandma Estelle.

Jay Cee wanted to teach me something, all the old ladies I ever knew wanted to teach me something, but I suddenly didn't think they had anything to teach me.

"Doesn't that sound like Grandma Estelle?"

Claire did not respond, her eyes fixed to the screen.

"Claire," Annene insisted. Jeff had turned his head so he faced Annene again. She was starting to get on his nerves.

"Annene, can you just watch the movie?" Jeff said.

"No, I can't. I'm going to go to my room. Why'd you pick this anyway? You like to torture yourself, you know? You like it."

Claire shook her head. "I've already read the book, Annene. I don't need to hear it."

Annene closed the book and walked out of the room. Claire called after her. "It sounds more like Grandma Bernie, Annene."

"Maybe that's why people keep reading it. It reminds them of the people they know," Jeff said.

Annene had stopped around the dividing wall between the living room and the short hallway to her bedroom door to listen to him. She just stood and listened.

EIGHT | Low Notes

"I think what the problem is, Judy, is that there is nothing interesting here."

Judy Berry ignored her daughter. She arrived home just moments earlier with time enough only to slip off the white leather nurse's shoes. Clogs with flower shaped punched holes. She wore green scrubs and an identification tag on a silver chain of linked ball bearings around her neck. Her wide hips were exaggerated by the poorly cut pants and shape of the boxy, v-neck top.

Annene wore a black sweater and jeans with holes in the knees, frayed across like cobwebs. They were marked up with Sharpie pen in varied colors but mostly black. She sat at the kitchen table where she ate Triscuits from an open box with one hand and held the dress in the other.

"I mean," she continued and chewed to get the words past the food. "I mean," she repeated and cocked her head to the side and smiled.

"There's Matzo Ball soup in the refrigerator, Annene."

"I know. I ate some."

"I hope there's some left so we can take it to Gram," Judy said.

"I didn't eat much. I just like to taste everything,"

Annene said. "It's boring anyway, Judy. Gram doesn't have anything to do in that place."

Judy inhaled deeply and settled her large purse, equal in size to a diaper bag, onto the table. The inside of the Berry home was covered in patterns; florals and plaid conflicted with each other and distracted anyone who walked in the door. One room was papered in a plaid of blues and another in a floral of the same color. There was light blue carpet and white shades. Judy chose the blue tone to cool off the house during the summer months.

Annene had asked Claire one day what she thought, honestly, about their home. Claire craned her neck around the living room where they sat since the Berry's did not have a den.

"It's very colorful," Claire said, trying to be subtle.

"It makes me dizzy. I painted my room white. I asked her if I could paint it black but she said no. You're lucky your mom knows something about... You're lucky your mom has good taste," she corrected herself. It was the first time Claire visited the Berry home. "It's the living room but we call it the den."

Annene wiped her hands on a towel then held up the dress. I think I'll take it to the home so Gram can see it. I changed the stitching around the bodice and waist."

Annene smiled and looked up at her mother who was partly hidden by the refrigerator door that she held open and hunched into. Judy looked over the open door and Annene noticed her flat eyes lined with still life shadows and pink whites and lids. Her cheeks were without the usual flush of activity or stubbornness.

"That would be nice, dear."

It was noon and Judy had arrived home later than normal. The night shift at the hospital made her tired but freed her days so she could visit her mother in the hospital. Judy would place her mother and her father in an assisted living home once Estelle left the hospital. A single parent and only child, it was the only option, but went so harshly against her innate skill to care for the infirmed, she felt guilty. Work made it impossible to do everything. Judy often hated herself for those limits.

"Alpharetta is boring, Mom. What if we went somewhere else?"

"We can't go anywhere else," Judy snapped then took in a long sigh. "This is where we live." She removed the large plastic container and closed the refrigerator. "Annene, I'm sorry. This is very difficult for me and I know you're trying to help." She inhaled again, releasing her breath slowly, and placed the container on the tiled kitchen counter. "I just didn't know how hard it would be. This is a very strange time and you're all I've got to get through it."

Judy left the container on the sink and walked briskly out of the kitchen. Annene rubbed the dress fabric between her fingers then touched the beads that hung from the trim that were stitched unevenly all over the bodice. When she held the dress by the thin spaghetti straps, she jiggled it back and forth so that the beads shook and the dress danced like a marionette at the end of its strings.

It was perfect. Annene smiled faintly then looked toward the hallway where her mother disappeared. Because she was her daughter, she knew the sound of her crying. She knew Grandpa Jack was in his room in his chair watching the small boxed-up world, but Judy avoided it and Annene would too. It had gotten so he only remembered Annene once a week, Judy moreso, but still not enough to make it so she could not feel hurt those days when she needed her daddy for support, to help her through a day she felt too exhausted to keep her family afloat. There was a time that Judy was buoyed by life, when Annene was young and their family was solid. When her dad was around and life was a fluid mix of a normal rush and ease.

Annene's dad was dead, though. A dead creep. A

creep before he was dead. She knew that in her teenage years, but not as a child. It explained things she would rather have not known. Mostly, it explained Judy, who needed time alone to cry.

An hour later, they pulled into one of the parking slots along the street, divided by long painted white slanted lines so that several feet of distance separated the sidewalk and cars driving past on the wide road. Bells rang from the Catholic Church steeple across the street.

Exiting the car, Annene held the Dillard's bag in one hand and combed through her straight black hair with the other. Her fingers functioned like a wide comb through the black strands. Judy shut the door and balanced a brown file-sized box on her arm. Rx was written on the side in black Sharpie pen. Annene's mother must have brought the box from home.

"Gram will be happy to have something to eat other than hospital food," Annene said.

The girl could not manage to get a reaction out of Judy. The last time her mother was that quiet was when she discovered a bottle of gin in Annene's bathroom cabinet. Two years had passed since then. This time, Judy was half gone to weakness despite the clinical training that distanced her. Estelle suffered. It was all bad and Annene felt a pang of guilt with the thought that she just wanted to get it over with.

"What was it called that she had done?" Annene asked.

"It's called a tracheotomy," Judy said.

She cleared her throat and quickened her stride past the nurse's station. Annene held a black garment bag folded over her right arm and followed close to Judy who nodded to the nurse on duty. Like Judy, the woman wore scrubs but was thicker all around. Her eyes opened a bit wider as she acknowledged Judy who chose to wear her nursing uniform for the sake of efficiency. She needed to get to work later in the evening.

"Hi," she said. "Judy Berry. I'm here to see Estelle Berry."

"Oh," she said. The woman smiled through an otherwise tight face that seemed unaccustomed to the effort. Her hair was a dull blond, dyed and in conflict with her age made obvious by the lines and sags to her face. Despite the similarity in dress and their strained expressions they were physical opposites. Judy looked like an older version of Annene, only with lighter hair. She was short but much thinner. Not a sign of fitness for Judy but one of stress. Everything about her revealed the hard edges of fatigue.

Judy, Annene knew, could negotiate her way through a hospital with ease. Despite the frequency of their visits, the head nurse did not acknowledge Judy or Annene. They passed a hunched over man in the corridor. Bones poked through his paper skin. His slippers scraped in a slow, rhythmic rustling sound across the white tile floor. The place smelled like ammonia and unwashed, acidic skin. Hints of too sweet floral deodorizer broke through areas along the hall as they passed the nurses station and open doors.

Estelle sat upright in bed holding long metal knitting needles that she expertly worked into knotted patterns. Her complexion was gray and more wrinkled with scattered age and sunspots, more than Annene remembered. Her lips were barely tinted blue. Round pink sponge rollers were twisted into her fine brown and gray hair, and Annene wondered if they were the same rollers that her grandmother used to style Annene's hair for her sixth birthday party. A tube was taped to Estelle's neck above the collarbone and connected to a large machine lit up with buttons and lights.

It was white. Everything was white, so stark it only further convinced Annene that hospital decor was the medical profession's way of preparing the infirmed for what most envisioned as heaven with its impossibly truthful light.

Estelle's hands shook slightly and more slowly than Annene was accustomed to seeing. Only a few days had passed since her grandmother was admitted into the hospital and had been transported from intensive care to a regular hospital room.

Estelle steadily wrapped the black fuzzy yarn around the needle, held the skein with her right hand and looped it around the needle in the same hand. She'd started the scarf less than a week ago at Bernie's house, coughing here and there and wheezing some at the time. The yarn was mohair and silk, she bragged, a cut above the usual quality Estelle was accustomed to. She seemed pleased.

Moments passed before she noticed Judy and Annene at the door. When she looked up, she dropped her hands to her lap and let go of the needles. With open palms she patted the pink sponge rollers in her hair. She felt the smooth pink plastic frame of the curlers with the tips of her fingers and tried to open one. The strained effort with old joints was not enough to open it.

Judy walked quickly to her side. She patted her mother's shoulder.

"Hi Mom," she said. "You don't need to do that. I'll help you."

Annene echoed her, "Hi Gram." She smiled and looked behind the door where she found a hook and hung the black garment bag from the plastic hanger.

Estelle mouthed the word, "Jack?"

And because Judy was her daughter she understood without the need for any more words.

"No mom, he's at home. I brought you some matzo ball soup for lunch."

Judy placed the plastic bag with the paper canister on the nightstand.

Estelle let Judy unfasten the curlers and brush through her thin silver hair that she wore just slightly longer than most women in their seventies. Under the floral pattern knitting bag on Estelle's lap where she stuffed the ball of yarn and needles was a pad of paper and dull number two pencil. Judy removed it from her mother's lap and placed it on the bedside table to the left of the bed. She pulled it closer to her mother so that it was directly in front of her.

"Here," she said, and handed the pen to Estelle. "Write it."

Estelle scratched out the words in cursive. The lines were unsteady but legible. *I hate not talking*, she wrote.

Judy and Annene shared a look and laugh muffled only by fatigue. Judy shook her head.

"I hate not talking," Annene read aloud.

"Honey, will you take these?" Judy bundled the curlers together between her hands taking care not to drop any and handed them to Annene who set the curlers in a pile next to the vase of a flower arrangement. She took care as she eased them away from the side of the already cluttered side table.

"Pretty," Annene said, and sniffed the roses so the sound of the air as it passed through her nostrils was audible even above the sound of the respirator. She inhaled a couple of short breaths and sneezed. Estelle smiled.

"Annene, cover your face. We're in a hospital."

"No kidding," she said. "How do you deal with it in here, Gram? It's so white."

Judy glared at her daughter. "It's white so they can keep it clean. You should feel right at home with the way you painted your room."

"I like it that way," Annene said. "It's not all white, anyway and it's easier to meditate without the distraction. It's very Zen. And, it's not black."

A loud shriek came from the chair that Judy pulled from the corner of the room to the side of the bed.

Annene took the seat already placed at the foot of the bed, her hands resting on Estelle's ankles. She and her mother looked across from each other with the almost blank expressions of languid cheer.

"You look tired," Estelle wrote. "Why didn't you stay home?" she wrote and pushed the pad toward Judy.

"I wanted to see you," she argued, getting up from the plastic and metal chair. Across the room and into the bathroom, she disappeared behind the door. "Mom, where's the mirror I brought you?"

Annene was antsy. She walked to the side of the bed and leaned over Estelle's adjustable hospital table on wheels. She pushed it closer and turned it so that the surface hung over the bed where her grandmother's extended legs were covered in a white sheet and thin, rough blanket. She then waited while Estelle used the more supportive surface to write. Her hand was slow and shaky but the words were legible.

Annene cocked her head to adjust her perspective and face the words upright. Again, Annene read loud. "Under cosmetics bag. Nurse put it there."

In the bathroom, Judy flipped on the light and took a moment to look at herself in the bathroom mirror. She shook her head at her reflection and found the opaque plastic hand mirror resting on the toilet tank. She flipped off the light, returned to her chair and leaned back into it. Annene pulled her chair from the foot to the opposite side of the bed averting the IV inserted in her grandmother's freckled arm. Thin EKG wires came from the loose hospital gown sleeve and hooked into another machine beside the respirator. The oxygen tube started at the opening in her neck then behind her head so she could move her hands freely.

"How many rows have you done, Mom?" Judy asked, almost fully reclined if not for the chair back.

Annene watched as her grandmother wrote out a number then held it up for Judy to see.

"Read it to me, Annene," she said. "I want to rest my eyes." Inhaling deeply, Judy's eyelids shut.

Annene couldn't help but think that her mother could probably use the oxygen mask with all of the deep breathing she was doing. Perhaps it would calm her nerves and give her a quick exit, the kind Neil needed every day now. Maybe sleep was enough for her.

"Nine hundred and fifty three," Annene read, surprised. "Gram," she said, "You knitted over nine hundred?"

Judy opened her eyes halfway and Estelle nodded.

"Don't you think that's enough?" Judy mumbled.

Estelle shook her head only slightly.

"She said no," Annene told her mother.

Judy threw up her hands in mock surrender.

Annene picked up a gauzy hospital mask and pretended to anesthetize herself. She fluttered her eyelids like she was ready to pass out.

Estelle smiled under all of that restraint.

"How many you going to knit?" Judy asked.

Estelle smiled and wrote, *twenty six thousand two hundred and eighty*, then included the division sign and the number two. *Two scarves*, she wrote.

"Mother," Judy said. She opened her eyes and sat up straight. "You can't be serious."

Annene giggled, pleased at Judy's outburst, her disapproval.

Estelle nodded, "Yes."

"Why?" Judy asked.

"Each day of my life equals that to seventy-two. Can't fit all into one," Annene read from the tablet. She spoke each word as Estelle wrote it out, carefully.

Mirror? she wrote on another line.

Judy still held it in her hand.

"She wants to see the mirror," Annene told her mother, and gestured toward it.

Judy leaned forward, blinked her eyes and strained her face, near tears. It was the same face she held onto just hours earlier at home. The rims of her eyelids were still pink.

Estelle held the white plastic framed mirror in her hands. Her reflection shook in it as she brushed her face with the palm of her left hand that passed over the age spots and lines. She smoothed her hair and coifed it at the ends.

Estelle put down the mirror and with her stable hand wrote, *makeup*.

"What?" Annene responded.

Estelle wrote just below it, *blush. I'm pale.*

"Let me, Gram," she said, and handed Estelle the mirror so she could watch while Annene applied a rose powder blush with a soft brush to each cheek.

Estelle nodded her approval and Annene put the brush and compact back in the bag. "Wanna see what I did to the dress?"

Estelle nodded yes.

Annene got up from the chair and unzipped the garment bag that hung from the hook behind the door. She held the dress from the straps in the bag and lifted it out, watching Estelle as it unraveled from the heap and hung from her hooked fingers. Judy breathed steadily from the chair and opened her eyes, when Annene asked, "You like it?"

Estelle smiled and nodded.

"She went and changed the whole thing," Judy said from the chair, breaking the silence in a room unaccustomed to her voice.

"Judy, I told you I'd change it. I think it looks much better," she added. She held it closer and let it move around her body as she swiveled left to right.

Judy's breathing quickly returned to a sleep state, her mouth open. The air passed in and out of her steadily interrupted by an occasional back up in her nasal passage.

Estelle wrote on the pad, *me too* and Annene repositioned herself on the bed, her arm hidden behind her back.

"I brought a book for you to read, Gram," Annene said.

She read to her while her own mother slept and Estelle listened.

NINE | Melting

Daylight came through the pinhole seams and the gap where the curtains failed to come together completely. Neil's mind drifted to her face and then to Farrah Fawcett beauty in the poster taped to the wall, the top right corner bending away from the imprecise adhesion. It was the attention she paid him that made him sticky, and that Marilyn Monroe appeal you see in the famous last photo of her on the beach, hair blown and all wrapped up in a terry cloth towel.

His hand found the way to his belly then to the elastic band of the cotton Hanes briefs.

Claire was beautiful but there was something missing to her slight frame and passivity. She was an agreeable girl.

He turned from the window. It was a game in this pitch black room to make figures out of the patches of light.

He imagined Claire with larger breasts and the pinholes as either stars or stadium lights.

Maggie held him close, his head buried between her breasts and the all-consuming wash of contentment that strung close his loose wires. Contained. Even a strong wind could be quieted.

Touching himself that way only stoked Neil's grief. She made him good, so he felt fulfilled, never quite knowing that a deep sadness could create such rage and that the smell of a woman could warrant such control.

He looked for it in Claire only he did not find Maggie there, and he knew it by his false efforts, too strained as he pushed forward into the delusion only to find it was a phantom with no feeling. Skin and bones. What he found was distance. Distance that already existed. It was a maddening, intangible reach, projected toward need and repelled by his shame. Every day that passed bordered on insanity.

Darkness was not Neil's truth but what Maggie wanted for him. She pieced it together for herself, wrapped it so well in nice clean folds and taped it shut. The box was entirely concealed to anyone but him. He remembered everything that was in that box but it made him feel less crazy to see the pieces of it himself. To see her face. That perfect face that he saw vaguely in Claire. Maggie's shadow.

Neil stood and fumbled with the curtains in his room, trying to make them overlap to block out the light. Against those memories on the reel in his mind, he could see her like he saw her just before that first time they were together.

Perfection graced Maggie as he watched while she wrapped his present to Claire and told her, "It could match the others under the tree."

"Very smart, Neil," she said, with conspicuous nicety. "Everything would coordinate. You just may have a knack for this."

Neil was pleased by the compliment and took it as no threat to his masculinity. Anything to impress Maggie.

"I don't think so, Mrs. Hinkley," he responded. "I think I'm better at raking leaves."

It was before anything ever happened.

"Fine," Maggie said. "You can rake them tomorrow when you come over. I'll pay you holiday pay even though it's two days before Christmas," she said, and placed the presents under the tree, arranging and rearranging, bent over at the foot of the squat and fat tree. She kneeled. Maggie wore a gray gabardine pants set with a fitted sweater under the suit jacket. He watched her move along the floor, placing the smaller presents on top of the larger ones, the silver wrapped ones and gold at every third present no matter how big or small the red and green plaid were in-between. Maggie could not see Neil's eyes on her back that faced him as she stooped then stood. Her hips barely shook with each movement and the curve of her teardrop backside was the only thing on Neil's radar.

She tucked in her belly and arched her sway back then reached around the tree. She kneeled and kicked up each leg bracing herself to stand. Everything that Maggie did was deliberate and whether it was cold or without maternal sense, it mattered to Neil. Everything. Patient, he watched her through lowered eyes, until she chose to turn around.

"Well," she said, and slapped both of her thighs. "I'll see you tomorrow then."

Neil had not formally acknowledged what seemed to be a command. There was no room for "no" and Neil did not think to back out of the arrangement. Mrs. Hinkley was Claire's mother, no matter how different the two were and no matter what Claire thought of the woman. Neil read her and the answer was clear. If he wanted to see her again, it would be under her terms.

It was the way she looked at him - saw through him like he was transparent. He had no choice but to be obedient.

"Okay," he confirmed, and lowered his head a notch.

Picking up her purse from the pink French wing chair Maggie walked out the door and left him in her own house, alone.

Neil squinted at the crease of light and turned his head. The curtains always left that little gap, even if it was momentarily closed. The fabric moved again. It fell straighter. It was Saturday afternoon and he hadn't yet left his room. He picked up the phone and dialed Jeff who answered in a voice, low and relaxed.

"Dude, I hope my grandma doesn't die before Christmas," Neil said into the phone.

He lay in his bed with the receiver propped between his ear and shoulder. The room was cluttered with sports paraphernalia in his favorite team colors; a navy blue Dallas Cowboys bedspread was bunched up at his feet and a lighter blue pillow folded in half under his head. He stared at the poster of the Dallas Cowboys cheerleaders just across the room as he held the brown, corded rotary phone.

Jeff froze for a second at Neil's words. At home in his own room he listened to Motley Crue and kneeled on the floor in front of his terrarium. His two fingers kneaded wood shavings in a plastic container where he extracted mealworms that he fed, one by one, to the spotted geckos inside the rectangular glass terrarium.

Jeff responded, "I know. Annene worships her grandma. I've never seen anyone so into hanging out with someone that old but, she says she tells a lot of stories. Your sister's pretty cool."

It was wrong to disclose himself to Neil unless Neil was the one to initiate any depth. Jeff did not know why he was doing it but it was too late.

Neil covered his eyes with his arm.

"Claire is the same way. Mrs. Hinkley and Claire only fought when she was around. Man, they used to get into raging fights. Claire would just be in her room and Maggie, I mean Mrs. Hinkley, would come in and freak out on her. But, then she'd be so normal when she'd chaperone the games."

He paused for a moment.

"Then she just fuckin' disappeared."

"Were you there, dude?" Jeff asked.

He lured the lizards to the other side of the glass cage. They followed his hand and the larger of the two propped themselves up on the side where its sand-colored and black-spotted feet tried to cling but slid to the glass until it took hold of the cream-colored insect in its mouth. The small, white mealworm squirmed once it had warmed in Jeff's hands, then writhed half-consumed in the Gecko's jaws. The lizard lowered its head and fell back on all fours to the sand-covered bottom where it chomped down on the worm and quickly worked it into its mouth and down its throat, the thing's head or tail squirming until it disappeared.

Jeff picked up another worm from a plastic container and lowered it into the cage. He held it for just a moment before the smaller lizard of the two, the female, took it from his hand. The only time they moved was to eat and get warmer. Jeff grinned then turned his attention back to Neil who began a description of a fight he'd overheard before Claire managed to hang up the phone.

"Mrs. Hinkley just started yelling at her one day. I could hear her over the phone. Claire barely said anything then started yelling back then hung up."

"Dude, Claire barely talks," Jeff said, fishing for more information.

"I know dude. She used to talk more, but she talks less now. After her mom left she talks less."

Jeff closed the lid on the terrarium and sat on the floor where he leaned back against his bed and replaced the white plastic lid on the container of mealworms.

Neil continued, "If Annene is bummed then Claire will be equally bummed. You know how chicks are."

"Yeah," Jeff mumbled. "I'm gonna ask Annene if she wants me to go with her to visit."

"You're going today?"

"I guess I better. Annene's grandma won't die though," Jeff said.

"I'm gonna call Annene and see if she wants to go."

"She's already there, dude. My mom took her. I heard them leave. Chill, okay?"

"Oh," Jeff said, downcast.

"How you gonna get there anyway? Your car's a piece. It won't make it out the driveway."

"Later," Jeff said.

He hung up the phone. He pulled a pair of worn navy blue Adidas running shoes out from under his bed then picked up the faded blue Champion sweatpants in a heap on the floor.

"Oh, fuck it," he said. The convalescent home was a mile away and he needed every opportunity to train for the track meet scheduled after the New Year. Winter break had left him with only Annene to think about, though he needed distraction badly.

Neil thought it odd that Jeff found his dumpy sister attractive.

"Dude, she's like a guy," Neil told him.

"You only say that because you're her brother. She's smart, dude."

"So is Claire. Claire is really smart. She's hot though. My sister's kind of beat."

"What do you talk about with Claire?"

Neil cut him off, "Whatever, dude."

"What do you talk about?" Jeff asked, his tone confrontational.

Jeff thought as his feet pounded on pavement like a heartbeat, thinking, thinking, thinking, but trying hard not to think. He reasoned... one, two, one, two, his shoulder barely rocked with the incessant pounding. One, two...

"Dude, your sister likes lizards. She finds them interesting," Jeff tried not to replay the conversation in his head but he did.

Running, Jeff thought about Annene. Who she was in terms of what was important to her. Grandma Estelle, couldn't be pinned down in a word. The woman was a firecracker from the stories she told. He liked that. Nothing to wonder. Just like his foster mother, it was all laid out. Claire, he knew, shared his taste for quiet. Both of them were introverts and both deserted. Jeff by his father. It seemed no matter how hard he tried not to replay this part of his history, the less he was able. He ran faster and thought of his adoptive parents. Nice and caring. Two lawyers who advocated for him and gave him everything though he was alone most of the time. Still, he lived in a virtual cocoon fortified long ago by his mother's mysterious death.

That's where the memory train stopped for him and he tried to focus on the future and what he could make of it. It was what he was taught by no one in particular yet everyone. Pain or no pain. It was easier to focus on the realities of a wound. Of how to heal rather than to stomp around in the past.

Despite his interest in herpetology and the circle of geeks, his taste for music somehow redeemed him. Amphibians, he rationalized, were survivors, virtually mute loners. He identified with this even though their blood ran too cold for him.

Jeff ran faster, his thin legs perfectly formed so his feet landed, rolling from the heel across the treads and the palm of his narrow feet to his toes. Vigorous strokes of his arms wound him up and made him run faster. Perspiration dripped from his forehead and into his eyes. He squinted at the salty sting. He'd forgotten the towel and had only the t-shirt on his back that changed to near translucent as perspiration marked his chest. He slowed for seconds with the thought that he had forgotten to put on another layer of deodorant.

The lizard boy would smell the first time he met Firecracker Berry.

Breaking his stride, Jeff shot ahead and ran faster but took steady breaths into his nose and out his mouth. He never chased his breath, only kept steady. He paced himself past the estates along the highway that he used as distance landmarks. His mind shifted from the hospital in the distance to the cautionary glances he made to the cars that approached from behind in dimming light.

Rounding the last bend, the destination came into sight and Jeff pushed a button on his watch that glowed neon at the touch and read seven minutes, ten seconds. He sprinted the last stretch, as his eyes narrowed in on the white, multi-level building with an aluminum rail around a porch and along the ramp and stairs that lead into the side entrance to the building. White louvered shades covered the plain, institutional windows spaced three feet apart and level around the weathered grayed stucco walls.

Jeff stopped at the corner and paced several feet back and forth just in front of the facility. He gripped the metal railing and leaned forward, bracing himself against it to stretch his Achilles tendons. Upright again, he stood with one hand on the rail, took hold of his foot and pulled it toward his lower back to stretch the quadriceps. He alternated right to left twice then, straight-legged and bowing forward, he touched the asphalt with the tips of his fingers. Keeping time with his wristwatch, he counted thirty seconds. His heartbeat slowed and his breathing returned to normal.

TEN | Mixing

"Open the curtains," Estelle whispered to Annene who was still seated on the bed. She shuffled through Estelle's makeup bag. Judy's breathing made the transition to a faint snore, barely audible above the steady exchange of oxygen in and out of her lungs. Annene looked up at Estelle who put her finger over her mouth and puckered her lips together. She gestured to her granddaughter and her eyes shifted to sleeping Judy.

Annene laughed. Only her grandmother could elicit laughter that came from her belly.

"You and Grandma Bernie are really wacky," Annene said, hushed.

It's an experiment, Estelle wrote. She held up the pad of paper. When she tried to speak it herself, each syllable was long and slow and choked by the release valve that let oxygen in and out through the hole in Estelle's neck. A shawl embroidered with pastel thread was pulled around her shoulders to conceal the hole in her neck where the tube was inserted. Only, the shawl had slipped so it covered nothing intended. Estelle pulled it up the best she could though her arms functioned like a marionette, with the tubes and wires.

Still seated at Estelle's bedside, Annene shook her head and smiled while Estelle went back to her knitting. The sprinklers clicked outside to a steady rhythm.

Don't they know not to turn the sprinklers on in the middle of the day? It'll kill the grass, Estelle wrote. The cursive was clearer as her hand got used to writing.

"I know. Judy said it makes it yellow," Annene said, then added, "Gram, can't you just make it twenty six and whatever hundred stitches instead of rows? That's a lot."

Open the windows, Estelle wrote, and raised her hand as Annene got up from the bed and pushed the curtains so that the front entrance came into view as did the vision of Jeff who stood just out of reach of one sprayed fan of water coming from the automatic sprinklers. His shirt hung off him like a wet rag hung on a clothesline. Framed by the borders of the window, he looked directly through the only curtains open to the front entrance and to public exposure. Annene returned the stare, squinting at Jeff who, eyes wide and full of false confidence, managed an apologetic smile. His view of Annene was blocked by the rolling table that functioned as a food tray but was pushed aside and decorated with a giant rounded coffee mug painted bright yellow with two black dots for eyes and a wide "u" for a smile. Yellow roses and daisies of the same color and white matched the happy face. The top of her head to below her waist was visible through the window. He stopped taking notice of the black outfits she wore, the detail lost to a prevailing black wardrobe: black hair, black shirts, black jeans, black Doc Martin boots. The frame of his view ended at her knees, but he could imagine. Could predict it. Anyone could. That particular day she wore a long-sleeved cotton shirt of gray and black stripes, he thought, to relieve herself of the thoughts of death the overwhelming black conveyed to most. Annene only did what she wanted to do, so it would have had to be her idea.

Stepping aside, Annene lifted the corners of her mouth

without opening it. With a suppressed smile she turned around and announced, "Jeff's here."

Estelle shrugged.

"The boy who asked me to that dance," Annene said, and moved out of Jeff's range of vision and to the bedside again.

Estelle turned her head away from the light of the window. Annene walked around the bed, passed the window without looking at him and threw her head back.

"Well, tell that boy. What's his name? Tell him to come in," Estelle whispered. Her voice was raspy and low.

"I heard that," Judy mumbled and fluttered her eyelids before she opened them. "Do you think I've been a nurse for fifteen years and don't know that anyone can talk after a tracheotomy? Especially you. No one talks more than you. Mom, you need to rest it or it won't heal."

"Smarty pants," Estelle said, softly to her daughter. The slipping sound of steam made her words into vapors and slurs.

"Tell that boy to come in," Estelle said. She looked around her at the tubes and shawl. She reached up to her hair and patted it again, self-conscious.

"His name is Jeff, Gram."

Estelle nodded, and took a deep breath to regain composure in a broken down state.

Judy got up from her chair then waved her hand and beckoned Jeff inside the room. Jeff smiled and ducked behind the building.

"Boy, he's drenched. Did it rain while I was asleep?" Judy asked.

"No. I don't know. What is he doing out there anyway?" Annene asked, mostly of herself. She walked back and forth, and twirled her hair.

She held up the mirror she had set on the rolling table and rubbed her cheeks then scratched away an eyelash coated with mascara on her nose. She paced at the foot of the hospital bed and waited for what seemed far too long for him to get into the building.

"What is taking him so long?" Annene asked, impatient.

"He," Judy began, but stopped herself when Jeff appeared at the open door. His hair was wet and slicked back and he wore doctor's scrubs. His breathing was just slightly heavy.

"Hi," he said, sheepish but loud with awkward confidence.

"Come in," Estelle said, and smiled.

"Where'd you get those?" Annene asked. She pointed to Jeff in the uniform.

"The nurse. I ran over here because my car isn't running and I got caught in the sprinklers." He looked to the floor for a moment then righted himself.

"Nice of you to visit," Judy said, poised upright in the guest chair.

Annene stared and Estelle freed her hands of the knitting to extend her right hand which Jeff shook gently.

"Jeff. Nice to meet you." He smiled and nodded to Estelle, then turned to Judy who took this as a prompt to shake hands with Jeff. Instead, he walked around the bed and shook her hand.

"Nice to meet you, ma'am," he said, again nodding.

"What are you doing here?" Annene questioned.

"I was talking to Neil and he said you were here so I thought I'd stop by. I had to go for a run anyway."

"That's such a nice thing to do," Estelle said.

Annene just looked at him, uncertain of his motivation to see her.

"On the phone," Jeff clarified. When Annene said nothing, he turned his attention to Estelle. "How long are you supposed to be in the hospital?"

"Not too much longer. She's feeling much better," Judy said.

"When do they take the tube out? Just a few more days, right?"

Estelle nodded mostly with her eyes.

"I won't be able to see you off to the dance like I wanted. Annene is going to look so beautiful."

Estelle blinked her eyes a few times.

"Oh, Grandma, come on," Annene said.

"You will. What a handsome couple you'll make."

Annene stood with her arms crossed.

"Don't you think so, Judy?"

"Yes. Very nice," she replied.

"So, Jeff. Annene says you want to be a doctor."

"Yes, Mrs. Berry," he replied, "I got accepted to Emory in Atlanta and Columbia for my undergrad. Just considering where I'll go for med school based on the acceptances."

"Really?" Judy said, impressed. "You know I'm a nurse, right?"

"Yes ma'am," Jeff replied.

Involved in the conversation with Jeff, Annene noticed a change in Estelle's eyes as she watched, marveled by Jeff's explanation. Her grandmother's social skills were far more refined and her interest, genuine. Despite herself, Annene studied her grandmother's manner.

Always act like you're interested in what he does for a living, she once wrote in her Alpharetta newspaper column. Courtship was the subject that week in a series of dating guidelines for young women. Guidelines that had fallen away in modern times. Later, Estelle adapted her column to function with a "Dear Abby" model that did not fare well with the Alpharetta Mafia, a group of gossips who seemed always to have a   conflict of interest with the existing advice column.

Occasionally, when Jeff bowed his head or looked up to the fluorescent lights, Annene managed a glance toward him then to Estelle's eyes that locked in her approval. Listening to him infused her with a foreign sense of pride that she tried to shake out with her usual cynicism but could not.

"So, tell me how you know my granddaughter."

"Gram, I already told you."

"I live next door to Claire."

"Our Claire? Claire Hinkley?"

"Yes, our Claire," Judy confirmed.

"He moved there right after Mr. Hinkley and Claire moved back to Alpharetta from Atlanta." It was her way of dodging the subject of the missing Maggie.

"My car broke down and Neil gave me a ride to school. That's how we met."

"That was nice," Judy said. She raised her eyebrows. Neil and she had not gotten along in months and it surprised her.

"How long have Claire and he been together now?"

"They started going out in the summer," Annene said.

"Wait a second. You live in the house next door to the Hinkley's? The Stones lived there."

"That's where I live then," Jeff said.

"Annene, I thought you said his last name was Smith," Judy said.

"I did," Annene said.

"You know what my last name is. Why'd you say it was Smith?"

"It *is* Smith," Annene said.

"Yeah, Annene, but that's the name on my birth certificate not my adopted name."

"You're the Stone's adopted son? I remember when that whole thing was going on. I just didn't think. Oh, I feel so stupid. Well, it's so nice to meet you," Estelle began, then stopped and scribbled. She took a moment to breathe and find her words. "How are you enjoying Alpharetta?"

"It's interesting," Jeff said. "I'm from New York. That's why I'm thinking about going back and the Stones said they'd help me with the tuition. They're really nice. I'm almost an adult by legal standards but they took me in. I lived with a couple of different families in New York before then."

Annene cocked her head. "I didn't know you were in foster homes."

Judy glared at her.

"One of my foster parents was a zoo keeper at the Bronx Zoo and I'd get in free to the exhibits, roam around. I spent a lot of time checking out the amphibian and reptile exhibits. So, I really got into it."

"He's got a couple of lizards," Annene said.

"That's interesting," Estelle said.

"It's a hobby. When I observe them I learn a lot about human behavior."

"By a lizard?" Judy asked. "I guess there's some merit to that."

"They're completely inhuman. It's the total opposite. Except the way they act when you're about to feed them. They have more energy at the thought of food than they do when they're actually eating it."

Estelle smiled and laughed, the loose skin on her face gathering in folds at the corner of her mouth. She was the only one who heard the laugh that felt stronger than it was interpreted by anyone else in the room. Like old age. The thought depressed her.

"How long have you been knitting?" Jeff asked.

"Years."

"My mom used to do that. What's this you're working on?" he asked, and leaned over. "Can I feel it?"

Estelle shrugged and replied, "Sure. Go ahead."

Jeff touched the folded scarf with the tips of his fingers then squeezed it like a ball of clay. "That's cool," he said. "What is it?"

"It's mohair and silk."

"Hmmm."

"Annene likes it."

"Its very girly. Who's it for?" Jeff asked.

Estelle opened her mouth. "I don't know yet. I just knit what I like then give it to whoever suits it most. This yarn is very high quality. Not girly. A man could easily wear this but,that's a matter of personal preference. This actually is a special project. It's different than anything I've ever done."

"The texture is interesting," Jeff commented. He rubbed it between his thumb and forefinger. "Soft but coarse."

"It's called ribbing. You do it by stitching four rows with regular knit stitch and another four rows with a pearl stitch," Annene said before Estelle, who was slow to speak, could respond.

Reaching again to the folded scarf in Estelle's lap, Jeff asked, "Do you mind?"

"No, go ahead. Take a look," Estelle said as Jeff unfolded the body of the scarf. He held the end and unraveled it from the pile on Estelle's lap then held it above his head so that it hung vertically from his fingers. He inspected it a moment before speaking.

"It looks like a DNA strand," he said.

"Jeff, it's a scarf," Annene said, petulant.

"I know it's a scarf, Annene. But, if you had two and held them up like this it would look like a double helix."

"Not bad, Jeff. You know your stuff," Judy remarked.

"I just finished an AP biology class and we studied genes. It's interesting stuff. Cutting edge."

"Tell me about it," Estelle said, wheezing. Her speech was getting slower.

"Well," Jeff began. He turned to Annene who sat watching, more at ease with his presence. Jeff, customarily resigned and withdrawn when he was with Neil, Annene and Claire, stood beside the bed and spoke with the calm assuredness reserved for the aged; his voice never wavered, his hands were steady and his eyes, once he made the connection, never faltered or fell but remained true and present. He looked Judy and Estelle in the eye. Annene had never seen him like that before and something inside her shifted. Jeff was definitely unique to the other boys she had known.

"You don't mind, do you Annene?" Jeff asked. "I really didn't plan to come her and talk but..."

Judy and Annene turned their attention to Jeff.

"You don't mind honey? Do you?" Estelle asked.

"No," Annene replied. She truly did not mind which was odd. "Go ahead. All I have to talk about is my dress for the dance."

"Don't let me interrupt," Jeff said. "I'm really sorry."

"She already finished. Besides Jeff, you're the guest."

"If you had two of these things it would look like a double helix. DNA makes up life. It's a code of proteins and..."

"That's it," Estelle interrupted, suddenly excited.

"What? What is it?"

Estelle swallowed hard.

"Take it easy, Mrs. Berry."

"Mom. You're going to wind up having to stay in here longer if you keep carrying on like this."

Estelle wrote: "I'm making two scarves, Jeff. Twenty six thousand, two hundred and eighty stitches for all my days here. Fitting it all in one will never work." She smiled.

"That's pretty cool. Twenty six thousand, two hundred and eighty stitches?"

"Personally, I think it's depressing," Judy said.

"Gram's just feeling her mortality, Mom. It's natural."

"Annene." Judy scolded.

"Well, it's true."

"Sorry, Jeff."

"No problem," he said. "Why don't we talk about your dress?" he said, smiling.

Annene felt chills at the back of her neck. Estelle looked at her granddaughter as did Judy, both feeling Annene's embarrassment. Her face flushed.

"You can wait a couple of days. I have to finish it."

"Annene's very talented," Judy said.

Estelle nodded and held up the needles to the scarf that was connected by loops to each needle.

"Can you knit too?" Jeff asked Annene. She watched his long fingers kneed it slowly.

Annene nodded. "A little. Gram taught me." Her voice was louder and her tone softened. It was getting easier to be around him.

"Mom, we better get going," Judy said, standing up from her chair then turning around to see the impression her backside left in the plastic covered seat. She straightened her blouse and smoothed her pants then let go of a long sigh.

"I'll tell the nurses to put the food away," Judy said to her mother. "Jeff, do you need a ride home?"

"Sure," Jeff answered. "I'd appreciate it, Mrs. Berry."

"I'll drop you off and if you want we can bring you over tomorrow so you can give the nurses back the scrubs."

"He's going to be a doctor. Maybe he should keep them so he can get used to the idea. Of course, it's your decision."

"It sounds like a good idea. That's very nice of you."

"Then, we'll see you tomorrow too," Estelle said.

Annene leaned over to kiss her. Jeff got up from the side of the bed and turned to the door. Estelle winked at Annene who followed Judy out the door shoulder to shoulder with Jeff. The configuration was an accident that gave him to opportunity to take her hand, a gesture that startled her at first but she relaxed into. Something had opened inside her. Jeff had won over her grandmother and her grandmother had won him over.

Estelle looked after them. She watched their backs suddenly struck by the distance in age between her and them. The distance in emotion. The distance of firsts. But, she was happy at the vision.

"Bye, Gram. See you tomorrow," Annene said over her shoulder.

Jeff's smile was wide.

"Come again tomorrow if you'd like," Estelle said.

She watched them leave in hospital silence before she picked up the needles again.

They did. He brought photos of his lizards, Rufus and Cornelius. Annene watched Judy and Estelle listen attentively to the young man, this time dressed in the white on black Specials T-shirt, explain the geographical differences between Rufus's tropical environment and the desert landscape of the Geckos, Bonnie and Clyde, and Cornelius, the Pyramid Agama.

"Rufus is a Water Dragon. So," he said, pointing to the long spine down his back. "He uses this fin for balance when he swims. Cornelius is a Pyramid Agama and his gray coloring and bumpy surface protect him from enemies.

Estelle was deeply interested in the lives of Jeff's lizards, and Annene, who had never been in the mixed company of Jeff and her family until the day prior, became increasingly aware of him. He was different, more different than any other teenage boy living in Alpharetta, Georgia. Wise. Sure of himself but not cocky like most of the jocks. Smart but not introverted. Silence seemed to be his choice. To listen. Despite circumstance, everything he did was by his choice. Oddly, he was a fighter and Annene could relate to that in her own way.

"Estelle and Judy are falling all over him. Since when do they care about lizards?" Annene said to Claire on the phone. She burned incense and kneeled in front of the Buddhist mandala set upon a low bookshelf. Her thoughts had interrupted an attempt at stillness and led her to call her best friend. Claire was her best friend now.

"They're just being nice," Claire said.

"I thought Jeff was so shy. Then, he went on and on about DNA the first day and then about his lizards today. I told Judy he usually doesn't talk this much. Judy said he must feel comfortable at the hospital because it's something he knows."

"I guess that makes sense. Kind of like my Dad when he would read a book he really liked and would lecture me for ten minutes straight."

"Yeah. But, Neil doesn't do that with your parents."

"My mom likes him though." Claire said the words that lingered with odd and questionable vibrations of lies.

"Yeah. But, he didn't go on and on," Annene said and rolled her eyes.

"It's not that bad," Claire said. Then, struck by the sudden thought of the feel and scent of her mother's wardrobe added, "Maybe it makes him feel closer to his family by being there with yours."

Annene was silent for a moment and cleared her throat.

Claire, then to save herself from an emotional pitfall, changed course. "My dad barely said two words to Neil."

"That's because your mom had him do housework and yard work."

"Dad said it was probably just an excuse to see me." Claire thought of the way Ernest examined, if not glared at, Neil whose shifting eyes would not connect with her father's. Ernest did not trust him for that. Claire shrugged it off as old-fashioned.

"How are you and Neil getting along?" Annene asked.

"Fine." Claire paused. She took in a deep reflective breath then continued. "You know what? I think the dance is going to be the first time that Grandma Bernie sees Neil."

"She hasn't seen him? " Annene asked. "I guess not. We're always at our house and he's stoned most of the time now. Not the material for meeting the family,"

Annene said.

"We're just busy. There's been a lot going on the past few months since we moved back to Alpharetta. Did she say something?"

"Estelle said Bernie said something. Don't worry about it. You're right. Anyway, you're pretty. They usually don't have to worry about you."

"That's kind of a shallow remark from a Buddhist," Claire said.

"It's not about being shallow, Claire. It's the facts. That's why I don't get why Jeff likes me."

"What? So you think Neil likes to be with me only because I'm cute? That's kind of an insult, Annene."

"Claire, let's face it. Neil drives an old Mustang, he's daytime television good looking. You're tall, thin, *pretty* and ride a Vespa. It's like Barbie and Ken. Then, there's me; short, ten pounds over weight and odd. Jeff drives a beat up car that runs only sometimes and he collects lizards."

"He has a good family, Annene. He's smart. He's also really focused on what he wants."

He wants me. Annene surprised herself with the thought.

Jeff never took pity on himself despite all that had happened in his family. She suppressed, tried to shove down into the base of her spine, the admiration she could not confess. Only there was this odd, internal conflict she could explain to herself only as a need to solve a mystery without a fully defined question.

"They're not his real family and he's creeping me out. I don't know if he should give me the creeps or if I should like him. I've never felt like this before. I'm very confused."

She shook her hands at her sides like she could drain the discomfort but did not.

"You know, one day I went over to your house and he was standing in the front yard just looking at the house. It was a while back. He just stood there."

"Maybe he was waiting for Neil to get home."

"No, this was a while ago. Your mom was already gone, obviously, but Neil's car, the Mustang, was parked around the corner. He was just standing there like a stalker."

The phone clicked and the high-pitched sound of seven digits sounded.

Annene held the phone away and when Annene heard the last of the seven touch tone sounds she said, "Neil I'm on the phone."

"Still?" he asked, impatient.

"Hi Neil. We'll be off in a minute," Claire said, her voice cheery and sweet.

"Oh, hi Claire. You getting ready?" he asked.

"Not yet."

"Not yet. I thought it took you all day to get ready. We can't be late."

"Oh, will you shut up and let us finish talking. God, you're a pain in the ass," Annene said.

"That's only because I have you as a sister."

"We'll be finished in a little bit, Neil. I'll be ready in time. Don't worry about it."

"Okay, Bye," he said. "Bye, Annene."

"You suck, Neil."

The phone clicked.

"Do you guys ever stop arguing?"

"No, I don't know why we fight so much. Judy says I take after my father."

"Did they argue a lot?"

"No, Dad yelled and Mom said nothing and only worked all the time so she didn't have to deal with it. She could have started working during the day. She didn't always have to work nights."

"I thought you said she had to."

"In the beginning she did but, then when I started going to Outreach and we met with the counselors at school, she told me she did it because she didn't want to be at home."

"I didn't know you did that. What? The Outreach thing?"

"It was when you were in Atlanta and Judy and I started fighting a lot. Sue and Carol are both pretty cool. I started going there when I figured out I could get out of class with a pink slip."

"Why didn't you say anything?"

"I didn't think it was such a big deal," Annene said, pausing. "Wait. Is Neil still on the phone?"

"No, he's off. I heard him click off."

"Maybe you should to too, Claire. It would help you, I think."

"With what?" Claire asked. She lay across her bed dressed in a gray, over-sized sweat suit and slippers. She supported herself on her elbows but pushed herself up to a seated position.

"For what?"

"It's not the easiest thing in the world, Claire, your Mom leaving. Don't you think it would be a good idea to talk to someone about it? It's not good to hold all of that inside."

"All of what? She's gone. What can I do about it?"

"I don't know. Just talk. I just started going in there when I felt like talking because I didn't have anyone to talk to. I mean, I couldn't talk to Judy and Neil's not exactly understanding."

"What about me?"

"Well, you're part of what I talk about."

"Really?"

"Yeah."

"What'd I do?"

"Nothing, Claire," Annene said. "I just worry about you. You're getting too skinny. You don't eat."

"Annene, thank you for caring, but I wouldn't worry too much about it."

"No?"

"No," she replied. Claire sat cross-legged on her bed. "I have to start getting ready now. Dad wants to take pictures before we leave and so does Bernie."

"All right," Annene said. "But you have to start eating, Claire. It's not good for you. You look anorexic."

Annene sat on the floor, her back was against the bed frame and the lights were off. The windows were covered with blackout shades.

"I've got Grandma's camera so she can have pictures at the hospital. She's so upset she can't go. You should have heard her yesterday at the hospital when Jeff was going on and on about the lizards. She made him promise to get a lot of pictures and bring them on Sunday."

"You can't get them that fast though. They don't develop them that fast."

"She has a Polaroid."

Claire laughed and rolled up her sleeves, then reached behind her head and twisted the coil of hair around and around, then tied it in a knot that unfastened almost immediately, letting her hair fall again to her shoulders.

"I'm getting ready now. I'll see you in a little bit," Claire said.

"You're getting ready now?" Annene asked, searching the room until her eyes steadied on the liquid neon numbers of the digital clock.

The phone clicked.

"You're not off yet?" Neil groaned.

"We're getting off now, moron," Annene barked, then added, "Bye."

She hung up.

"Bye," Claire said.

She sat on her bed for several minutes, reclined on the pillows stacked against the headboard. Extending her legs, she gathered the pants material over her thin legs until it was so snug that she could see the actual outline of her thighs, then slapped her hip a few times to watch the flesh jiggle.

She dismissed Neil's behavior since they rarely spoke on the phone.

"Hmm," she said to herself. "Look fucking fat to me."

Claire tossed her legs over the side of the bed. In the bathroom she removed the sweat suit pants first then hung it over the back of her vanity chair with the iron, heart-shaped back. The cushion was dusty rose with white and yellow flowers, and the frame, a rough and bumpy antique iron, was painted white.

Opening the glass shower door, she reached in, turned the pressure knob and let the water run over her fingers as she rotated the handle toward the hot indicator. She let the water run and closed the door then turned to look into the mirror above the sink. It covered the wall almost entirely, from the top of the white tile set in a backsplash to the ceiling. To her left was a mirrored medicine cabinet that Claire opened to an angle that allowed a side view of her body. Milky white and tomboy thin. She dropped the towel to the floor and felt the skin over her ribs. Her hip bones protruded. Her chest was flat and merely verged on development though she had passed puberty. She was an adolescent on the threshold of being a woman. She knew her growth was stunted and stifled. She knew it was true.

Steam billowed out above the shower door opening between the metal glass frame and tile. Claire pulled the silver handles and reached into the shower again to turn the dial to the left and cool the water down. Steam quickly clouded the glass mirror. Thinking again, she closed the door and dropped the rose-colored towel to the floor. She walked to the scale and stood on it. It read one hundred and one.

She stepped off then into the shower, satisfied with the temperature to touch.

ELEVEN | Additives

Neil lay in his room in the dark. Both he and Annene had gotten into the habit of sleeping through daylight hours; Judy needed a dark house in the middle of the day to sleep either off or toward her night shift. Light came through the blinds and crept across the denim bedspread that covered half his body. His legs lay exposed to keep cool. He brought the phone to his ear and, hearing the dial tone, set the phone to his stomach. Tilting it toward him, he lifted his head and dialed.

Two rings came through the receiver and Neil lay inhaling deeply, his heart stepping up a few beats. A woman's voice answered the phone.

"Hello."

No response. Neil held his breath.

"Hello," the voice repeated, impatient.

Neil cleared his throat before he spoke. "Maggie?"

The phone clicked and Neil lay there, his ear to the receiver until the loud hang up signal blasted into his unguarded ear with the cadence of a car alarm. He pulled the phone away so it was muffled by the blankets of his bed. Through his nose, he took a long breath and caught the musky scent of Annene's Nag Champa incense.

He shot up straight when he knocked the phone off the

side of the bed. The sound still blared. He flung open the door, squinted at the light then yelled to the door directly across from his and just past the bathroom door.

"Will you put that shit out? My allergies are making me feel like shit."

The door opened slowly and Annene appeared. "What? Pretty boy thinks his nose'll run all over your dress?"

"Oh shut up you tub. It gives me a headache."

Annene drew back and closed the door enough to reveal only a sliver of herself.

"Neil. Who has allergies in the middle of December? No one."

"Whatever Tubbo, Buddhist, weirdo. You're such a freak, Annene. Why do you have to burn that shit?"

"I'm meditating."

"You can meditate all you fucking want to. Dad's not coming back either."

Annene's face went blank.

"You're such a shallow imbecile, Neil. You don't give a shit."

Annene slammed the door and continued yelling. You can't even tell Claire is starving herself to death. She's so messed up. Did she tell you her mom finally served divorce papers? She didn't even mention her in the letter that came with the papers. You don't give a shit."

Annene withstood Neil's teasing in the past, but the last stung and she had to work hard to keep herself from crying.

Neil walked across the hall and stood at his sister's bedroom door dressed only in boxers and a Hanes under shirt, listening.

"I'm sorry, Annene," he said. "I didn't mean it."

"Leave me alone, Neil. I have to get dressed. Go back to your room and smoke some more of that shit. At least when you do that you're too stupid to be an asshole. You already fucked up my night."

Neil returned to his room and closed the door. Faucet water ran in the bath, then a pitched squeak and the light drizzle of the shower came down. They had to be at the Hinkley's in two hours and Annene was starting to get dressed. At the side of his bed, Neil rested his head in his hands, slouched over like he'd seen a football player pray before a game. Unable to resist the urge, he leaned over and slid a shoebox from under the bed that he set beside him. Still off the cradle, the phone had finally gone silent. Neil replaced it on the base and put it on the hardwood floor beside the multicolored area rug. He flicked on the light and pushed on the button next on brass doorknob to lock the door.

He took the box off the bed and sat on the floor where he leaned against the frame. The royal blue on white cardboard box was printed with the "Vans" logo. The corners were frayed soft. Neil's name was written large in all capital letters, penmanship that sloped to the left. Several rubber bands were wrapped around it, two lengthwise and one around the girth.

Inside, the box was half-filled with photographs that he flipped through fast like it was a stack of LP's. He knew what he was looking for and when he found one he lingered on it. There he was photographed, young and dressed in a Hang Ten T-shirt and shorts, tube socks with blue stripes and trendy checkered canvas slip-ons. Judy squatted to his left wearing a blue tank top and jeans. Her hair fell across her shoulders and her smile was wide and real. Her face was young and tanned, not old and dragging. Also squatting but positioned in the photograph to his right was a man in a plaid, short-sleeved, button-down shirt with a front pocket. He wore jeans and sneakers, held a player's mitt tucked over his left hand. A baseball cap hugged the circumference of his head. His unshaven, shadowed face was fringed with a layer of wavy dark brown hair. His right arm held Neil's shoulder into him by his side. Under the dark moustache was a wide smile. His eyes were concealed by dark, aviator sunglasses with a thin gold wire frame. His father looked like Burt Reynolds and was often mistaken for him by many women in Georgia who impressed their movie star fantasies upon him. The Alpharetta Mafia was late with even new styles of men so images and fantasies of him hung around long after the coasts let him go for someone else.

Neil sat looking at the photograph of his dad, then put it back on top of the others and sifted through the papers, envelopes, old baseball cards and more pictures toward the bottom where he found a photograph torn in half. It was a younger Maggie dressed in a black formal gown. Blond hair and blue eyes with a soft and full smile. Perfectly curvy, Neil imagined the softness to her hips, the warmth, and he swallowed hard against his excitement. She held a man's hand but the portion of the photograph had been torn out. The portion with Ernest had been discarded. Like him. She did not need either of them anymore.

The screech from the pipes cut off the flow of water abruptly. Annene was out of the shower.

Back to the bottom of the box, Neil replaced Maggie's picture, then resealed it and slipped it back under his bed. Bracing himself with his lean arms, he pushed himself off the floor and went to the door. Wiggling his toes, he tried to remove dust and lint from the bottoms of his feet. It gathered on the hardwood floor and embedded itself to his damp soles. Balanced like a flamingo, he rubbed his feet against his bare shins. Weeks passed without Judy nagging him to clean his room.

Annene stood in the hallway, her hair in a lavender towel turban and another wrapped around her chest.

"You done?" Neil asked, squinting. His head was thick and heavy.

Annene looked at him hard and shook her head. "I'll need to get back in but I'm done with the shower."

Her brother rubbed his eyes and Annene thought she noticed pink circles on his eyelids. Wet eyelashes. Only they could not have been tears of sadness or of remorse but perhaps tiredness. Fatigue. Allergies. She studied him. Neil never cried. He was a jock like their dad.

"Listen Annene, I'm sorry."

"Just get dressed, Neil. We have to get over there and I don't want to be late."

She weakened to the sight of his vulnerability but shut down the feeling, unready to engage with him again.

"All right," Neil said. They passed each other, Annene heading to her room and Neil into the bathroom.

The door was half closed before she added, "Make sure you lock it, Neil. You don't know who might try to get in."

"You're so sarcastic, Annene. I just want my privacy."

"Uh, huh," she said. "I'll close my door."

Neil undressed and let the water wash over him as though it would wash away the memories, easier to leave than be left.

TWELVE | Botanicals

Claire stood in the living room where she looked out the window while her grandmother rearranged items on the kitchen counter to make room for the appetizer trays on the kitchen sink.

Bernie mumbled instructions to herself. Dressed for her guests, she wore a peach silk sweater and cream-colored pants. Her gold lame shoes had a modest heal. Claire, Annene and Bernie spent that morning at the salon. Bernie's hair was curled and teased full like the thin strings of cotton candy then brushed smooth with a comb.

"I'll put this here and this... This. Claire, help me move these things out of here," Bernie said louder. Rushing, she pushed the flour and sugar tin canisters to the corner of the linoleum counter to make room for a bag of wheat rolls, the coffee jar and apples. She placed them all in a large stainless steel pot.

"Claire," Bernie called again. She held the pot by the handles.

"Just a second, Grandma," Claire replied. "I'm coming."

"Good. Good. I need your help, honey." Bernie thought again. "Don't rush. I don't want to rush you."

It was exciting. Claire was doing something normal and that took Bernice back in time to a life very distant where the firsts of youth are surprises.

She left the pot on the kitchen counter and walked into the living room where Claire stood and faced the window to the front yard. Her hands fumbled at her sides.

Before her granddaughter could say anything Bernie opened her arms wide and said, "You look beautiful, dear."

She hugged Claire who returned the embrace a bit stiff but genuine. Nerves, adrenaline and anticipation overwhelmed Claire with anxiety. She was never good at the dog and pony show. She thought of her mother's grace and the comparison to her lack only made her feel more awkward.

"Oh, what a good job we did picking that out. "Turn around."

Claire teetered a bit on the two-inch black-healed shoes and smoothed the black satin dress over her waist and hips.

"This thing keeps slipping down." She scowled and pulled the dress up by the bust line. It was a fitted strapless black dress hemmed at the knee. Swept up into a French twist, strands of hair fell and tickled her cheeks.

"No, you look lovely, honey. I love the style you chose for your hair."

"I got it out of a magazine. You sure I don't look like a surfboard?"

"A surfboard? What do you mean, a surfboard?"

"Flat," she replied, pulling up the bust line of her dress.

"Of course you don't, honey." Bernie shook her head and turned up the corners of her mouth. "Why do you say that?"

"Grandma, I didn't inherit your bust line."

"Oh, come on. Where did you hear that expression? A surfboard?" She smoothed the sides of her waist that continued to thicken as the years ticked forward.

"Neil's friends." Claire followed her grandmother into the kitchen.

"Not so sure I like the sound of that," she sighed.

"What do you need help with?" Claire tried to change the subject.

Bernie cringed. "Hmmm," she said, and felt a surge of anger that locked her jaw tight. She cleared her throat and controlled her voice. "Boys that age can be cruel. Don't listen to that. I certainly hope Neil is a gentleman and doesn't talk like that. Not to you."

Claire looked to the floor. "No," she replied. "What did you need help with?"

"This stuff. I got some things for you and the boys to munch on," Bernie said, and gestured toward the counter.

"Thanks." Repelled, she pushed the thought of food away in her mind like it was poison to her body. Saliva came from her mouth and she wanted them then hated herself for it, for the lack of control. "We're having dinner at Benihana before though," Claire said. She put the clean, washed, soap-making pot in the cabinet below the sink. Food before would ruin the night. It would ruin her maximum calorie intake for the day. "You didn't have to do that, Gram."

"It'll give you something to nibble on while we take the pictures," Bernie replied. "If you don't like this, I'll just put out the vegetables and dip. Just a little something."

The front door opened and both Frank Hinkley, Claire's grandfather, and her father, Ernest, entered the house through the living room.

"Hello," Frank said, his voice cheery and at home though it was his son's home. Ernest followed behind him and said nothing.

Sensing Claire's detachment, her stiff composure braced against nerves, Bernice changed course and used the excuse to arrange appetizers. She spread them from one side of the sink to the other: a crudités platter of cut carrots, celery sticks, radishes, broccoli, and cauliflower florets arranged on a glass serving dish with a glass bowl in the center filled with poppy seed dip. Wheat Thins and Ritz Crackers were arranged around a wedge of Jarlsberg cheese. Several drinking glasses and both Diet and regular Coca-Cola cans and a pitcher of water were set beside a black ice bucket.

"We're in here," Bernie replied. She pulled apart the sides of the pretzel bag so it opened at the seam, then tilted the contents so they spilled into a big wooden bowl.

She turned around with the sound of her son and husband behind her.

"So, where's the gang?" Frank asked. He stood in front of his wife of forty years, over two feet taller than Bernie. He wore a short-sleeved, button-down shirt of neutral plaids. A pen hung from its silver clip and clung to the breast pocket. Flat front khakis and loafers. Simple. He had a long face and blue eyes. His gray hair was thinned. Expressionless though his face was most often, Claire was his joy. His only granddaughter.

"I thought they'd be here at five thirty," Ernest said. He looked around the room for any signs of the boys as though they were hiding somewhere behind the furniture or drapes, buried between the sofa cushions.

Claire turned around to face her father and grandfather and noticed that her father and grandfather both looked and dressed the same. She tried not to laugh. Ernest wore beige pants, Topsiders and a short- sleeved, button-up, blue, plaid shirt. A pen stuck out of the front pocket. Frank wore the same, only brown loafers.

"Holy Moly," Ernest said. "Claire, you look great. I didn't even recognize you."

Claire looked away. The corner of her mouth lifted and her eyebrows narrowed.

"Get a load of that," Frank said. "You letting her leave the house like that?" he said.

"Oh, Frank, come on. I thought you were going to dress up for crying out loud."

"You going to let her go out like that?" Frank repeated.

"She looks great, Dad," Ernest said. He realized he had already said the wrong thing by Claire's reaction and extended his hand as if to block Ernest from crossing the street into oncoming traffic. The light of the kitchen revealed more of Claire's figure. A waif in a little black dress looked less than what she was. She took hold of her boxy left shoulder with her right hand, her arm a shield across her chest.

"Honey, you've gotten so thin," Frank said, instantly at her arm.

"It's just the dress, Grandpa," she replied and took the spoon from Grandma Bernie's hand.

"You'll ruin your dress though," Bernie argued.

Claire stirred the insides of the bowl at the center of the crudités platter in several circular sweeps that left a thin coating of onion dip on the spoon.

Frank regarded Bernie for a moment. The room was silent.

"What?" Claire asked. She tossed the container into the trash can, a large woven basket, then froze like a rabbit seized in the woods at the sound of a twig snapping. She recognized the sound of the Mustang engine.

Within seconds, Annene's voice spilled into the living room. "We're here," she shouted though everyone stood within a few feet of each other in the Hinkley's living room.

"Oh, rats," Bernie said. "I haven't even finished."

"Gram, we're done," Claire said, and set the spoon into the sink.

Annene instinctively walked into the kitchen.

"Tah, dah," she said to Claire who just turned around.

Annene modeled, her hands prim and straight to her sides. The purple spaghetti strap dress clung to her full figure. Stacked glass beads strung in twos, threes and fours hung from thread attached in an even pattern throughout the dress bodice. A sheer piece of lavender fabric wrapped around her neck and fell in a cascade down her back to her bottom. She raised her hands above her head.

"Well?" She asked, her eyes wider than usual. She wore false eyelashes and black mascara with bright red matte lipstick. Her black hair was bone straight.

"Where's Neil?" Claire asked.

Annene flopped her hands to her sides in mock defeat.

"Neil," Claire blurted. "Yeah, where is he?"

Annene put her hands on her hips. Her buoyant expression was vivid with a full-lipped smile that transformed her pale face but it dropped when the focus again turned to her brother.

"He's parking the car. He'll be in, in a minute," she said.

Claire walked on the toes of her short heels as she looked Annene up and down with removed admiration. Annene had no problem with attention. Claire, on the other hand, hoped she would blend in, self conscious and teetering in black satin heels that were an entire two inches lower than Annene's.

"Claire, what's wrong?" Annene asked.

"Nothing," she replied. "I just want to get going."

Aware of the shift in conversation, Mr. Hinkley motioned Frank toward the appetizers at the kitchen sink. Neither feared the emotional tone of female conversation, but they knew when to allow them space and when to relieve themselves of the discomfort of its depth. Bernie handed a tray to Frank and looked over her shoulder at Annene whose disappointment rendered itself as a smile that lacked emotion.

It was the only time in Annene's history that she worked so hard to get ready for the kind of group function normal for kids her age. Despite her otherwise grand entrance, the disappointment was obvious and she was ashamed at her need for recognition. Hadn't they known how hard she'd worked for this?

Bernie immediately understood and felt for Annene. Grandma Estelle was still in the hospital. The girl was fragile and Bernie knew all of this, ever the caretaker with also a grandmother's intuition.

Annene, you look lovely. Doesn't she look lovely, Frank?"

Annene lowered her eyes to her shoes. Her C-cup breasts were exposed but decently covered by a veil-like material where Annene had also sewn a few iridescent plastic beads.

"Frank took the crudités platter. "Yes. Yes," he agreed, nodding.

"Your dress looks great, Annene." Claire looked her up and down. "Your face though. It looks like… It's a little white."

"It's rice flower. The Geisha's do it and I like the look. It's very contemporary. Of course, no one would know that in the South."

"You don't have to get all snappy with me. I was just asking." She was already exhausted and wondered how long she could last in the heels. Annene wore black stilettos. It was going to be a long night.

"You're just ahead of the times, honey. Your grandma is the same way. It's very unique," Bernie said.

Ernest walked to the door, opened it and looked out at Neil's nineteen-eighty-six convertible Mustang parked on the street. He sat inside with the motor running.

"What's he doing?" Ernest asked his father who joined him at the door.

"Annene said he was parking the car," Frank replied.

"It's not like he hasn't been here before," Ernest said.

"Here you go." Bernie handed the pretzel bowl to Annene. "Will, you put this out for me, dear." Then, changing the subject she added, "Oh, I can't wait to get those photos for your grandmother. She's going to be thrilled."

"You look beautiful too, Grandma Bernie." Annene lowered her eyes to Bernie's gold lame shoes to the top of Bernie's head. Wearing three-inch heals, Annene stood a few inches taller than the woman. "Is that a new outfit?"

"No. I've had it for some time."

Claire looked away from the window and smiled at her grandmother.

"Where's Neil?" Claire asked. Inches from the glass, she tried to find him in the car but he was gone.

"I'm here."

Neil stood at the door wearing a standard black tux cut wide to his shoulders. At eighteen, he filled out the uniform enough to be mistaken for a college freshman. He patted his hair, slicked back with Aqua Net hairspray. Strands were stuck together and stiff like it was still wet.

Claire took a tentative step back. Neil smiled wide and his eyes were clear which Claire was glad about. Ernest approached him and shook the young man's hand.

"Neil, good to see you again," he said. "It's been a long time."

It was a reminder of things he'd rather not imagine but Neil inhaled deeply and smiled wider.

Claire moved from the window to her father's side.

"Nice to see you too, Mr. Hinkley," he said.

"Well, hello Neil. Nice to *finally* see you," Bernie said. Though she tried not to, she raised her chin and looked down her nose.

"Neil, you remember my Grandma Bernie," Claire said.

Neil nodded and extended his hand. "Nice to see you again too, ma'am."

Annene stood over the plate of crudités, picking out the carrot sticks then reached for a handful of pretzels. "Where's Jeff, Neil? I thought you said he was going to meet us here."

"He's on his way. He should be here any minute." Neil cocked back his head like it was a rubber band on a slingshot.

"Well, come in honey," Bernie said.

Neil stood on the porch, awkward. When he took the first step through the door his toe caught on the metal plate that stuck up just slightly and caused him to trip into a two step. Neil's face flushed and Annene turned her head to hide her smile.

"Frank, I thought you were going to fix that," Bernie said and cleared her throat. "I'm sorry, Neil. We keep meaning to fix it but with all there is to do around here, we haven't had time."

"Mom, don't worry about it."

"Don't worry, Bernice. It's on my honey do list."

"What is *that*?" Annene asked. She still sat on the sofa cradling the pretzels in her hand, eating them one by one. "What's a honey do list?"

"You know. Honey do this, honey do that."

"Oh Frank," Bernie squawked.

"What?" Frank threw up his hands.

"Mom, don't worry about it. It's my house. I'll get to it," Ernest said.

"But you're so busy. Your dad'll do it."

Claire looked over to Annene then exchanged a knowing look with Bernie.

"Why don't we sit down?" Bernie asked. She put her arm around Claire who leaned her head down to Bernie's shoulder where she caught the smell of honeysuckle oil dabbed behind her ears. Claire was too tall to rest for more than a moment, but Bernie got the effect and rubbed her granddaughter's arm.

"You smell nice, Gram," Claire said.

"Thank you, honey."

"You going to make soap with that smell?"

"It's the same thing I've worn since you were a little girl. I'm using honeysuckle, magnolia, lavender."

They sat down together.

"Lavender?" Annene turned up her lip.

"Bernice, I don't think our guest wants to hear about

145

your soap making tonight." Frank smiled at his wife attempting to couch the issue while Ernest came in for the save.

"Please Neil, have a seat." He gestured to the wing chair where Ernest usually sat most nights reading under his lamp.

"Lavender is a nice smell." Bernie cocked her head at Annene who finished the handful of pretzels and leaned over toward the coffee table. Frank and Ernest sat down at the dining room chairs Frank brought in from the adjacent room. Claire gave her father a hopeful but blank look.

"Old ladies smell like lavender," Annene said, chewing the last of the pretzels. "Grandma Estelle wears it all the time so I hope she gets some of your soap for Hanukkah."

"You're celebrating Hanukkah this year?" Bernie asked.

"Yeah, Judy will. We get a Christmas tree too though. She said we could keep doing it even though my dad's not around."

"Aren't you a Buddhist though?" Bernie asked, picking up the plate of vegetables.

Annene shrugged.

"Anyone for some vegetables and dip? Neil? Here, have some. You have a while until dinner and you must be hungry."

Neil took the plate from Bernie and placed two or three pieces of cauliflower covered with dip on it. As he chewed, he realized he was hungry despite the tension.

"So, Claire says you play sports," she began.

Neil nodded, still chewing. He swallowed and wiped the corners of his mouth with his thumb and index fingers.

"Football. Our team is doing well this year but I hurt my back so I haven't been able to play much." It was a well-practiced lie by then so the delivery was natural.

"Oh, I'm sorry to hear that," Bernie said. "Frank here injured his ankles playing basketball years ago. Tell Neil about it, Frank."

"Oh, he doesn't want to hear a bunch of stories from me," Frank said shaking his head.

"Fine," she said. "Ernest, my son here played football. He was the star of his team senior year in high school. He was quite the athlete back then. Maggie was…," she began, but stopped herself. "Well, I guess you don't really want to hear a bunch of old stories. Frank's right."

Neil looked to the open door willing Jeff to arrive so they could leave. Claire angled her eyes to Annene who, distracted by the urge to eat more, wondered if Jeff would stand her up.

Moments of awkward silence passed.

"Why don't you call Jeff?" Claire asked Neil and pointed to the phone. He stuffed the last piece of cauliflower into his mouth.

"Mmm hmm," was all he said before he got up from Ernest's chair and went to the phone. He picked it up then placed it back down on the cradle.

"I'll just go over there instead."

"Oh, no need to do that," Bernie said.

"Gram, he lives next door. It's not going to be that much of a problem," Claire said.

"Well, I just thought it would be easier is all." She patted her breastbone and rolled the round, polished quartz stones linked together like pearls between her fingers.

"I'll be right back," he said, and took a brief look at his sister who grew visibly disappointed. She pulled strands of black hair just in front of her face to examine the ends. When Neil turned, she watched his back as he walked out the door, and let go of the one split strand. It was a peace offering whether or not Neil understood.

"You really like it, Grandma Bernie?" Annene asked when he was gone.

"It's beautiful, Annene," Bernie said. She put her hand flat over her heart and cleared her throat to suppress the emotion. All that feeling made her glad for the rote actions and stifled emotion of ceremony.

"It is," Claire nodded.

"What is?" Jeff asked. He stood in the entryway beside Neil. He wore a purple cummerbund and bowtie. His normally shaggy hair was brushed back but not held in place with any hair product. Annene was struck by how handsome he appeared. He held two plastic containers with white corsages in each.

Neil stood behind him where he cradled a small camera case and pack of film.

"I'm sorry I'm late," Jeff said. "The florist was pretty crowded. My apologies, ma'am. Sir."

Frank and Ernest stood up and Bernie glanced over to the girls insinuating with her firm eyes that they should stay put. Claire crossed her legs, and seeing this, Annene crossed her ankles.

Carefully, Jeff opened the clear, plastic corsage box and took out the small bundle of white flowers; tiny buds of baby's breath surrounded one large white rose. Delicate, he handled it carefully but let it go. The plastic box fell to the floor and Jeff bent to pick it up.

"You look like you have your hands full," Ernest said, leaning down to help him.

Jeff smiled and felt his face warm into what he knew was a deep flush. If he suppressed it, it would be worse.

"Here, let me help you out," he said.

When they both stood, Jeff handed the clear box with the corsage to Neil. In his other hand, he held the elastic wristband attached to the short stem of the rose intended for Annene. Ernest held the empty, plastic box.

"Thank you, Mr. Hinkley," Jeff said. "Very nice to meet you sir."

They shook hands.

"Nice to meet you too, Jeff. Claire's grandmother has only good things to say about you. This is my father, Frank Hinkley."

"Did you bring the camera?" Annene blurted from the

sofa.

Jeff peered around Ernest's shoulders, an obvious gesture to see Annene.

"Hi," he said.

"Hi," she replied, and crossed her arms.

"You look really nice, Annene."

"Doesn't she?" Bernie agreed.

"I'm sorry I'm late. The flower shop…"

"That's okay. I heard. It was crowded," she blurted and rolled one of the beads between her index finger and thumb. She pointed to his bowtie and cummerbund. Both a deep shade of purple. "Nice touch," she said and looked down at her dress.

"Thanks. Do you want to wear it on your wrist or should I pin it?"

Annene self-consciously touched the bust line of her dress. "Wrist," she replied.

"Good choice, honey. You don't want to ruin that nice material." Bernie patted Annene's hand. "Oh, let me get the camera so we can get going."

Annene shook her head.

Ernest removed the camera from its case and loaded the film. "It's ready," he said, and put the camera to his eye with the lens pointed at his daughter. Before she had the chance to object, the flash went off.

"Dad, not yet," Claire whined.

Ernest laughed. "Neil, why don't you go ahead and put the corsage on Claire and we can get this show on the road." It annoyed him to tell Neil this.

Still seated, Bernie watched as Neil pinned the corsage on Claire's black dress without asking. A satin trim folded over at the bust line and allowed room for the small bundle of white flowers.

Both Frank and Ernest shifted.

It was in that moment, the two of them together, that Bernie froze in her private realization. Her memory never failed even in these later years. The pieces came together when Neil and her granddaughter, whose ski slope nose and long, narrow face struck Bernice in what was a sudden remembrance mixed with insight and a collision of facts that suddenly trap the truth. Silently, she choked on it and stopped breathing for seconds that tallied quickly to need.

Claire smiled as everyone watched Neil without knowing that his confidence was already giving way to the beer he already drank and fatigue, his energy lost to a tired act.

Bernice had an inkling of something to come. She was too old to ignore it but wise enough then to keep it to herself. She felt a deep pain in her chest, tearing through weakness toward anger, again. That woman always made her angry though she always tried to be polite.

Judy left her father in Estelle's hospital room after a short visit she paid to her mother the night of the high school dance. When the late afternoon arrived, Judy drove Annene to Claire's house to gather with their dates. Jack joined them for the ride as Estelle asked to spend the evening together with her husband. Judy was unsure of the plan. She questioned her mother. Jack forgot most things and that was part of the reason. He had started to wander too, his mind failing at the pace of a young boy descending a slide. Nothing made sense anymore and Judy had to honor her mother's request. Estelle was finally old enough, and ill enough to ask Judy without much argument. Surrender finally found the room to leave it alone and let it go. Exhaustion and a life on the verge of great loss, even death, she worried, could do that.

Estelle bombarded Judy with questions about the dance preparations once Judy arrived with Jack. He nodded to Estelle and sat in the chair that faced the television that hung from a metal arm attached to the ceiling. Before Jack had the opportunity to confuse himself, to use the wrong words, to babble the ridiculous, he pointed the remote control to the television that lit the box with the evening news anchors to her touch.

"Why is the television hanging from the ceiling?" he asked and tapped the plain wooden arm of the chair.

When his daughter did not answer, Jack repeated, "Nurse."

Judy nodded her head to a rhythm of thought that brought her to the answer. "So everyone can see it."

Satisfied, he sat motionless aside from his right hand that tapped the chair arm, his eyes drifting from focus to the blank stare, in and out but mostly out of the cognitive fluidity of the working brain. There was the recognition but misspoken identification of his surroundings. The end of the day was the most susceptible to his slips. Those slips were continuous. Estelle knew not to prompt him with any demands but she had to stop herself. It had been so long since her husband inhabited that body. Judy kept him clean though his beige golf shirt was wrinkled.

"You told her I wanted to be there, didn't you?"

"She knows," Judy said, patting her mother on the shoulder and kissing her good-bye. "You'll be out soon, Mom." The words surrendered to fatigue.

"I hope that young man remembers the camera too."

"He'll remember." Judy kissed her father on the top of his bald, freckled head and followed his glassy-eyed gaze to the television that hung above them.

Closing the door behind her, she left them in the hospital room and told the nurse with the thick, large glasses, goodbye. She would return home alone. The last few years were about the type of loneliness that snuck in and loomed like the vague, pungent scent of something burned. Estelle's surgery used the last of her capacity. Drained her. And, Annene was changing so that Judy teetered between the perfect understanding of her daughter and the imminent loss of her. When Judy blamed herself for it, she tried to calm herself with the understanding that she could not make everything right.

Annene's youth prevented her from seeing things the same way. Her little girl was nothing like her mother and nothing like her father. She was Estelle Berry, a bit eccentric already at age seventeen.

Neil looked exactly like him. Like his father. Youth provided a sense of readiness but prepared that youth for nothing real. Judy, left alone and an only child herself, found strength enough to care for her ailing parents. She saw to her children's immediate needs: food, money and proper clothes. The nights passed more quickly when she worked at the hospital and the days of sleeping and hospital visits disappeared so quickly with repetition that she often forgot the details. And, she was glad for that. Greif and anger resided in those details. Rage fueled her efforts when grief held her down. When love and loss made her weak, apathy was the bridge she found with constant work.

She turned on the ignition in the Jeep Cherokee and left the hospital parking lot. At the light where the highway crossed Peachtree, a convertible black Camaro stopped beside her. When the light turned, a boy wearing a tuxedo laughed and shifted the car into gear with one hand then quickly grabbed at the bare knee of the girl beside him, her floral skirt lifted several inches above her knee. He was no older than Neil but he did look younger. The rear of the Camero lowered as he skidded through the intersection before Judy realized the light turned green. The driver could not see the road slip away underneath the body of the car, but she could. The kids were out. It was Neil's last year. He was held back a year in preschool so both he and Annene would leave her at the same time. All at once her life would be empty.

Life sped by fast and without grace. She feared that no matter what she would miss something.

Jack spent the night in the hospital beside Estelle as she

knitted with concentration and urgency. She stitched rapidly to escape sadness, poking and looping and turning the long scarf after each completed row while Jack watched Georgia newscasts repeat themselves like war stories told by fading old men.

Silence.

Estelle watched as her husband dozed, unaffected by the visible discomfort of the machine that fed her lungs air. His hair thinned at the sides and the crown was bald. She did not see his age but remained devoted to the brave man in the post World War II photograph. Frozen in time was Jack, decorated in stripes colored with valor. The former Cavalry man returned from war after a four-year absence from his wife and daughter. She understood that his mind slipped away a bit more each day keeping pace with her body that became less whole. His memories of shared moments were removed one by one while Estelle was faced with a barrage of them. His recall became distorted like lenses too strong that so confuse the vivid.

At least this is what she told herself.

Judy thought the man was her hero, and to Estelle, he would remain so. The thought pleased her as she looked up again to see Jack's eyes closed, head resting back against the wall, his mouth hung open.

Estelle spoke into the speaker phone. "Please, can you have that young man, David, fix the remote for me?" she asked. The pile of knitting lay on her lap. "I can't change the channel. It'll only be a second."

A woman's voice responded, flatly. "It's not a problem. It's only that he's not in this evening."

"He told me that he would be here so he could hook up my program. My daughter taped it for me. I need to take my mind off this place and I can't switch it from the news channel. I'm going a little crazy in here."

"Mrs. Berry, you won't be here much longer."

"Oh, rats. Now what am I supposed to do?"

Estelle looked over to Jack, his breathing softer,

rhythmic. Estelle picked up the knitting needles and continued with the basic pattern, stopping only to try the remote again. When it didn't work, she resisted the urge to throw it against the wall and instead placed it on the nightstand where Annene had left the bronze-covered copy of *The Bell Jar*. Age spots covered her bony hands that held the copy of the book. She opened it to the tabbed page and began reading. Black wire-framed reading glasses rested at the end of her nose. She read through the passages Annene underlined in blue pen, laughed quietly, and every now and then, looked over her shoulder at her sleeping husband. She barely heard his breath over her own wheezing and the valve release of the oxygen machine.

I found it strange that the nurse should call me Lady Jane when she knew what my name was perfectly well.

Tears pooled at the bottom of her pink lids and trickled down her cheeks as she returned to her knitting and cast on the stitches for the second scarf. Sighing deeply and long like a cat stretching, she relaxed into the sheet and bedspread. She laid her head against the raised hospital bed mattress, set down the needles still in her hands and turned to her husband in the chair beside her. He was oblivious to the sound of the newscast that called for clear skies.

She surrendered to sleep with the awareness that one life was too much to examine in a room with white walls.

Jack awoke to loud bells ringing the next morning. He lay in the recliner beside his wife's hospital bed where he shook off sleep slowly without understanding his whereabouts and Estelle's condition. He did not recognize the woman who lay in the bed but needed to find his wife.

Suddenly protective and confused, he left the room without a word and shuffled past Estelle and several people who rushed past him in the opposite direction

toward the noise and the woman who lay prone and
hooked into various machines in the room he just left.
The digital clock read five-o-seven and the streetlights
outside the hospital room window were still lit like fireflies.
Was it summer? Did he care? What did he have to care
about in that moment besides the family out of sight.

Despite the shadow of sleep, he moved with a sense of
urgency past a nurse talking into a phone, then through the
sliding doors that parted as he stepped onto the padded
plastic mat.

He wandered into the dawn. Instinct and automation
led him home like a hungry, tired dog.

Judy found her father wandering alongside Peachtree
Road where he walked along the sidewalk with his head in
his hands, lost. Tears wet his face but he forgot moments
after crying why it was that way. Then it started again.
Helplessness could have been the trigger that allowed the
memory of his daughter to comfort him. To save him.
He went with her without a fight. Without panic.

Annene sat in the passenger seat of the Pacer. Her face
was clean and eyes wide open in naïve terror. Shocked.
She wore green cotton sweatpants with a hole in the knee
and a black hooded sweatshirt. Her hair was still smooth
from the night before, snarled only slightly in the back
where she slept on it. She sat erect as her mother ushered
Grandpa Jack into the car.

Judy still wore her scrubs. The call to the hospital in
Atlanta where she worked came close to the end of her
shift, only twenty minutes prior. No one knew he had
disappeared. She needed just one night to be alone and
rest but all this had transpired. Her own denial kept her
from the acceptance that her dad could not function.

Judy held Annene, sobbing, caressed her back and hair
like she did when her daughter was a little girl.

Bernice arrived with Frank just short of an hour after

that and returned home to her thoughts of the night before. Her suspicions. Suspicions that receded into the background.

Christmas day fell on a Sunday that year, two days after the dance, and Bernie knew to finish her preparations for the holiday between all that had to be done to plan the memorial.

Bernie thought and thought about that night.

Bernie did not speak at her usual pace for the remainder of the winter formal evening, but stood back and watched as Ernest snapped photos of two couples. Like everything at Bernie's age, life passed too quickly only to be stored among the fragments with other dim images.

The next day she woke earlier than usual to receive the call about Estelle. Christmas preparations would have to wait. It would be the first Christmas in forty-three years she would spend without Estelle Berry.

Bernie, who always turned to the kitchen first, out of habit, turned off the faucet and left the pot in the sink to soak, to loosen the bits of soap still in it. She left it there and walked to the living room where she lowered herself onto the sofa, next to Estelle's knitting bag Judy gave her to take home.

Then, like a child who clutched a blanket to her face for comfort, she let the long black scarf absorb the tears that came fast and even, like steady hands that worked the yarn into one perfect strand.

THIRTEEN | Soponification

Jeff sat at the bus stop across the street from the club as he listened to The Doors through the headphones of the yellow Walkman he held in his hands. The Stones were away so he was on his own to get to the funeral, the memorial service, for Estelle Berry.

Just one week earlier girls in white paraded single file into that very large dance hall of the Thursday Club and one by one onto the stage where they curtseyed in long white, almost made-for-bride dresses. White beaded busts and fluffy taffeta sleeves strung the line of debutantes together. Like bells, the big tea length dresses swayed at their hemlines.

Jeff watched like he studied animal behavior. It was his entertainment as he waited for the bus. Life in New York, foster homes and group meals made his new life mysteriously reliable to him.

He never knew quite how to live. Not anymore.

The contrast of the Alpharetta debutante ball and the funeral was stark. It suited his experience and his mood and made him angry at formulaic joy. He and Annene agreed about that. Even Claire.

Jim Morrison sang, "I am the lizard king, I can do

anything," and Jeff mouthed the words.

Jeff's eyes shifted from the closed club door to the church entrance. He looked at the time on his Swiss Army wrist watch with the brown leather band. It was a gift from the Stones.

Three o'clock.

A police car and two black cars arrived and partially blocked the view of the church door main entrance located less than a block away from the Thursday club. One was a hearse. It was getting a little too real.

Moments after dead air the play button popped up and the tape deck wheels stopped. Jeff pushed the eject button and turned the tape to the "b" side. "Rush, Moving Pictures" was written in black capital letters on the label.

"Analog Man" blared in his ears. He reached into the pocket of his black pants, took out a small bottle marked, "meal worms," then replaced it and took out a cassette case. He looked at the play list then replaced it in the pocket.

More cars arrived in a line. Lead by two motorcycle cops, the cars passed The Club then the church and turned right to park behind the two buildings. Moments later people, or what Jeff knew to be mourners, filed into the church dressed in black and gray and some navy dresses. The women wore hats that covered mostly their eyes at least from Jeff's view. It occurred to him that the funeral was yet another social grace, though he found nothing graceful about it.

He saw Annene for only a moment as she turned the corner to the church entrance where she stopped and stood by herself, invisible. She watched the proceedings just as Jeff did until she vanished into the swarm of people who arrived at once. It was the first time he had seen her since the dance. Less than a week had passed.

Cars drove past, one after the other. Jeff watched catching brief glimpses of the back of Annene's head as she walked away from the church entrance. Briefly, he noticed a woman who stood to the side of the building. Jeff's observation skills placed the women Estelle's age in the circle of her newspaper colleagues. They were older but not as old as Estelle. Maybe in their late fifties and early sixties. One particular woman dragged on a cigarette between dramatic arm gestures that conjured loops in the air made by her burning cigarette. Sky writing. A white bow trimmed the brim of the black hat, a black skirt suit and two-tone pumps. There were pearls on the three of them, all conspicuous against their black suits and dresses.

Jeff removed the headphones from his ears and stuffed them into the inner pocket of his jacket. He brushed his coat with the palms of his hands and jogged across the street.

He watched Annene duck around the opposite side of the building where the gaggle of women left.

He found her.

She rolled her eyes when she saw him.

"Hey," he said, forcing a soft smile. Not hard to do because he was glad to see her. He couldn't help but think about the kiss she allowed at the end of the night just days earlier. "Why don't you come in with me?"

"I don't want to go in. I can't handle this," she said, and looked up and over Jeff's shoulder. He wore a suit this time.

"Annene, you just have to be there. No one expects anything."

"Leave me alone, Jeff. You and your DNA bullshit. You know what? You should be glad you were adopted because at least you didn't get hurt by not being the perfect clone of someone who's just light years apart from you. I just lost the only person I could ever talk to and I can't go in there," she said, and wiped under her eyes.

"Go away, please."

Jeff stepped back just as Neil turned around the corner.

"Judy said you're not coming in," Neil said.

"She just needs a minute to get herself together."

"I can speak for myself, please," Annene said.

Neil and Jeff exchanged a look and Jeff nodded.

"I'll see you in there then," he said, and left Neil and Annene to talk.

Annene lost control then and started to cry.

She quieted herself with deep inhales and removed a handkerchief from the black satin handbag. It was white with lace trim. "I don't know how Gram used this thing. It's white. It'll get disgusting."

"That's what it's for though," Neil said.

It was the smartest thing she had heard from her brother in months.

"Yeah," she said, examining it as she turned it by its corners.

"You better blow your nose. You sound like you just sucked in a balloon full of helium."

Annene laughed, raw, and slapped him on the shoulder. He smiled, strained.

"I wish Dad would come back, Neil. I know that's not going to happen, but it would make this a little easier. I sort of thought he'd be here today."

"Come on. Since when are you hopeful?" Neil joked.

Annene cocked her head.

"No one really cares, Neil. I think that's the thing really, you know? I think..."

Neil interrupted, "We should go in now, Annene."

He frowned and rubbed his eyes. "Put on your big girl pants and just go in. Jeff did. He wants you to sit next to him."

Annene realized it must be the first funeral for him since his parents died.

"It's not like it was Grandma's choice to die," Neil said.

"Since when did you get so deep?"

"I've been stoned for about two months now," he replied.

Annene shook her head.

"You're right," she said. "I suppose there's a first time

for everything."

PART TWO

FOURTEEN | Safety Tips

Television stations flashed on screen one after the other as Neil pushed the "up" arrow on the remote from two to thirteen then back down at a robotic rate. Perched on the glass top coffee table, his feet swung alternately. He wore white socks, faded jeans, unbuttoned once at the waist for relief, and an Atlanta Braves jersey that he only wore inside. He held a Coors Light beer can in his other hand that he drank from at intervals of approximately four surfed TV stations per drink. Lit only by the television, the room was dark with the blinds closed. The volume on the television set was just loud enough to hear.

Annene walked in the front door, still dressed in the black dress she wore that day to her grandmother's funeral.

Neil barely moved when he heard the keys jingle outside the front door and the wood scrape against the doorframe. It was just past midnight and too early to be his mother who worked into the morning and was not yet due home.

She stood in the living room silent and slipped the man's suit jacket off her shoulders. It was Jeff's. The black dress, a remainder from the Contempo Casuals formal collection that she got on sale. Clutching the bag in one hand and her black pumps in the other, Annene closed and locked the door behind her.

"Is Judy here?" she asked, looking straight on at Neil who didn't respond. Annene's face was bare with only a trace of black smudges under her eyes. She had washed her face with Mrs. Stone's cleanser and Jeff sat with her since Claire wanted to be with Neil. Annene wondered if she regretted that decision now and it worried her.

"Well, I guess that means, 'no,'" she said, a bit angry. "I guess I thought maybe she would be home tonight."

Silence. Neil flipped through the TV stations.

"Judy'd be pissed if she saw you on that," Annene said. She pointed to the glass top kitchen table. "I mean, why? I have to police you when she's not home."

He shook his head and exhaled. The glass was thick enough to resist his weight but he realized through his drunkenness that he had gone from leaning to sitting so he slid off and took his usual spot on the very end of the overstuffed yellow brown colored sectional.

"I'm moving to New York in the fall. I just wanted to tell you. I made up my mind and I'm going to go to the Fashion Institute in Manhattan."

"I thought you got accepted to Virginia." He made eye contact with her for the first time.

"I did."

Neil looked at the television screen. "You know, Marcia Brady's a lesbian?"

"She is not, Neil. You better mellow out on the drinking or you'll end up just like Dad."

He stared blankly at the television. "I broke up with Claire today."

"What?" Annene said, confused. "You serious? Why'd you do that?"

Neil shrugged. "Maybe it's Jan who's the lesbian," he said, and turned back to the television. "Wouldn't be able to figure it out though."

"I'm tired. I'm going to bed," Annene said. "I'm going

to check to see if Claire left a message.

Neil didn't respond, only flipped through the channels and drank from the can of beer.

"We're having a party for Jeff's birthday at his house. His parents are going out of town next weekend."

Annene turned around, her hands at her sides. "I don't think I'm much into partying, Neil."

"It's Jeff's eighteenth birthday, dude..."

Annene interrupted him. "I was just with Jeff. Does he know this?"

"He will," Neil replied and smiled.

"I can't talk to you right now. I don't think I need to know much more. I'm going to bed. She turned into the short hallway.

Neil tilted back his head and the can chased his open lips. When he found it empty but for a few drops of foam, he flipped off the television. In almost total darkness, he got up from the sofa and gathered beer cans from the mahogany coffee table and glass top breakfast table and placed them in a large paper grocery bag that he carried to the refrigerator in the kitchen. The refrigerator light made him squint as he reached inside and removed the last can. He pulled off the six-pack ring and dropped it into the paper bag. He proceeded to bed, his head thick and dim.

It was always easier to deflect Annene's quest for truth with bullshit. It was the only way she would leave him alone.

That day he sat through the funeral and viewed the ceremony from the front row as he fought off fatigue from the night before. The nights were long, extending well into the morning and beer was his only exit to sleep. Every day he needed more.

"Just like Dad." He heard Annene's voice say it. It was not the first time he had heard those words.

Alpharetta, Georgia was tolerant of stray husbands and fathers distracted by alcohol. From a purely biological perspective, it was in his genes. Jeff, the medical genius, told him to be wary of it. But he knew it was Maggie and Georgia and everything. It was this blind wandering through life that happened when she disappeared. He wanted her back so badly and gave a silent prayer to nothing that the last beer would bring on sleep and silence to the suffering he hated himself for.

Bernie held Claire to her chest, and coddled her granddaughter's head like she would an infant while she cried. Her hair smelled fragrant, almost too much so. Bernie thought of the baby shampoo on a downy baby head of hair. She had long since passed that part of her life and the scent felt like a much-needed hug.

Bernie rocked her back and forth all the while whispering, "Shh, shh, it's okay, honey. It's okay. Let it out," while her own mind spun and strung together the events of her life, looking for some comfort, some healing. She held Claire close, held down the shakes as though she restrained an epileptic seizure. How could God shake the truth from a girl now so fragile? How could that boy be so cruel?

Once solid, the fissures easily broke.

The voice in Bernie's head said, *She's gone. I can't believe she's gone. What do I do now? One day she was there, talking, knitting, spitting fire like she was able to go up against the devil himself. And, then she vanished.*

That day in the kitchen came to mind as they talked about the dress when Annene insisted it was bad luck.

"Bad Karma," she had said.

Bernie rocked Claire and listened as the sobs lulled to a vague strain on her breath. She thought of the sum of the ingredients that reacted poorly the day when the four of them stood, sat, spoke about things in that moment she could remember like it was scented. It was. She made only three bars of soap worthy of her own use. It was a first effort interrupted by the thing she least expected and most feared.

Estelle did not complain about her emphysema and her strength that drained day by day. Her voice faded. Bernie knew that silence was protection from the truth, that if made real, that honeyed Georgia peach fragrance in the air – that pleasant omission - would be sabotaged by the stink of the occasional overflow of the Alpharetta septic tank.

Bernie placed the memories together in her mind like loops on one of Estelle's knitting needles. The memories intertwined and made her friend young again. Age shocked the afflicted elderly but the young were clueless. There was a reason for that. There was a reason for everything. Bernice traced back through the details as the truth rose to the surface. She rocked Claire and imagined Estelle seated next to them automatically working the yarn in her hands.

It revealed itself to her in pieces. It answered questions. Little by little Bernie summoned the suspicion forward. Anger forced it out but the power of that emotion kept the subdued any sadness. She felt strong. Strong in her isolation. Strong momentarily so her need to talk it through could be stifled. Her one true confidant was gone. She stopped breathing when the brutal truth came to mind.

Why did Estelle have to be gone now? Why did Neil turn his back on Claire, an action so malicious and alienating and of such dreadful timing? Why had Maggie gone? Why, at age seventeen, had Claire been thrust upward and onto the thin tightrope of life? She hung above the ground. It was odd though, really. The girl's protections were so fortified by warped survival instincts that asking "why" would put her in danger of bending. Controlling the answer was the thing that starved her, a collision so perfect that it shook her thinning body to sleep there in her grandmother's lap.

When Claire's breath slowed, Bernie let the tears fall, feeling the death of hope in the girl.

Still, there were some things Bernie had to keep to herself. For the time being.

FIFTEEN | Fumes

Neil shoved the pointed end of a slice of Dominos Pizza in his mouth, biting off half of it and chewing with stuffed cheeks. Orange grease dripped from the sides of his mouth down his face. He leaned over the paper plate held below his chin and cracked a beer with his other hand. He focused on the Falcons versus Jets game on the television set into a console. Black VHS tapes filled every otherwise empty space not occupied by the electronics within it.

It was a clean break.

"You want any of this, Jeff?" Neil asked, as he stuffed a less ambitious bite of pizza into his mouth, chewed then choked back several gulps of the Coors.

"Yeah, I'll have a piece," Jeff said. "Dude, you should slow down. You're gonna be wasted by the time anyone gets here."

Jeff stood in the living room of his parents' home wearing his Rush Live T-shirt and jeans. No shoes. His hair was ruffled and he was in need of a haircut. Neil's hair was groomed, shaved close at the sides of his face and stiff with Aquanet hairspray. The muscles in his cheeks flinched when he chewed.

"You wearing that?" he asked Neil, pointing to the Atlanta Braves shirt he knew Neil never wore outside.

"No, I've got another shirt. I'm just not changing yet. I brought it so I wouldn't have to go back home."

"People are going to start getting here soon," Jeff said.

He took a paper plate from the kitchen and walked into the living room where he reached into the white box with the red and blue Domino's logo. Melted cheese dripped over the side of the pizza crust as he pulled it away from the larger pie and placed it on the paper plate.

Neil leaned back against the burnt yellow sofa. He wiped his mouth with a flimsy paper napkin then tightened his fists and bent his arms in toward his chest, flexing his biceps that he admired, touching them. He spent a few days a week lifting weights despite what had become poor habits and excuses. Mesmerized with himself, he looked over his shoulder toward Jeff then shouted and stood straight up, letting the paper plate and pizza crust fall to the carpeted floor.

"Shit, what's *that*?"

Jeff laughed, his cheeks stuffed with pizza.

"What the fuck is *that*?" Neil's mouth full of food was muffled but still conveyed the sight that startled him lucid.

He pointed to the large green lizard that had perched itself on the sofa back behind Neil's head. Its thick long tail hung a third of the way between its clawed feet and the floor.

"That's Gwendolyn. Gwendolyn, meet Neil. Neil, Gwendolyn. You can call her Gwen. She's one of a pair."

"How can you let them roam around the house like that? Don't you keep them in your room? They're supposed to be in your room, dude. People don't let lizards walk around their house."

"When the Stones are away, I let them roam around. It makes them happy."

"A happy lizard… Great. They reek too." Neil shook his head.

Jeff took another bite, this time without the paper plate as a net. Red sauce dripped from the slice to the carpeted floor.

"Oh man. They smell better than you," He walked briskly, almost ran, into the kitchen and returned with a wet rag. "Not good. They're going to kill me."

"What?" Neil asked.

"I just got this stuff on the floor. The sauce on white carpet."

"It'll come out. Don't worry about it," Neil said as he watched Jeff on his hands and knees rubbing the rag against the floor.

"Dude, stop. You're being a woman."

Jeff looked up at him and scowled. "It's not funny. We can't let people in here when they come over. Only upstairs and the kitchen. If I get this carpet dirty, if I mess up this house, they'll kill me."

Jeff could not explain to Neil that he was more concerned at letting them down. They had some faith in him, faith enough to help him.

Neil shrugged and took another piece of pizza. He sat on the other side of the sectional, in the place where it bent into an "L" shape.

Jeff scrubbed the floor, got up to go to the kitchen and returned with a bottle of Woolite, a rag, wetter than before, and a liter of Mountain Dew that he set on the glass table.

Neil looked hard at the bottle and chewed with his mouth open so Jeff could see the bits of pulpy pink mush. He smacked his lips and swallowed before he spoke.

"I have the perfect solution. We'll put the keg on the balcony upstairs and only allow clear beverages downstairs."

Jeff kept scrubbing and noticed that Gwen had walked from the back of the sofa to a potted tree set in the corner of the living room to take in the warmth of the sun that shone through the sliding glass door.

"God dammit," he yelled. "These guys are getting worse and worse. Can you believe this shit? The Cowboys are the best. Falcons suck. I hate Atlanta teams."

"I hate football, Neil," Jeff said, his face sullen, conflicted.

"How can you hate football?" Neil asked.

"I just don't like it," Jeff replied.

"Dude, do me a favor, okay? Will you?" Neil urged.

"Tell me what it is, first and I'll decide if I want to do it."

"Ask Claire if she'll come over and help you get that out. She knows how to do that kind of stuff."

"You're kidding me? You just broke up with her. She's not coming over here."

"Yeah she will. Dude, it's fail safe. She wasn't putting out so I had to do something."

Jeff closed his eyes and shook his head back and forth.

"Come on Dude," Neil said, whining. "People are going to start getting here and you won't have any more time to get it done.

"Why are you so worried about it?"

"Because I know you. You won't be able to relax at all tonight if you don't get that shit off the floor. Just go over and ask."

Jeff got up off the floor and wiped his hands on his pants, palms first, then the backs.

"Fine," he said, and heaved a long breath then moved toward the door. He opened it abruptly then shut it behind him leaving Neil and his dumb ass game, its cheering fans, grunting players and the thuds of colliding shoulder pads that, in concert, composed one beating, animalistic noise blanketed with thunder claps. A civilized ritual.

He jogged down the steps, his spirits lifted, glad to be

out of the house. At Claire's front door he smoothed back his hair and realized he should have showered and changed. His heartbeat quickened as he knocked twice at the door.

"Who is it?" Bernie called from inside. Her face peered through one of the two long windows that flanked the door.

Jeff smiled to appear cheerful but lowered his head, unobtrusively cowed when the door opened. Bernie stood in her slippers and purple velour sweat suit. The top and bottom matched. It was a few years old Jeff noticed, not by the style or the level of wear but by Bernice's reaction. Self conscious, she smoothed over her pants and looked over her shoulder where she took a quick inventory of the kept house.

"Well, hello, Jeff. Come in." Her voice shook. It cracked slightly and she cleared her throat. Jeff realized that she barely spoke in the last few days.

"Claire, Jeff's here," Bernie said and looked over to the sofa. "Well," she continued and brushed back her slightly disheveled silver hair held back from her face by a thin gold headband. "What brings you here?" Bernie waved him inside. "Come in."

Jeff stepped into the doorway and looked over to Claire who sat undisturbed and consumed in the pages of a book. She wore her usual blue Jordache jeans and a gray Chattahoochee High School sweatshirt. Her slender feet were bare and her toes, painted red. Next to her was Estelle's unfinished scarf. Anyone who sat on that sofa, sat next to the bag and the scarf like it was embodied by its maker.

Claire's eyes reluctantly left the page and she raised her head just enough to see Jeff with the tops of her eyes. Her face was without a trace of makeup and her eyes appeared hallow. She finished the paragraph in the book.

"Hi Jeff," she said.

Jeff's back straightened when she spoke and he averted

his eyes, trying to read the cover of the book. She lowered it so it lay almost flat. An uncharacteristic dark aura loomed around her. Sadness. Strange and hallow.

"I'm sorry to bug you Mrs. Hinkley but, I'm having some people over for a party ..."

"A party?" Bernice interrupted, excited. "What's the occasion?"

"It's my birthday, actually, but it's no big deal."

"Really? Oh, of course it's a big deal," she said, putting her hand on his shoulder. "Come in. Have a seat. I made some iced tea. Would you like some?" Bernie had the ability of most Southerners to be hospitable at a moment's notice, brushing off a quiet day with her granddaughter to be instantly attentive to Jeff's needs. Her light disposition outshined her, always.

"No, that's okay. I don't want to bother you."

"Oh, don't be silly. You're not bothering me."

Claire let out a long sigh, closed the book as she kept her thumb in place and held it down with the other hand on her lap. Jeff caught sight of the title, *Wuthering Heights*, and took the seat where Ernest spent his nights reading, located a safe distance away from Claire.

"Okay," he said. "But, I'm fine. I really just came over to ask Claire if she wanted to come over."

Claire studied him now, as he sat, calm. There was nothing disingenuous about him and she trusted him. Gaps of silence were allowed to Jeff who never talked about his past.

"What is it?" Bernie asked, then intuitively licked her teeth so that a small fleck of red lipstick disappeared.

"Actually, Mrs. Hinkley, I feel kind of strange asking this, but I spilled some red pizza sauce on Mrs. Stone's carpet and can't get it out."

Bernie and Claire shared a look and Bernice restrained a smile.

"And, I was wondering if you or maybe Claire could tell me or help me out because I can't get it out. Some people are coming over and..." He stopped himself then continued. "I'm sorry, this is really lame. I just know you're good at that kind of stuff and thought you'd know something I could do. Actually, Neil's over there and suggested it because he said Claire may be able to help."

"Neil's there?" Claire asked, as she put a bookmark of pansies pressed between plastic into the pages of her novel and set it beside the knitting bag still on the sofa.

"Would you mind, Claire?" Jeff asked, tentative.

Bernice looked at her without much expression and grinned timidly. She raised her eyebrows. Her granddaughter hadn't been out of the house for anything other than the necessary in a week's time. Bernie spent every day with her.

"It'll just be a few minutes, Claire," Jeff assured her.

"You know, honey," Bernie said. "Just use seltzer. You have some seltzer don't you? And, soap? You have cleaner, don't you?"

"Yeah. We bought a bunch for the party tonight," Jeff said.

"What, soap?" Claire asked. The conversation lost her, her mind deep into another story, distracted by it. She was used to her grandmother leading conversation even with her friends. She was not lazy, but malnourished and sad. Her body and mind froze. Covered though they were, her arms were chilled, the skin puckered around small hairs. She felt the downy skin with the tips of her fingers. Fine little hairs had formed on her arms and felt like a thin, light, feathered, down coat of a duckling. She read about it from the website shared by the community of girls starving too. She learned things from them, and while she knew it was wrong, it amazed her that so many others found their strength in that deprivation.

"No, seltzer," Jeff replied. Awkward, he shifted his feet in the doorway to make room for Claire who sidled up to her grandmother.

When they arrived next door to the Stone's house, Neil was laid out on the sofa, unconscious.

"Neil," Jeff shouted, and pushed him slightly on the shoulder. His mouth was open and, his eyes partially exposed under his forearm that rested in what was his usual sleeping position. The white slits of his eyes made him look creepy, half dead or undead, but his friends were used to it. Neil could fall asleep anywhere in that position.

"It's weird that he can fall asleep that fast," Jeff said.

Neil inhaled deeply through his nose and released his breath through his throat so that it made a hissing noise like the sound of a cap as it came off the valve to a pressurized container. Claire eyed the empty beer cans and an open pizza box on the table. She smelled the melted cheese, sauce and bread and felt the taboo linger there in her mind that shut like a trapdoor against it.

"I think he's out," Jeff said, his hands on his hips. He combed his hand through his hair. "Shit."

Claire took a seat at the end of the sofa. She stared at Neil. One of his feet dangled off the side, his shirt exposed the black hair around his belly button. The top Levis button was unfastened and his hand rested on the television remote control that he held to his stomach. He looked sloppy to Jeff who should have been anesthetized to it.

"Now what am I going to do?" Jeff asked.

Annoyed, he looked at the television and tilted his head back, walked over to Neil and slid the remote out from under his hand. When he pushed the power button the screen went to black and he placed the remote on the coffee table.

Claire removed an issue of Vogue Magazine from the bottom shelf of the coffee table where old issues of Tiger Beat Magazine and Seventeen were stacked. She flipped through the pages. Jeff just stood there, nervous, and ran his hand through his hair like a middle-aged man held onto his history amid hair loss.

"Relax," she replied. Just leave him there."

She shut the magazine and got up from the sofa.

"Okay, where is it?" she asked, then took the bottle of seltzer from Jeff and lowered herself to her hands and knees where he handed her the towel.

"You really doused this thing, didn't you?" she said, humored. "Did you put any water on the rug or just the soap?"

"I wet it but it wouldn't come out."

"It didn't come out because you put so much soap and no water. You should know that. Isn't that something they cover in chemistry?"

Jeff cleared his throat.

"Do you need help?" Jeff asked.

"Yeah, get me a glass of water," Claire said, her breath a little heavier. "When's the party supposed to start?"

"Soon," Jeff called from the kitchen.

"When?"

"Claire, I'm sorry I didn't invite you, but I didn't think with everything going on with you and Neil that you'd want to."

She leaned back and sat on her knees trying to conceal her hurt. No one seemed to let her make her own decisions anymore with all of the effort they made toward protecting her. Ernest, Bernie and now Jeff. The thought reclassified him into the people who loved Claire. Neil and Maggie filled the other category. The people who left Claire. She wondered why she needed the ones who left her more than the ones who loved her. It was a thought far away, removed even but acknowledged enough that she held it in her mind for a few seconds before she set it down. Protected or abandoned, she felt hurt. Neither gave her any kind of a chance to be herself. To be accepted or trusted.

"You were right. I'm pretty good staying with my grandma. So, why don't we just finish this so I can go home?" she said, taking the cup from him. "When's soon?"

"Eight."

"That's an hour from now."

She poured the glass of water on the spot and worked through the large, round, pink smear on the floor and continued rubbing in short, fast strokes against the nylon fabric that scratched and squeaked against the thin cotton towel. Breathless, she worked as her words came out jarred and spastic.

"See, the soap pushes the dirt, the sauce in this case, to the surface but it needs the water because these little suds act like worms and squiggle to the top. That's what gets the dirt out."

"How do you know that?" Jeff asked, impressed. He stood above her watching.

"Just do. Grandma Bernie explained it to me one day when we were in the kitchen. She read it to me from her book on how to make soap. It explained it. It said something about how the Romans discovered it by accident. The place where they slaughtered cows was close to the place where they cleaned their clothes in a river. The fat mixed with the soap and water and got the clothes clean. She's kind of obsessed with it right now. I think she's bored and knows I don't like cooking."

"The slaughter place must have been upstream then," Jeff said.

He glanced over at Neil who made a grunting noise as he shifted on the sofa. Glancing back at Claire who knelt and scrubbed the floor, Jeff recalled Neil's comment that the job was woman's work.

"Let me help you," he said. He kneeled down next to her, moving his hands and fingers, straining to insert himself to fix it.

"I can do it," Claire snapped. "You said you wanted help. Now I'm trying to help you. You guys are so stupid, I swear to God. I can't win."

It felt good to say it even though it was misdirected. She threw the pink stained rag in a heap on the floor and moved to get up. Jeff instinctively took her arm as he raised himself to stand at her side. When he took hold of her wrist she pulled away.

"What are you doing? Jeff, let go."

"It's not your fault all of this, you know. I'm sorry," Jeff said, as he released his hold on her. "I'm sorry. It's none of my business. I just want you to know that none of this is your fault. It's not your fault that all this happened to you." His eyes, though averted, implored understanding but Claire read it as pity.

"What do you know?" she snapped.

Neil dozed, and Jeff looked over his shoulder, aware of his friend asleep on the sofa. She whispered.

"I know that your feeling isn't real. It's not the truth. I know that because I've never really felt anything but those feelings. When the Stones came along and took me in I still felt really bad even though I knew none of it was my fault. I still felt like it was. I never thought I'd stop feeling lonely. But, I did. The feeling mostly went away. I think partly because I got used to it. I found ways not to feel so bad. They tried to send me to a shrink and all the shrink did was criticize my survival skills. But, they're there for a reason. To help you survive. It's when you don't need them anymore that it turns on you. It gets hard. I don't know. You just got to adapt. Like a lizard, I guess."

Claire listened to him, her large, round eyes still on him, open wide and offset by her remarkably smooth skin, pale skin that made the shadows under her eyes darker. Her cheeks were pink, flushed from the help. He touched the side of her face, pushing back the strands of hair at the corner of her mouth. She was still and listening. His words settled on her like fragrance.

It was too long, his eyes on her face but she smiled. "Lizards?"

"Yep!" He replied, with sarcastic pert enthusiasm. He

mirrored her lips with effort into a grin but wanted them. Reason fell away and the plane, the glass slide that contained that perception of Claire Hinkley, shifted. He wanted them, suddenly curious, his focus clear. Vision from the periphery of his eyes, ears and mind ceased function and he felt himself pulled toward her but controlled.

The jackass on the sofa just dumped her. The girl has problems and I don't need to be one more.

Taking it in, she lowered her head. "When did it go away?"

Jeff withdrew his hand and picked up the towel from the floor, looking at the place where the stain was wiped clean. "You're right. It worked," he said.

"Jeff, when did it go away?"

He stared at the wall where photographs of the Stone's extended family hung in simple, wooden frames. One showed a family reunion before Jeff joined the family. His eyes remained fixed on the wall as if in a trance.

"I think it really went away when I met you," he said. He nodded his head at the sudden realization. "Yeah, that would be it." Nodding again, he looked into her eyes and repeated himself. "That would be right. Yeah. That's what made it go away."

Claire took a deep breath. She felt it, the draw, like a rope had been tossed to her after she fell into a deep hole that gave her almost everything she needed. To be alone.

"I have to go," she said.

Jeff watched Claire walk to the front door and close it behind her. He sat at one of the chairs set around the glass table and stared at the Stone's picture. When Neil came to several minutes later, Jeff was still lost in it. Lost in his own mind.

"You still doing that?" Neil asked. "I thought you were going to call Claire and get her over here." He pushed himself up to shake off fatigue. "Shit, how long was I out?"

Jeff waited a moment before he responded then leaned down and with a sudden fit of anger that exploded in his chest, he grabbed the wet rag and threw it at Neil.

He caught the rag in the face.

"What the hell?" he said. "What'd you do that for?"

"Shut up, Neil. Just *shut up*." He yelled.

Music blared from Jeff's bedroom over a dull yet infrared buzzing of fluorescent terrarium lights. Rush, "Subdivisions" played through the two speakers mounted at the corners of the room. Posters covered the walls: The Specials tour and another of the Rush, "Moving Pictures" album cover.

He had gone there to calm down leaving Neil to drink more and lay around in the living room. He pondered the playlist for the party, careful not to expose anything of himself with his choices. He would not bring himself down with dated Journey songs that took him back to the four years prior to his life with the Stones when he lived with a zookeeper and his wife.

He spent most of high school with them in New York. His foster father could have been a herpetologist but he looked after the Bronx Zoo reptile exhibit. His wife was a biology teacher who wore pancake makeup and dyed her hair black. Jeff enjoyed the amphibian silence of that house. Uncomfortable at first by the cold-blooded creatures and the smell most closely likened to urine, he slowly learned to enjoy their company. Like him, they did not need much, just the occasional feeding of insects and pinky mice. Once he saw how the feeding made any visitor's skin crawl, he made a point to do it himself and found a slight pleasure in their disgust. Misunderstood creatures. Jeff left that house when his foster parents were determined by their excessive drinking to be unfit parents.

Jeff stood in front of the sink and mirror. He wore blue and white plaid boxers, scratched his behind and ran his hand over his lean, long arms. He was a skinny kid before age shaped his shoulders. The least bit of remaining baby fat was shed in track. A distance runner, he trained at a quick but steady pace. He had to finally get rid of his hair. It was slowing him down.

Electric hair clippers buzzed as he glided the device through his hair, close to his scalp. He started at his forehead and resisted the urge to bob his head in time with the music that blared from the bedroom into the small bathroom. Off key, he softly sang the words instead. He was starting to feel better and tried to shake off the confusion of Neil, Annene and Claire. There was no confusion with Claire. No push and pull. No rejection and misunderstanding. It was weirdly calm and quiet.

As he sang along with the words to the song, he let them embrace his mind like it was a gospel that wrapped around his heart as a protection. Jeff believed in his own God. It was simple. It was the promise he made to heal who and what he could.

Neil walked in just as Jeff scooped the last of his shaved dark hair into the small black trashcan. Against gravity, too light to stick to the ground, some of the black wisps floated back onto the light blue tile floor.

Neil looked at him in the mirror and clenched his face in disgust. His eyes were groggy and glazed.

"Dude, what are you doing?" Neil yelled over the music.

Jeff bowed his head again and, back to front, shaved off a missed row the size of a small knife. Neil watched in awe as Jeff shed his hair. There was a pile at least an inch deep in the trashcan.

The song ended and Jeff placed the sheers on the bathroom sink then walked from the bathroom into his room, shuffling his bare feet across the beige carpet. He sat on the bed covered with a patchwork quilt of blue, red and tan.

Neil flipped on the light and gawked at Jeff's buzzed

head.

"I can't believe you just did that."

"What?"

Neil pointed to the trashcan.

"I needed a haircut. So, I gave myself a haircut, dude. Easy."

Neil shook his head. "You could've just gone to get it cut like everyone else does, you know. " He picked up the cassette cover from the top of the stereo, held it up in front of his eyes and read the back. "You just do things weird. Your room smells like shit, dude."

Jeff leaned over the trash can and squatted. He cupped his hands around the bits of hair on the floor as he swept them into one hand then brushed them with the other hand into the can. Several stray hairs remained on the tile floor. He replaced the can beside the toilet and turned the one shower dial to "hot." Deep in his belly, he felt relieved of his need for Neil's acceptance as though someone had turned off a switch. He turned on the shower that hissed as the drops fell with splatters and sounds like whistling rings against the tile.

Barefoot, Neil walked out of the bathroom and across the remaining hairs on the tile floor. Seated on Jeff's bed, he kicked back his feet and wiped the hairs from the bottoms with his hands.

"Claire came over when you were passed out on the couch," Jeff shouted. His voice echoed from inside the three white tiled walls of the shower. "She helped me clean up, like you said she would."

"Why didn't you wake me up?" Neil asked, his voice drowned out and groggy.

A white mist began to cover the shower door and Jeff wished he had not planned any of it.

"Hurry up, dude. We have to get this place ready," Neil shouted behind him as he left the bedroom.

Jeff dressed and fed worms and crickets to the bedroom menagerie that consisted of three terrariums; two flanked the stereo and desert landscapes that housed the pair of Leopard Geckos and the pair of Dwarf Tegus. The largest was set on an old wheeled television stand to the right. The floor of the glass house was covered with a few inches of water and several green branches. It belonged to the Water Dragon. Next to the large sliding glass door that lead to the balcony, was a large terrarium, empty except for a large terracotta feeding bowl set in sand and water. The top of this one was left open.

Neil stared at it for a while before realizing there were two empty terrariums. Still drunk and half-thinking, he decided to keep it to himself. Uncertain but knowing he should know.

Jeff shook the bag of crickets into the smaller tropical cage, then picked meal worms out of a Styrofoam cup filled with sawdust and squirming white insects that he handfed to the lizard resting on the topmost branch. The effort relaxed him into subtle thought.

A blind chameleon still changes colors to match his environment.

SIXTEEN | Aroma

Annene heard the door close behind Neil and let an
hour pass unattended as she dressed. She knelt down in
front of the altar and opened the Gahonzan's tabernacle, a
wooden birch box with two hinged doors she bought bare
but painted a glossy white to cover it. She examined the
perfectly attended altar. Fruit filled a white, porcelain bowl
to her right. Palm fronds sprouted out of a black vase
from the opening that shone brighter with its gold painted
rim. Just below the mouth of the vase was the gold image
of the crane with a circle around it. A lotus, also in gold,
faced the opposite direction, elegant and bright with the
strength of a family crest. The white box with the double
doors protruded from the wall. She had used her father's
drill from the garage and installed the tabernacle with two
very large screws.

Nothing could shake it loose from the wall.

Resting her backside on the miniature stool, she took
hold of the string of sandalwood beads in her left hand
then tapped the black and hammered bowl-shaped bell
three times with the mallet.

Monotone, she repeated the mantra, "Nam Myo Ho
Renge Kyo," her hands clutched in prayer around the

beads which she occasionally rubbed like dough rolled into a tube shape. Trance-like and hallow, her eyes locked onto the paper scroll of Japanese letters painted in black against jade and ivory filigree parchment.

A faint trail of smoke made its ascent from the short incense stick. Judy allowed her daughter to burn only the Morningstar smokeless incense or Nag Champa, even though Neil complained that it aggravated his allergies.

"It clarifies the air," Annene told her mother.

Annene placed a new photograph of Estelle on the altar. Annene's sitting time increased from fifteen minutes to an hour as she became more withdrawn. Days lapsed since the funeral and Annene hadn't spoken with either Jeff or Claire. Neil called it her daily ranting and left his sister alone. He was oddly fearful of her uncharacteristic silence. Nothing was the same.

Neil's attempt at pretense melted under the weight of his memory as the days passed. Annene's eyes became sharper with each passing day and made Neil shift with discomfort. Annene knew more than she was letting on.

They said when you chant you should chant for what you want. It was the truth.

The ashes from the incense settled onto the mahogany tray and left only the stub of the long stick fitted in the small hole that held it, suspended. Annene said the words, "Nam Yo Ho Renge Kyo," slow and long and final. She tapped the bell again and it rang like a tuning fork. She struck it three times, set down the smooth fat wooden stick and bowed. Then, reaching behind her, she slid the small, unfinished wooden stool out from under her and settled back onto the floor cross-legged, setting the dark, stained prayer beads beside the small singing bell. Inhaling deeply, she extended her legs to each side kneading her thighs. She ran her palms to her calves, repeating the motion until the pins and needles began at the pads of her feet and climbed up her legs. Awakening.

"I hate this part," she said to herself, her eyebrows

narrowed. She shook her legs so that each flopped like a fish on dry land.

"I don't know if I should do this," she told herself in a whisper. "I don't know."

Her heart sped a little faster, racing against the pace of her mind. In the past week, she'd spent more time alone and with her thoughts, and in that time, came upon a few conclusions of her own that needed confirmation. Estelle had told her to always trust her intuition and meditation got her closer to it. It crept into her like the pins and needles, misunderstood as pain rather than awakening.

Her brother always locked his door, and though she pushed away the truth, silence allowed for her to observe by listening. Daily, several times now, she heard the door latch and the floorboards creak under Neil's weight as he closed his bedroom door across the hall. Often she thought she heard him cry. He hid something apart from the usual adolescent boy derelictions. It was all too unusual.

She rose to her feet and quickly surveyed the vacant living room. Two steps across the hall, she stood at his door and turned the knob. In his haste to leave the house for the party, Neil neglected to lock the door. The pitch black bedroom was unchanged in all the years they'd lived in the house.

By the hallway light Annene lowered herself to her hands and knees and groped under the bed. Her fingertips picked up a thick coat of dust, then aligning her shoulder for a deeper, longer reach, she gripped the pointed corner of a cardboard box. She pulled it towards her and deeply inhaled the musty scent of the worn comforter then got up and moved to the door where she could both listen for the door and browse through the contents of the box by the light.

Second-guessing herself, she got up and went to the front door, closed the curtains and locked it. Neil left his keys in the tray beside the sofa. Relieved, she returned to the bedroom, leaned against the wall and slid into a squat position where she inspected the box. Her heart slowed. She had not noticed its rapid beating until it returned to normal.

Buried beneath Neil's box of momentos - birthday cards, team photographs, buttons, and dated family photographs - was a picture of Maggie Hinkley and a note written in black ink on monogrammed stationery. Her initials were scripted in very curvy, fluid, raised, blue ink.

Dear Neil,

I've decided to leave Alpharetta. I know you'll be fine. You're young with so much ahead of you. Make the right choices.

Love,

Maggie

Annene studied the handwriting of perfect loops and lines, fluid like paisley patterns melded together. Each letter was drawn with loops and sways to form the perfect connections and revealed a person who gave time away to scripted reception seating cards.

Outside the loud crash of a dumpster lid closed and she jumped, startled. Her mind sped in reverse like images project onto a white wall, one after the other.

She placed the card back in order, then picked out another half torn photo of Maggie.

It was true. It was the truth. It was what she had thought.

She packed up the box then, careful to leave it as she found it deep under the bed, and hurried out of the room.

Across the hall in her own room, she flung open the closet doors, tore the purple dress she'd worn to the school holiday party from the padded hangar, and both ran and walked briskly into the kitchen where she ripped a white garbage bag from a cardboard box, pulled several times at the opening to separate the sides and give an opening to the dress that she stuffed inside. Without tying off the top, she proceeded outside to the dumpster where she tossed the bagged dress inside.

She stood, her hand braced like a car jack against the top of the lid. She looked inside at the few white tied-up garbage bags collected at the bottom of the dumpster, emptied just the day before but still smelling of the week's disposal, the low rancid notes. Months of waste caked inside. It was all black unless the food that caked it was not old enough to be that dark.

When she slammed the lid, a small burst of putrid air gusted into her face. She turned away from it and toward the development of ranch style homes with their perfectly groomed lawns and stucco walls. A deep anger swelled inside her and gutted all other thoughts. It was sudden, deep hate. There were times she resented Neil for his selfish lack of sense, for his vanity and base misogynistic need. His glory and pride. His drinking that increased progressively with the resultant apathy he displayed toward everyone. At times she pitied him. His one-dimensional self was half a man's shadow.

Her grandmother was gone. There was no net to fall into though she wondered if it was something she could confide to Estelle. How would she be able to tell her, regardless? Even if she was alive, how could she check it against what was always the barometer of her truth?

Annene snuffed the urge to run full speed away from her house. She had nowhere to go. Where could she go? There was nowhere to go with the secret and she regretted the decision to look for evidence. She found it. Found the truth. But, it was the kind of truth that separated character from soul and reason from instinct.

Annene was estranged from the only other human being to whom she felt close. She felt completely alone. Annene was suddenly helpless against the clamor inside her head, like she was locked inside a house with an alarm that set off without cause. Left without the proper code to disarm the clamor. Nausea rose up at the back of her throat.

Dizzy, she walked back to the house where she poured

herself a glass of water that she took to the sofa. Reclined there, she closed her eyes against the mismatched wallpaper that gave only chaos to her eyes. Her head spun as she breathed in deeply.

An hour passed when Annene awakened on the sofa, her head still vague and her stomach relaxed just enough that the tearing inside ceased as did the nausea. Grandma Estelle told her a couple of months back when the symptoms began after the eyebrow incident that anxiety often aroused nausea in the family and she must have inherited the tendency. When Estelle referred to "the family" she meant herself. This Annene realized as she lay prone on the sofa at eight o'clock in the evening.

The party was due to start though no one would arrive until at least nine, after dark. One hand on her stomach, Annene picked up the phone and dialed Claire. It rang three times before her friend answered.

"Hello."

"Hi," Annene said, with a deep breath and forced cheer.

"Oh, hi," Claire replied. "What's up?"

"Nothing. Just woke up from a nap. Lazy day," she lied.

"Me too," Claire said. Before she could decide whether or not to bring up the party she heard the music next door. Shifting in her seat, she leaned on the sofa arm and looked through the window to the Stone's house. A group of three young men stepped from the brick front steps and stood on the porch for just a moment. One pushed the doorbell button. All were dressed in jeans and collared shirts of different colors and patterns.

"What are you listening to?" Annene asked.

The white door opened and the three stepped inside. It was Neil who greeted them.

"Nothing. It's the music next door. Some guys just went in. You going?" Claire asked, tentative, as she peered through the curtains.

"You're kidding."

"No, I'm not kidding."

Claire watched as Bernie got up from the sofa, an attempt at distraction to subdue the pang in her chest. She held the phone to her ear, listless, and waited for her friend to speak.

Annene was never at a loss for words but she choked back the thoughts that flooded reasonable speech.

Claire's pretty dark eyes followed Bernie's movements as she put down the knitting and moved away from the sofa. Claire watched her grandmother's sides jiggle under the chenille fabric as she walked, placing each foot ahead of the other in perfect alignment.

"Why doesn't she come over?" Bernie asked over her shoulder. She opened the cabinets under the sink and brought out a pot. "If it's alright with you, I'm going to move my little factory over here, honey. Your Grandpa doesn't want me messing up the house anymore. He says if I keep goofing up we're not going to have anything to eat from. But, I keep using the same pot over and over again. I wish he'd find something else to do besides stick his nose into things he doesn't know about. God bless him, but I wish he had a hobby. Something besides that garage. What do they do in there anyway?"

"Claire, are you listening to me?" Annene barked through the phone.

"You're not talking. My grandma's talking so I'm listening to her. She's going to start making the soap over here now. Grandpa is getting mad at her for messing up the house. She's been working on finishing the black scarf though. She's almost done. She said your Grandma told her who she'd planned to give it to."

Silence.

"You can come over if you want," Claire said, still listening as Bernice mumbled to herself in the kitchen.

"Hold on," Claire said into the phone, then faced the kitchen.

Kathryn Merrifield

"Gram, if you just wait a minute I'll go over and get the pot from your house."

"What's she doing?" Annene asked.

Claire laughed.

"What? What's so funny?" Annene asked, too alert.

"She's ransacking the kitchen. She's been here every single day. I know she's trying to be helpful but it's getting on my nerves. I'm the only person she talks to anymore."

A loud crash came from the kitchen.

"I'll call you later," Claire said, and hung up the phone.

"Oh, rats," Bernice muttered, loud enough for Claire to hear.

She found Bernie hunched over, her hands gripped the sides of a large aluminum pot on the floor. Embarrassed, Bernie let go, pushed herself up then turned away from Claire who leaned over easily and raised the pot from the floor. She held it under her arm and on her hip.

"Be happy you're young, Claire. This getting old business is for the birds."

Claire examined her grandmother and noticed for the first time the silver gray roots at her scalp. Claire touched her hair, full without looking like starched helmet head that left some women her age with hair that was like gauze, the downy strands stiffened with hair spray to the scalp.

"You should grow out your gray hair, Grandma," she said, struck suddenly with her beauty.

"Oh, I know. I look awful. I already feel old enough though, you know? It would make me feel older."

"It only means you're wise. That gray means you have stories to tell."

Bernie sighed. "I thought I was boring you. It's good to see you smile, honey. I just want you to be happy."

"I think it'd be great then. Go gray. It's very fashionable. You can have this wonderful mane of silver hair."

"It's a flat gray though."

"No, it's not. Look." Claire took her by the arm and

192

led her so that she faced the mirror on the wall between the hallway to the bedrooms and the kitchen. A large vase was placed on the table to the right of the mirror, framed in white carved wood with faint gilded accents. To the left was a photograph of the Hinkleys and another in black and white of a woman. Bernie pointed to the picture.

"My mother wore her hair gray," Bernie said.

Bernie had not given herself a moment to cry since the funeral. There had been tears but survival won out. Sober training gave women of her generation grace to withstand suffering. Mothers, women alike, wrestled grief to protect their sons and daughters. They moved forward despite it.

The corners of her mouth quivered and tears streamed down her face.

"I miss her," Bernie said, tilting the framed photograph in her hand. "I miss both of them," she said, and closed her eyes.

Claire watched her grandmother who stood vulnerable, without the usual composure and dignity that steeled her. Tears fell as she held the framed photograph of her mother.

"I feel so alone, Claire," Bernie confessed. "It's hard when you get this old to let things go. You get used to it and then the mind flits around and wanders and you think that maybe it's because your body doesn't have the same notions, doesn't get so restless. But, then you know suddenly that it just wants to be free, and at the same time, hold it all so close because you know it'll pass because you're old. Nothing stays the way it used to. Your hair, your face, your body," she said, trailing off, then shook her head. "I don't mean it's so bad being old. I guess you're right," she continued, her eyes fixed on the photograph. "My mom was gray and I thought she was the most beautiful woman in the world. Maybe you're right, Claire. You're young and there's so much for you. You should be who you are like I should. Just be who you are."

Claire nodded, and lowered her head averting her eyes

to give her grandmother space to cry and ease her own discomfort at it. She walked Bernie over to the sofa, sat her down and put her arms around her.

"I'm going to go over and get that stuff so you can do your project here, okay? We can do it together, alright?" Claire said, her voice low.

She placed both of her hands on Bernie's shoulders. Bereaved and listless, Bernie nodded. Claire handed her a box of Kleenex and Bernie took it. Next to her was the fabric bag and yarn that she picked up and automatically set on her lap with one hand as she stifled more tears with a tissue in the other.

"You do that and I'll go get the stuff," Claire said, with a false assurance. She looked again over her shoulder to the Stone's house. The music faded in and out, louder then soft as the front door to the house opened and closed with each arriving guest.

Bernie cleared her throat and asked. "Is Annene meeting you there?"

"She doesn't seem to want to be around right now. Ever since the funeral, she's just angry and won't talk to me."

"She's always been a bit, I don't know," Bernie began, blowing her nose into an already used tissue stuffed in a ball and removed from one of her velour pockets.

Claire interrupted, "Edgy."

Wiping her nose, Bernie smiled. Nodded.

"I'd be angry if I was her too, Gram. Everything is so different now," she said. There's this link missing now. I feel like everything is falling apart."

"Oh, honey. You are not going to fall apart. Things bring two people together and it's not always what keeps them together. It's like they cross the street at the same time on the same road and maybe one of them needs directions and the other someone needs to talk on the way, and they discover they're going the same way. It changes and there may be a rough patch, but when two people, man or woman, really care about each other, they stick together like glue. You find a way."

"Uh, huh," Claire said. She stood with her arms tightly crossed and clenched in front of her, guarded, when they suddenly released and hung prone at her sides as she listened until a silence fell between them. Bernie took out the ball of black yarn, stabbed through with the two, thin metal needles, and picked up a first stitch.

"We'll be okay," Bernie said.

Claire walked to the closet and removed her thin, wool coat before she opened the adjacent front door and stepped onto the porch.

"Gram, it's not that cold. I'll be back in a little while. Grandpa can give me a ride back later. I need some exercise anyway."

"Okay, honey. If you're sure."

"I'm sure. I won't be long," she said, watching the front door to the Stone's. She waited until the small crowd gathered at the door and all of Neil's friends had disappeared into the house. "Figures he'd only invite his stupid friends," she mumbled to herself.

"What?" Bernie asked. "I can't hear you."

"Nothing, Grandma. I'll see you later, okay?"

"Bye honey. Be safe."

Claire closed the door and walked around the side of the house to the street. Several cars had already lined up on the side streets, a short distance away from the Stone's and toward Bankhead along Peachtree Street. She was glad the curtains and shutters were closed so she could escape the attention of any of those boys, especially Neil.

A brisk walking pace warmed her as she took in the familiar sights of the homes along the road to her grandparents' house. The Ruppert's black Labrador Retrievers sat barking at the side gate; the Watrous' McMansion was barricaded with an electronic gate and trees to block the view to his car collection. Scott Watrous played tennis with Jim Calvert and owned the real estate company where Maggie began work a few years back. It was the year that Claire began high school. Maggie thought it would give her something to talk about at the dinner table but it became her ticket out of Georgia.

Claire walked on, determined to get the thoughts of her mother out of her mind. She needed to clear her head and pulled the jacket closed but unzipped around her body, arms crossed and hands clenched over the lapels. Every few steps, she looked over her shoulder at the cars shooting by. She made a left at Northside Parkway, crossing the street so that she walked toward the traffic. She counted the steps in her mind to steady her thoughts with rhythm. Grandma Bernie's house was only a short distance away but she stopped short at the sight ahead.

Stuck in the ground was a sign at the side of the road. It read Watrous Real Estate, and just above the black lettering was a slot that held upright a white metal sign that featured the listing agent with a photograph. "Contact: Maggie Hinkley" was written below. The phone number was the Watrous' main number.

Claire brushed from her eyes the few strands of hair released from the banana clip at the back of her head. She focused and took in a long breath. Her heart beat fast. Hung from metal chains at the bottom of the crossed wooden planks was a "Sold" sign. It had been there for the past year but the remembrance of it was lost in the emotional upheaval of the day.

Each time Claire passed it she wondered why no one had bothered to take it away. Maggie had been gone over a year. Maybe they were still using her face. That pretty, perfect face. Claire wondered why she had not removed it herself. Cocking her head, she took a deep breath and pushed up her jacket sleeves then stepped over the street hedge that bordered the edge of the lawn. She took hold of the sign then let go and ducked behind it, hiding in plain sight from the oncoming headlights like an ostrich would. Once the taillights disappeared around a corner, Claire stood up straight and braced her legs in a slight squatting position and took hold of the crossed wooden plank of the sign. She pushed against it and strained her arms and legs tugging it from the ground. The pointed end slid out of the dirt and revealed the grass and dirt stained, pointed tip. Satisfied, she let it drop on the brown and yellowed lawn.

Claire ducked around the side of the house when she saw another set of approaching lights afraid that the sign, faced down on the lawn, would attract the attention of the neighbors. Everyone's business was everyone's business. Squinting, she watched the maroon Cadillac Seville with the sloped trunk back vanish around another corner further ahead. There was little to hide behind in the grated, flat Alpharetta development. She wondered briefly what it would be like to live in the woods.

She walked faster, propelled by a rush of energy and some glimmer of fear. Anger and elation quickened her pace. Smaller steps, sharp and fast.

She thought about Bernice at home and wondered about her father as she always did. The man would not be alone for long which is why he stayed with his father, Frank. They behaved like bachelors, which was fine since Bernie only wanted to be with Claire, hovering over her like a guardian angel. Bernie returned to her home to sleep as did Ernest. It was what they needed. Though Bernie claimed her presence was for Claire, she needed her granddaughter, the assurance and smell of her. Bernie needed to care for the girl so she could care for herself.

Each night that Bernie called home Frank reported, "We're watching the game," as if there was no other game but that game. The one that looked the same to Bernie every night despite the different players and uniforms. She tried to take notice, to mention the score, but it could never capture her attention.

"What game?" Bernie asked.

"Braves."

"Baseball? In January? I know just as well as you do

that baseball season isn't until the Spring. It's…"

Cheers came from the television, interrupting her. Ernest shouted something and Bernie knew to give up.

"Well, at least you're having fun."

"Mm hmm," Frank replied, chewing soft food. "Repeat."

"What are you eating?" Bernie asked.

Muffled, he responded, "TV dinner. Hungry Man."

Claire sat alone at the table, eating, and Bernice was glad for that. While they both felt the vacancy in their lives and resultant misplacement, they shared grief. It was an atmosphere of patience and silence and Claire wanted to get back there.

She turned the corner at Bankhead toward her grandparents' house on the corner ahead. It was lit by a front porch lantern and a living room lamp that glowed through the window. Taking a short cut, she walked across the lawn, alongside the house to the porch which she stepped up and onto. Rarely did she take the time to walk around to the front door that always seemed too formal. It was lit by small lights along a curved path that ended in three white painted wood steps up to the porch. As a child, she would rock on the porch swing.

The burgundy Cadillac was parked in the driveway.

Maggie left behind Ernest's gift, the exact type of car Claire had just seen pass the house where she got rid of Maggie's face. The Sevilles were all over Alpharetta. It was different but it was ugly.

At the door, Claire turned the knob and softly knocked as she entered unnoticed. The small sounds of her entry were concealed by the blaring television. Frank and Ernest sat on the sofa; aluminum TV dinner trays were left empty except for brownish goo on the coffee table. Gravy. The television was set to football.

"Hi, Dad. Hi, Grandpa. I just came by to pick up some stuff." Her hands were still stuffed into her pockets. "Can I get a ride back after I get them together?" she asked then walked into the kitchen where she filled the cooking pot with dried botanicals and jars of lye, boric acid, lard, and the tray of vials filled with essential oils.

"Yeah, honey. Just a second," Ernest replied as he pushed himself off the sofa and into a standing position, his eyes still on the TV. "I should get going anyway."

He patted his father on the shoulder then stacked the aluminum metal trays on top of each other and gathered the knives and forks in his right hand. His eyes returned to the game for just a moment before he walked away.

"I'm going to get going, Dad. Going to drive Claire home. I'll be back in a bit."

Frank turned his head to see his granddaughter standing, her arms wrapped around a large cooking pot. He spoke as if he just woke up. "How'd you get over here anyway?" Frank asked.

"I walked."

"Walked? At this time of night? You could get run over by one of those Saturday night maniacs," Frank said. His eyes returned to the game. "I'm serious, honey. You should have called. I'd come get you. Or, your dad."

Ernest nodded.

"I'm fine," Claire said, and shrugged. "I just needed a walk. I needed to walk."

I needed to do something on my own.

They drove home in silence except for the Glenn Gould piano music that Ernest never took out of the cassette deck. He pushed in the "stop" button only to get the score report on the radio.

"Oh, it was Hungry Man, by the way."

"What?"

"The TV dinner. Hungry man."

"It was good?"

"Yeah."

"I saw the tin covers in the sink."

"You're like a little spy, you know?" Ernest said. "Fried chicken and mashed potatoes with gravy."

"No Tator Tots?" Claire asked.

"That was last night," Ernest said. "I think we ate the last of them. I'll have to pick up some more for tomorrow."

Claire watched the side of the road as the car moved, steady just below a street lamp that cast both shadows and light on them as they past beneath it. She wondered where the sensors were hidden.

"I can't wait until summer and the fireflies come back," Claire said, her mind drifting with the scents, subtle, sweet, high and low tones released from the capped vials in the pot on her lap. She held close the aromas Bernie so carefully selected to blend her soaps. Her grandmother was obsessive but it came to something. She made things and kept trying.

"Remember when I was little and we'd try to catch fireflies?" Claire asked.

Ernest adjusted his grip on the steering wheel and turned the corner from the Highway to Peachtree, "Yeah," he began, leaning into the corner as several lights flashed across the lenses of his horn-rimmed glasses. Squinting from the misplaced flood of headlights and signals, he focused on the swarm of people gathered around a fire truck and ambulance parked outside the Stone's home. Claire slid the pot from her lap onto the floor in front of her.

"What's going on? What happened?" She searched the corners of the house with her eyes. She turned to the door then to her father then to the windshield. The crowd of people was calm and kids folded their arms talking in tight circles. Boys stuffed their hands in their pockets, against the cold. Girls wiped their eyes. Black mascara leaked and stained their faces. The red truck somehow cancelled their importance and lessened their distinctive features. They all looked the same; confused and sad. "Is it a fire?" Claire asked.

"Just stay calm," Ernest said. He put his hand out in front of his daughter by instinct. He held her back like she was thrown forward in an accident or crossed the street too soon before the light changed to green.

"What is it? What happened?" Claire repeated, reaching for the door handle of the crappy Seville.

"I don't know. Just hold on a second. I'll park the car and we'll go look together."

Ernest carefully turned the car slowly toward the curb averting the few young kids and adults in bathrobes who lingered at the periphery of the crowd that had gathered. Their wide tired eyes stared. Red, wet and squinting eyes proved that some had been crying and cried. All looked toward the house where two paramedics appeared from the porch. Each held a gurney at the sides. A white sheet covered a body they carried down the steps and toward the ambulance.

"Oh my God. Oh my God," Claire said. She pushed back her hair with one hand as she gave a hard yank at the handle and shoved against the locked door. She hit the black switch with the picture of an open padlock on the armrest door and opened it.

"Wait, Claire," Ernest said. He pushed on the brakes just as Claire emerged halfway from the car that only tripped her up for a moment. The door slammed. She ran toward the human wall of clenched shut and unaware bodies. As she pushed through the crowd of people she scanned their faces until she found Annene's expressionless and limp. Her eyes were pink and wet. Bleak contemplation clouded her as she fidgeted with the three silver rings on her two fingers and thumb.

Two police officers sandwiched Annene between them and to the right of the one with the thick neck, bulbous cheeks and moustache, stood Judy. Bereaved, she held a Kleenex in her hand and spoke automatically the police officer, but without the clinical separation of a nurse. His bronze nameplate read, 'Harris.' He made notes in dull, small writing while another officer plied Annene with questions. Dazed, she ignored him like only Annene could do.

Claire pushed through the blond and narrow twins, Molly and Ashley Olson. Dressed in pretty little flower print dresses despite the cold, they opted for the feminine choice for a party that had been planned indoors and relocated out.

"What happened? What's going on?" Frantic, Claire asked Annene who shook her head, dazed.

Judy interrupted. "There's been an accident." She moved beside Claire and put her hand on her bony shoulder that appeared sharp even though it was covered by the padded jacket. Claire stood, waiting for an answer and watched the paramedics open the doors to the ambulance then collapse the gurney so that it slid inside.

Ernest appeared behind Claire. "What's going on?" As always, he was levelheaded.

"Neil's dead, Ernest." The words, strained from her mouth and the tears fell. She sobbed and Ernest pulled her close into his chest. She muffled the sobs and the violence that her clenched fists insinuated but loosened as she held onto Ernest's. Incomprehensible even to Annene were her mother's words.

"Oh my God," Claire said. "Oh my God."

Ernest stroked Judy's hair. She buried her face into the crook between his neck and shoulder. "It's okay, Judy. It's okay." Her body hurled sobs at him so that it felt as though she was choking in his arms.

Claire felt her heart race and reached out to Annene who stared with what would otherwise be read as cold, distant eyes. But Annene was numb and severe as she watched the white ambulance doors close and the bolt lock in place.

Jeff appeared at the front door. Listless, he descended the front steps. He'd changed clothes since earlier in the day and wore a plain, black zippered sweatshirt, black jeans and black checkered Vans.

"Jeff called the house when it happened," Annene said. "I answered the phone and had to tell Judy. We came right over."

Claire inhaled deeply, her eyes frenzied and wide with shock. "What happened?"

Claire's eyes darted between Jeff coming from the house and Annene shut down in her silence - her words were flat, not anchored in her usual concrete opinions but faint and hopeless. Words floated.

"Jeff knows what happened. Ask him. I can't talk about this anymore. These creeps have been making me talk about this and I wasn't even here," she said.

"Annene," Judy interrupted. "You ready?"

Judy had stopped crying and wiped her nose between sniffles with a balled up tissue. She stood next to Ernest who still had his arm resting across her shoulders. Mrs. Berry blinked her puffy eyes unnaturally fast as though a piece of dust had gotten caught under one of the lids. Annene remembered her doing that once when her mother had to explain that their "father wouldn't be living in the house any longer." It was only five weeks later that he died, having collapsed from a rare condition; a halo of fluid had formed around his lungs. It was not pneumonia; but he passed out in his living room after a morning run. He stopped breathing and died.

Jeff sidled up to Claire as Ernest walked Judy to the ambulance, his arm around her as the emotional pain within bombarded her psyche like a tornado.

Ernest opened the back door of the police car and gently held Judy's arms as she ducked inside. Annene entered from the other side of the car and Claire stood by waiting as her father made his way back through the swarm of familiar faces. School kids. All of them. Too many faces in the tragic cacophony that both separated and united strangers.

Jeff closed his eyes and ran his fingers through his hair only to feel stubble at the top of his head. He looked at his hand then rubbed his eyes.

"I cut it before the party," he began. Then, taking her cue if only sensing her need for an answer, he added, "Neil fell off the roof, Claire. He climbed up from my bedroom balcony and fell off. He hit his head on the concrete and the impact... The impact killed him."

"Why was he on the roof?" Claire asked.

"I don't know. I was downstairs letting people in the door and Neil said he'd be back. He was gone for a while then Jason said Neil fell off the roof. He went up there with me a couple of times. I told him I go up there to think. He was drunk. He'd been wasted all day."

Claire stared at his mouth. The words came out without her clear comprehension of their meaning.

"He fell off the roof." Claire repeated, as she looked down at the ground, then eye to eye with Jeff. She nodded her head up and down.

"I don't know what happened. I don't know why he went up there, Claire. I swear. I don't know. It's not even that high up but the way he hit the ground. They said it killed him instantly. I'm sorry. I'm so sorry. This was just a bad idea. All of it. I knew it."

Claire searched Jeff's eyes and found them hazel but flecked with little pieces of light like gold slivers. Answers came to her senses as she watched him. It was nothing she could articulate. His face did not change to please or adjust her mood. But, Jeff's presence then was a glimmer of light that gently shed the darkness with a slow burn. She was not alone.

SEVENTEEN | Molds

Maggie held the phone to her ear.

It was her lawyer, Bart Walker, a thin man with banker's horn-rimmed glasses. He sat in a slump of exhaustion in his office chair, the phone to his ear and his pinkie finger extended. A titanium wedding band with five tightly and sequentially aligned inset diamonds was slung loosely around his ring finger. Seated at his desk, he rose above the surface into a man, tall but slightly slouched. It was a position familiar to him - looking at the computer monitor screen, flipping through papers. Those wide shoulders created a shelf for an average but large head. Dull brown hair swept to one side in a perfect part - he looked like an old boy with puffy cheeks on a long, otherwise thin face. Narrow set, his eyes were regular. His face, shaved clean. His voice was his most attractive quality and it conveyed only assuredness and trust. The redemptive quality of his voice made him good on the phone, convincing to most. It made most anyone forget the look of his eyes.

"Yes... Maggie, I just got them in the mail today." He took off his glasses, and paced the floor. The phone cord uncoiled and stretched across the room. Bart tempered his

speech with deliberate calm and paced his words with
legalese confidence. "I also got a call from Ernest. He
said you'd know what to do. He said that Neil Berry died
two days ago. He said it was an accident, that he fell off
the roof. His feet slipped out from under him and he died
instantly…"

"Is that all he said? He told you this?" Maggie asked.

"He gave me more to tell you, Maggie. He said that
Claire was pretty shaken up. He said…"

"I don't want to hear anymore. Maggie blurted. "I
can't believe he told you all of this."

"He said," Bart began again. Through the phone, he
heard water splashing.

"Hold on," Maggie said, then pushed mute on the
phone and pushed herself out of the bathtub holding onto
both sides of the tub. The bubbles settled into small
mounds; flat patches of white drifted like snow caps across
the water that was tinted slightly blue. A box of Calgon
was set on the woven blue mat that covered the bathroom
tiled in white. She drew back the white curtain of the
antique tub and reached for a plush, blue towel hung on
the rack bolted to the back of the door. Two windows
slanted open were covered over in steam even though
Maggie turned on the fan and the space heater that glowed
red; it was just below the medicine cabinet and warmed her
as she applied makeup. The winters in Los Angeles were
colder than Dick made them out to be. Maggie's skin,
more suited for the warmer climates, felt the slight sting of
damp air encased in the tiled walls and floor. California
was cooler than Georgia. It was nothing like Georgia.

Maggie wrapped the towel around her chest and
fumbled with the phone. Wet by her dripping blond hair
she wiped it with the towel and pushed the mute button
with her left thumb, held up the towel with her right. She
stepped on the doctor's scale and read the weight, one
hundred and twenty-five, down two notches from the red
mark she drew just the day before when she started the

Hollywood Juice Diet.

"He signed the papers, right?" she asked.

"Yeah. He signed them," Bart replied. "He asked me to tell you that Neil's memorial service would be five days from today. January fifteenth. He said that Claire needed you there. You have to meet with him. It'll look better if you meet with him face to face. You have to talk through this. We all do to get it done quickly."

"I didn't hire you, Bart, to be my marriage counselor, you know? I need a lawyer to dissolve my marriage."

"Maggie, I'm only the messenger. Don't shoot me. I'm doing the best with all of this. My job is to make certain you get everything that you can out of this. In my professional opinion, going to the memorial would be good for your image, overall. I don't think Ernest is going to make things difficult, but I do know that if anything gets sticky it will be better all in all."

"Bart, I don't give a shit about my image when it comes to all of those backwards people. I just want this to be over with. He's signed the papers and that's that. Do your job." It swelled up before she could push it down. The anger that lashed toward Bart. Bart, who she needed. Who she needed to ply so he would fight for a clean slate. She left and Ernest did not have it in him to fight for a thing. She could just be gone from all of it.

"Maggie, I'm just saying that this divorce is a little messy in the first place. It doesn't look good when a mother abandons her daughter."

"I didn't abandon anyone," Maggie snapped, as she looked at herself in the mirror, shifting her head so that she stood in different angles. She folded the corner of the towel between her breasts so it stayed in place then opened the medicine cabinet where she took out eyebrow tweezers that she set on the sink then a pill bottle. She pushed down on the white top and turned it, removed two pills, placed them on her tongue, and replaced the top. A cup of coffee was set beside the sink and she sipped from it.

The wet tangled ends of her hair dripped down her back. A few strands that had fallen from the elastic band hung alongside her face. Her dark roots were barely visible. She sipped from the coffee cup and spoke slowly while she tried to grasp and yank each small, brown hair that strayed from her perfectly arched brows. Her hands shook and she tried to hide the fear from her voice.

"Besides, Maggie, with all that's going on in your career, it wouldn't hurt you to do a little good deed for someone."

"I am doing good, Bart. Dick has me signed up for a few charity events next month. I've got the Caring for Babies with AIDS dinner and that save the dolphins group.

"Hollywood hates to see dolphins killed," Dick said.

Maggie lifted her eyebrows and opened her mouth as she tried repeatedly to pluck out one brow lash that strayed from the arch.

"Dammit," she said, in a whisper away from the phone.

"What? I'm only doing my job. It's my job to counsel you through this divorce. You know, your husband could very well press charges against you. He could make this very difficult."

Maggie listened, replaced the eyebrow tweezers back in the medicine cabinet and pulled and repositioned the towel wrapped around her chest. She cradled the phone between her ear and shoulder as she applied foundation. Half-listening, she dabbed the sponge, working it around her hairline suspended by a thick black cotton headband. Halfway through, only one side covered, she released the towel wrapped around her chest and let it drop to the floor. She examined herself in the mirror. One pregnancy left only very thin and barely visible stretch marks alongside her full breasts. Her hips were wide enough that she appeared in proportion to the long legs that brought with them attention. Her waist was small and slightly pinched. Over her shoulder she studied her backside, round and fallen only slightly since her cheerleader days when she wore chonies, the closest garment a teenage girl could get to wearing ruffled diaper covers.

"Are you finished?" Maggie asked. She patted her face with the triangular sponge. Her attention was split between that and the conversation with Bart. "I have to finish getting ready for a reading I'm doing this afternoon. It's that role in Mike Nichol's new film and Ellen got me an audition."

"I don't know how you deal with her. She's such a bitch."

"Who, Ellen? She's an agent. She does her job."

Bart shrugged, turned and walked across the floor of his office in six long strides until he was stopped by the taut phone cord, shortened by the twists of his pacing. "Will you at least consider it, Maggie? Just consider it, will you?"

"Fine, Bart. God, you're a real pain in the ass, you know that? A real…"

"That's why I'm the lawyer and you're the actress, right?"

"Right," she replied, breathing in a deep gut of air. She put the sponge down and removed the headband from her head, then ran her fingers through her hair again. "I'll get a flight by the fourteenth but, I'm not staying any longer than I have to. Understand?"

"Good girl," he said.

Maggie hung up the phone, resting it back on the cradle mounted on the wall.

"Shit," she said, and took in another long breath. She shook her head while she stared at herself for moments before she picked up the towel and gathered it under her armpits and over her breasts. She reached to open the mirrored medicine cabinet. Inside, bottles of Jean Nate body splash, Apri Apricot Facial Scrub and other bottles and tubes, including toothpaste and a razor, all set on the glass shelves. She withdrew a plastic sepia bottle with the white cap, not childproof, and flipped it off with her thumb. The white label read her name, changed to "Maggie Wilde," and "Xanax" prescribed by her internist to calm stage jitters that had lately turned to suffocating panic attacks. She spilled two of the pills onto the white tiled bathroom sink counter and replaced the top with one hand. Between her thumb and the outside of her bent index finger, she pinched both pills and placed them in her mouth. She swallowed then chased the pill with the tepid coffee. She winced at the bitterness of it. She opened the towel and wrapped it tightly right then left and tucked the corner of the long terry cloth fabric between her breasts. She resumed, smoothing a flat round puff drawn from the compact across her face.

The clock read ten twenty nine. She pushed the beige liquid deeper into her face. Hurried by the sudden awareness of the time she flipped back her head, shaking her head without response from her hair that she had just cut and dyed lighter than before so it was closer to platinum than blond. She was angry that her only choice was to follow Bart's suggestions. As her lawyer, he had become her only confidant. Dick knew nothing of Claire or Ernest or the unresolved issues of her past and Bart was bound to secrecy. That was the way it was. Maggie made sure of it.

Panic dissolved when she remembered that Dick kept the clock ahead one half hour. The sedatives began to calm her as her mind and body slid slowly into numbness and her arms and legs relaxed and allowed the thoughts and feelings, the anxiety, the panic, the anger to subside so that she could focus on the present. Numb was always better. No feelings, she cleared her mind of distraction.

Maggie dressed with the speed and efficiency of a runway model. Since every wall was mirrored in the bathroom and others hung throughout the house, Maggie was able to have a three hundred and sixty-five degree view of herself at most times. Closed, the bedroom closet face was a reflection of the bedroom except when open to reveal fine and pressed clothing that hung from rods on each side. She faced it. Dick's suits, pressed slacks and long-sleeved, button-down tailored shirts hung to the left. Polished loafers, unlaced dress loafers, Mephisto walking shoes, K-Swiss tennis shoes, and Sperry Top-siders were arranged in the shoe rack built from the ceiling to the floor. Maggie examined her own selection of Ferragamo pumps both high and low, loafers, strappy heels and ballet slippers that made her feel like a dressed-down Marilyn Monroe when she slipped on the shoes. The favorites were arranged in a row at eye level; below were her Mephistos for the long walks never taken in Los Angeles, gold painted metal thongs for the beach, K-Swiss whites for tennis, and the deck shoes she bought on the chance she'd be invited to go out on the Berg's boat if Ellen Jacobs, her agent, advised her to go. It had not yet happened but she remained hopeful.

Quickly, she selected green slacks and a thin white blouse with flecks of yellow and green and, her ivory closed toe mules with the crisscrossed strappy back. She'd always gotten compliments in the outfit and was called back for a second reading before she got cast as the ghost of some dead soap star the week prior. Things were actually working in her favor now, she thought. No more of that blank existence in Alpharetta with all of its big things and small people with hopes flattened by the landscape. Life began to move forward when she met Dick, a Hollywood producer who not only bought the house she showed him just weeks before moving in with him but, who praised her for her classic Faye Dunaway looks and figure.

"That's better than saying I look like King Kong," she teased then. "I was always told I should be an actress," she lied.

"You're a natural. You should act. I should know. I've been in this business since I was a kid."

Dick was from old school Hollywood. He was born in

the Bronx and left at age eighteen to bus tables at
Dantana's in Los Angeles. Later, he found himself
working as an assistant to Frank Sinatra and surrendered to
the business of entertainment like it was an artery needed
to channel blood through his body. It was his life.

He'd stopped chasing women out of boredom (they
came to him) and intervals of incapacity. At age fifty, he'd
recovered from surgery to remove the beginnings of
prostate cancer. The impact on his sex drive was so
significant that all of his energy was diverted into work.
Those ten years were the most productive years of his
professional life and allowed him to brush shoulders with
A-list filmmakers and actors. Dick was a straight arrow,
bottom line producer who dedicated his life to telling
stories on screen. So, when he said Maggie had talent,
when he said she was a natural, he was not stroking her
ego or coaxing her into bed. His estimation was entirely
genuine, so she thought.

Maggie was an outsider to all of that. When she
entered the picture the lights came on.

"I feel like I've got another ten years of this business in
me," Dick told her.

Friends commented on the change, the apparent calm
that came to a man so secure in his life that his moods
were even, his smile solid and, if a level was placed even
against his temperament, the bubble would rest in the
center tilting to the left or right only slightly. Yoga and
Maggie's insistence on a post-holiday season diet helped.
The doctors said he'd begun to function again sexually
with time being the only solvent if mixed with the proper
care of a good woman.

Maggie left out the details to her life before Dick. She
had a way of finding good men that could fulfill her needs
for a while. She knew Dick in a way that no one else knew
Dick. Like Ernest, he was easily manipulated.

"How'd it go?" he asked, as he put the car keys in the silver tray on the marble top stand next to the front door. He moved behind her where she stood at the stove then kissed her neck. Dick was only an inch shorter than Maggie who stood barefoot and moved a spatula around inside a skillet full of cut zucchini, tomatoes, and onions while they sizzled.

"Okay," Maggie said, feeling his hands move along her waist to her hips. She wore jeans rolled up at the ankle and a fitted white T-shirt that clung tight to and across her full breasts. Dick removed his baseball cap that butted up against the back of her head, pushed aside a large wooden salad bowl and placed it to the right of the stove next to a ceramic vase filled with wooden spoons, a whisk and ladle. All were new. He scratched the top of his head where the thin patch of hair was before he shaved his head completely. He always wore a hat, his favorite being the Yankees cap he'd managed to hold onto for ten years, frayed and faded to a patina of the original navy blue.

Maggie turned around to face him. "Do you like it?"

"Do I like what?" Dick asked, his eyes closed.

"My hair," she replied.

Dick opened his eyes and blinked like moth wings fluttered against a bright light.

"Wow," he said.

"You like it," Maggie asked again, only the second time more confident.

Dick stroked her hair at the sides and back. "It's so short now. Curly. How'd you get it so curly?"

"That's the way it is naturally," she said, as she sidestepped away from him, wounded. "What? You don't like it?" Her tone was defensive. She unconsciously touched the hair at the back of her head, patting then twirling several strands that she wound and wound.

"Of course I like it," Dick replied. "Honey, it's a great change. It's just a very big change."

Maggie felt the ends. Pulled at them.

"Bart said I should cut my hair because I looked like I was married. So, I went this morning and did it before the rehearsal. Looks kind of like Meg Ryan's hair, right?"

"Good for you," Dick replied. "Bart gives good advice. He's got it."

"You think?" Maggie replied.

"Yeah, he told you what he thought, you know, would help your career."

Dick had turned his back to Maggie who stood in the kitchen with her hands prone at her sides.

"He also told me I need to lose five more pounds."

Dick stirred the sauce in the pot on the stove then moved the zucchini around in the skillet, plucked a cherry tomato from the salad bowl and started chewing. Placing his cap back on his head, he cocked it to the side.

"If you lose any more weight, Maggie, you're going to disappear."

Maggie shook her head and lowered her eyes to the floor, fixated on her red painted toes. She disengaged from him, backed away while the phone conversation with Bart weighed heavily on her mind. Dick feared he had dug himself into a hole and pulled her closer. She stepped back when he moved near enough to touch her. Maggie, cold, lifted her head and placed her hand on his chest.

"Honey, let's get dressed. The Sheyers will be here in an hour and I have to get dressed.

Dick kissed her on her cheek and walked past her into the living room and toward the stairs that led up to the bedroom. "I'll be upstairs if you change your mind," he said, his voice trailing off as he turned away and started toward the living room where the stairs led up to the bedroom.

Maggie stirred the zucchini. "Hon, Bart got me a reading for a film coming up. Richard Gere is attached. It's happening pretty quick so I have to leave quite early tomorrow."

"Uh, huh," Dick said. He stopped at the foot of the

stairs. "Something you're interested in, I hope. Has to be worth it."

"Yeah. It sounds good. I have to get all the details but he's pretty confident about it. I'm not so sure Ellen will like it, though. Him horning in on her job."

Maggie laughed and Dick was put at ease for the moment. His wife's distance, mysterious as it was, was both intriguing and unsettling. It pulled him closer. It pushed him away.

"Can I take you in the morning?"

"I knew we'd be out late tonight and I didn't want to bother you." So sugary sweet she was that he did not even ask where she was going.

She puckered her lips to a pout of sexy but sweet pity and he fell into the illusion of Maggie. The Maggie everyone collapsed into.

Except Claire.

EIGHTEEN | Batches

Maggie boarded the plane the next morning carrying one piece of luggage: the Tumi black wheeled overnight case with the red ribbon tied around the handle.

She settled into the window seat for a nap, covering her legs with a standard blanket large enough for a small child. Confined space was a comfort that gave her mind room to roam. She closed her eyes. The parameters of thought dissolved with the imposed restriction of space that contained her thoughts and gave her mind reprieve from its work to organize her internal life.

A vague sound of spinning machination steadily built as though it approached from afar while Maggie, who briefly allowed the soundness of sleep to settle on her mind, was jolted from the drifting place by the sound of engines that fired and jerked the plane forward. Her mind wandered, content with the first moments of safety as she watched out the window to her left where the road sped away under the metal belly. The wheels and wings partly blocked her view.

Once the plane lost its connection with the ground, Maggie pushed the attendant button while she looked out the window. She was not cold but pulled the thin, red blanket up to her chin. A tall, thin woman dressed in a navy blue uniform with a large burgundy, white and blue bow tie placed her hand on the backrest above the seat next to Maggie's. Black liquid eyeliner traced both lids and her hair was sandy blond and teased.

Maggie acknowledged the person seated next to her then, for the first time: a young man the same age as her daughter. She vaguely heard the back beat of the sound thumping through her headphones. Next to her, a young man's gangly legs butted up against the seat in front of him. He was too tall to fold into the space but clean-shaven, dressed in a white starched oxford. His blond hair was feathered back.

The flight attendant wore red lipstick and moved her lips too much for what were very simple, very common, very expected words.

"Can I help you?" she asked, quietly as though speaking in confidence. The young man turned to Maggie then back to the in-flight magazine.

"Yes. Could you please bring me a glass of water? I have to take some medication and need to do it now."

The attendant nodded before Maggie finished her explanation.

"Oh, of course. You just stay there. I'll be right back," she replied. Her heavy Southern speech made Maggie suddenly conscious of her own altered dialect, which flattened words with the help of a speech class. Once a rhythm of peaks and valleys her words unnaturally drew out long syllables like a dry desert highway. The young man beside the girl smiled to reveal his large, gapped teeth. He held the magazine a notch higher and snickered.

Maggie watched the clouds fall away as the plane rose above the white tufts.

"Here you go," the attendant said, gently, as she leaned over the tall young man. Maggie caught him looking at the attendants breasts as the woman bent over the young man. Maggie took the water and placed it on the tray in front of her.

"You're not really supposed to put that down during take off but the captain is just about ready to turn off the seatbelt light so I'll let that one go, darlin'. My name's Rosie if you need anything else."

"Thank you," Maggie repeated, flashing a strained smile at the woman. She reached under the seat in front of her and removed the prescription bottle from the black bag. Placing two pills on her tongue, she drank the water and handed the cup back to Rosie who exposed more of her bleached white teeth with a Vaseline smile.

Maggie pulled the shade down and asked the young man, "Do you mind?"

Guilty, he shook his head. Maggie turned her back to him and pulled the blanket to her chin while she rested her head on the window shade.

Hours later she awoke to a firm nudge on her shoulder and the immediate silence of shut engines. She first mistook the touch as turbulence then discovered it was the woman poking her fake nails into Maggie's shoulder. Groggy, she barely showed the whites of her heavy eyes when she opened them. Her head was so full of sleep that open eyes would release a flood of unattended remorse.

The doctor told her the pill could put a horse to sleep. The side of her face was numb from sleeping and the lashes adhered together by the thick mascara. She'd slept through the six-hour flight and descent. The pillow between her head and the window shade fell so the moment she straightened her head upright, pain clenched between her ear and shoulder. The attendant and a male steward took hold of each arm to assist her off the plane and into the car just outside the baggage claim. The driver stood with a sign that read, "M. Gilardi."

By the time Maggie arrived to the car she was conscious enough to duck into the back seat.

"Welcome to Atlanta," the driver said.

Maggie cringed.

"Careful with the baggage. It's worth a small fortune," was all she said before she slumped back into the leather seats of the black town car. She assumed he knew where he was going. Sleep would take her back to numb so she did not ask, quietly hoping they would arrive lost by the time she woke up.

Jeff watched the Hinkley's house through the window of his bedroom as he turned over the events in his mind. Since the night of the party he kept the sliding glass door closed and locked, unable to bring himself to walk outside. To step foot on the terrace where Neil climbed up to the roof, would be like Jeff stepping into his friend's shoes. He feared for his own safety as he recalled the police officer's explanation. Neil either jumped or slipped and fell. Beyond that instant came details of the injury that described the impact to the skull through the temple region as it hit the cement planter while kids milled around the back yard, drinking. Several stood in a circle in the dark, smoking weed. They were all high when they heard Neil fall to the ground. Clouded by dizzy elation they questioned their eyesight until Jeff leaned over the balcony railing and looked below him where Neil lay twisted on the ground. He could have been passed out. Only blood - a lot of it pooled around his head.

Sam, Russell and John, part of the circle of stoners, inched toward Neil on the ground. They called his name, aware of the proximity of the Hinkley's home next door. The girls from the group released panic and fear in shrieks and yelled as they ran toward the back of the house.

Though he still stood on the balcony, Jeff bent down as he tried to draw himself closer to his friend who lay unconscious. Instinct thwarted the initial shock and he realized that Neil lay close to dying. It was a twitch under the skin. It was a certain understanding. A genetic understanding. It was the raw truth that tugged from his belly, hard won with experience in loss.

NINETEEN | Seizing

"Gram, it says here that seizing is, 'The process of soap quickly becoming solid before the soap batch is poured into a mold or hand-shaped into soap balls." Claire stood at the kitchen sink next to Bernie, her hair done and make up applied tastefully. She wore the velour sweat suit and an apron. Claire wore makeup after several days of keeping to her preference to be bare faced, something her mother would not have liked. Bernie never said a word about it.

"Let's just do this then. Get going, okay honey?" Bernie said.

She put her hand on her granddaughter's shoulder just as Claire gripped the handles on the large pot, lifted it and let the liquid pour into a mold that resembled an ice tray only five or six times larger. A pale thick yellow mixture covered the dried botanical leaves and petals in the tray. They were decorative and would be preserved by it, like wax on a Georgia peach.

Claire spoke without taking her eyes off the mixture. She smiled. "I love the little sunflowers the most."

Bernie picked up the soap making reference book Claire laid on the counter and squinted. "It says it may take several hours to harden depending on weather conditions.

It's pretty cool so I'm guessing that it won't take that long."

Claire watched the liquid flow into the first tray, righted the pot to cut the flow of liquid soap slightly, then moved onto the next slot.

"This should fill the whole thing," Bernie said, and watched Claire pour the remaining mixture into the molds. Without a task to occupy her hands and mind, she drifted and her interest changed to a distant stare.

"I'll be just a few minutes, Gram. Why don't you change your clothes? I'll go get dressed when I'm done. It'll only take me a few minutes." Claire smiled and nodded to her grandmother, a gesture unfamiliar to each of them because Claire was the one who needed the reassurance. Discomfort lingered for a moment before Bernie returned what was barely a small grin, partly lost in her own world and partly disoriented like a small child unable to find her parents.

Claire turned on the faucet water and watched as it ran into the pot. The steam rose first gradually then in a cloud as the temperature turned from tepid to scalding. Her face and neck attracted the tiny beads of moisture and coated her with a sudden warmth to the usual chill she felt to her bones, never mind the weather.

Bernie patted her granddaughter's back with a stifled affection that acknowledged a switch in their roles as granddaughter and grandmother. It was a reversal to their understanding of caretaker and nurtured. This first moment of quiet reciprocity startled each of them. They nodded, Claire looking from the pot to Bernice and back as she watched her grandmother pat the front of her apron out of habit, though her hands were clean. She untied it behind her and lifted it over her head so it barely touched the teased, combed and sprayed hair. Held by the loop that hung from her neck just moments before, she rested it on the cabinet door handle to the right of the stove.

Clearing her throat, she just nodded again, and held

herself together, trying hard to suppress tears but cringed as the pain came to her nose as a warning to let go. She could not. Not yet. Not with Claire there. Her need to hover over the girl was acute and frenetic, and crying would only make Claire more nervous. More uncertain.

Slowly, Bernie put each foot in front of the other, placed carefully as she held onto the handrail and half pulled herself up the steps to the little guest bedroom next to Claire's room where she left her toiletries on the bureau. She and Claire shared the bathroom.

It was a neat little space with a double bed topped with a plain beige comforter and white dust ruffle. The frame was brass and the little nightstand bare wood. The lamp was also brass with an ivory lampshade. The walls were white. It was plain and barely significant. Ernest did not expect guests, but he appreciated his mother who took care of Claire to a fault.

But the world was caving in on everything and everyone. Bernie was suddenly aware that Estelle would never know about Neil, how he died. Something bigger than all of them had saved her from that but had left Bernice with a weight to bear alone. She let herself sit on the little bed, her arms crossed tightly against her chest, only a few moments before she had to get up and start moving again.

She pulled off the sweat suit and removed from the back of the bedroom door the black dress last worn for Estelle's funeral. She quickly glanced at herself in the full length mirror which completely covered the closet door, smoothed the loose cotton and polyester knit over her wide waist and legs and slipped on her shoes, black and open-toed. Dressing was a task that required more time at her age, so she did it in pieces: a bath then hairdressers in the late morning followed by the clothes then makeup. She had done it so many times before but the many distractions and lack of sleep tripped her up the way that Jack was tripped up in his dementia. She stopped and took a deep breath. Did she have it too? She hung in the space between things real and not, the present and the anxious future.

The sound of rushing water came through the thin walls. Bernie became suddenly aware of her reflection in the long mirror. Of her age. Who would she talk to now? It had finally settled in, the knowledge that Estelle was gone, when she was struck by the sudden truth that there was no one to tell and there would never be anyone else to tell. It was not her plan to bear this. To bear the secrets and the words alone. She could talk to her only one true friend and be heard. Bernie was not the most social of people but attached to her family and Estelle. They were honest with each other and her heart ached knowing that this part of her would be remembered but had disappeared.

In the other room was her granddaughter, and that girl was also a piece of her.

She was old enough to know that people stayed with you in pieces, whether or not they still embodied the whole person to be seen and touched and felt. They were gone but their lives lingered. It happened that way when her parents died but this was less thought to be inevitable. Estelle's character was inside Bernie too, and Estelle would have told her, "Chin up, girl." Then, obeying everything else her friend would do, she put her makeup on oddly aware of every movement. Aware of the lines in her face, the difference in her eyes, her hair, her body, everything that changed in the many years of their parallel lives. Young women with little babies and lonely if not for each other. All the hours at the kitchen table together talking about the same things over and over again but remembering nothing. Judging sometimes. Forgiving always. Being there. They had been so lucky.

She took her time with every brush against the little folds in her face. When she heard the bathroom door open and the floorboards from the hallway squeak, she stepped out of the guest room and into the hallway where she lingered outside of Claire's bedroom door, listening. She heard nothing and knocked softly.

"You need anything, honey? Any help?"

The question felt odd and inappropriate, but Bernie needed to keep her eyes on Claire. She found her in the girlish bedroom, too neat for a girl her age. Everything so well kept and clean throughout the house. Claire would spend afternoons after school cleaning unless she was with Annene, but there was little of that while Annene dealt with the preparations for the memorial service.

Claire stood in front of the white vanity in a white terry cloth bathrobe, her hair in a towel turban. Lights on the painted white shutters were closed to the daylight. Her face was drawn and pale against the thick robe.

"I can tell you're coming before you walk in the door. The floorboards squeak just outside my door."

Claire spoke to her grandmother into and through the mirror then turned to face her.

"You have good hearing."

"I can hear everything. Too much. It's not good. Because I can't sleep," Claire said.

"Me either," Bernie replied. "It's a tough time, honey. You shouldn't have to go through all of this. None of us should."

Claire ignored her out of habit then wiped her mouth with the back of her hand and shook her head. "I tasted it."

"That's not good," Bernie said, as she breathed in a deep sigh. That's toxic. You could get sick."

"Then why do parents always threaten kids with washing our mouths out with soap? Mom always told me that she'd do it if I didn't watch what I said. I told her I hated her once and when she tired to pry my mouth open I bit her finger so hard that she smacked me across the face and ran out of the room. I think that's when she started hating me. I mean, other stuff happened, but that was the first thing."

Claire felt nothing when she said this but blinked several times over. "I shouldn't have done that."

She took her granddaughter's hands and led her to the side of the bed. "Come here, honey," she said.

She pulled back to a tension that hung on. "Gram, I need to get dressed. Dad's gonna be here to pick us up."

But, Bernie latched on to the words and refused to let go.

"I just worry about you, honey. I just want you to be happy. I know all of this is tough but I just want…"

"It's okay, Gram."

"No, it's not okay. You're too skinny and you never eat anymore and that's the only thing you've said about anything that's happened."

"She's going to be there today," Claire said, flat, as she looked toward the door. "I don't know why I know but I know. It's what I know."

"I know, honey."

"I don't even know what I should call her now. Mom? Maggie? What am I going to say to her?"

"I don't know. You can say whatever you want to say. You don't have to say anything."

Claire drew back but her grandmother's freckled hand held onto Claire.

"I just want you to know that…" Bernie began before Claire interrupted her.

"What? It's not my fault she's like that?"

"Well, that's not what I was going to say but that's true too." She patted Claire's hand and lowered her head.

"I just won't say anything to her unless she wants to talk to me."

Bernie blinked her eyes a few times then closed them, damming up the tears with anger. Claire needed her support. Claire was too young to shoulder it all.

'You should say whatever you want to say to her. I don't care what she says. She lost the right to you. She lost her right. Mothers don't desert their daughters."

"Mom always told me to be quiet and be a lady and not talk back. I mean, I don't know how many times I embarrassed her and it was because I forgot to put on some lipstick or my nail polish was chipped or I just didn't say the right thing to one of her stupid friends."

Bernie nodded. "I know. Maggie just changed. Some people do that. There's something wrong with her. Some people change for the good and some don't. Some change the right way. Some don't. Estelle… She didn't change, but Neil did," Bernie said.

Claire looked at her grandmother without a shift to the contours of her perfect young face. It was not the right time to lure Claire into that truth but it lingered between them as a test and Bernie was sure she had no idea. She was oblivious and it pained her to know that someday, someday soon, she would understand the extent to which both her mother and Neil had let her down. Bernie let the thoughts go so they would turn back to her friend. "I miss her so much. I'm so sorry you have to go through all of this. Life is dirty and not easy. But, if there's one thing I know, it's that no matter how much you try to protect your children, you can't. Life happens to everyone. My mother tried to protect me, but she couldn't and I tried to do that with your Dad. There are just no guarantees. The only thing you can do is try. There's so much beauty, honey, and so much goodness in the world. You just have to take it all in. You are a beautiful young woman who is so, so loved. I love you so much."

Claire put her arms around Bernie who, consumed by her own words of hope, managed to lift herself out of the prevailing sadness that could have consumed her with grief.

"It's just a tough time right now, honey. One thing you know when you're an old lady like me is that if you can get through this stuff, and this is really, really hard stuff, you can get through anything. You can appreciate happy times even more. You just have to talk about it, or it will whittle you away to nothing. No running away. No starving yourself. None of that stuff that feels like protection. You can't be numb. We have each other, honey. We have each other and we need to be glad about that because it's all you need."

Claire nodded. "I know, Gram," Claire said. Bolstered yet repelled by the words, she got up off the bed. "You look pretty."

Bernie brightened. "You think so?" she asked. "Estelle hated the way I looked in black. She just hated it. I almost brought a blue dress instead, but then I'd be socially inappropriate. That woman never minded a single fashion code that she espoused in that column, and yet she always had an opinion. God love her." She threw up her hands.

Claire shook her head and left the room.

Bernie sat on the bed and listened to the floorboards creak as Claire descended the stairs. Her delicate size seven feet managed to avert every forgiving board but the one at the very bottom, avoided only if it was skipped altogether. Claire stepped right over it.

Bernie could not have avoided it herself. Not at her age. And, at her age she did not care.

The funeral took place at Good Shepherd. Ushers removed the remaining limp flowers from Estelle's memorial and the florist delivered new and fresh bouquets though fewer and mostly carnations in blue and yellow to match Neil's football jersey. Each side of the entrance was flanked by enlarged photographs mounted on foam core that leaned against tall otherwise flimsy easels. In one, Neil wore a teenage chiseled smile against his tanned and fresh face set off by the vibrant team jersey colors. A football was tucked under his forearm. The photo was over a year old. His eyes were bright then and without the shadows that had become the norm, like it was residual eye black. Another photograph, the one to the right of the double doors pictured Neil, age one, leaning up on his elbows and dressed in a railroad uniform and cap, smiling. Proud. Another two or three steps inside the vestibule at the church door entrance were two more photographs, to the left of the door was one of Annene and Neil together. Annene was dressed in a pink sleeveless shirt with a ruffled fringe and cotton bell-bottom pants with a matching ruffled hem. Pink bow barrettes held her hair away from her face but had become loose and limp. Her eyes were focused on the ice cream cone that dripped over the hand that held it. She stood next to Neil whose broad grin stole the attention from both his discontented sister and the man dressed in a bunny costume that stood behind him. He wore a Hang Ten striped shirt and white Ocean Pacific shorts.

"I just want to make sure that it looks okay," Judy said to Annene.

Both wore black dresses. Judy's linen shell with the short three quarter inch sleeves jacket was already wrinkled. Annene's was soft with capped sleeves and strings that tied into a limp bow at the bust like a medieval corset. The length fell just below her knees and a black sweater was draped over her right forearm.

Annene stifled the urge to object to the photograph that conveyed a bad disposition and failed to take into account her finer attributes apart, that is, from her sense of style. She sidled up to Judy who stood dead center in the entrance to the church. The Berry family photograph was positioned to the right and included Annene's dad. While it made them conflicted and uncomfortable, Judy chose it as one of the four photographs.

"Judy, let's go in, okay?" Annene said.

Judy shrugged and shook her head without taking her eyes off the photograph.

"Mom, let's go in."

Judy said nothing for several moments before she responded. "You think it looks okay?"

"It looks fine," Jeff said. He stood behind them and wore the same dark suit from weeks before when he attended Estelle's funeral. Judy smiled reflexively at the sight of him. He was a good kid and she was suddenly happy. When she reached up to hug him around his neck, Jeff found her waist with his hands to prevent himself from falling forward.

"I'm so glad you're here." Judy said, as she let go and patted his shoulder. She was unexpectedly needy.

Jeff nodded, respectful.

"Hi, Annene," he said.

"Hi," Annene replied, cordial.

Judy wiped her eyes and nose with a balled up handkerchief.

"Nice dress."

"Thanks," Annene said, straining a smile. Unconsciously, she rolled the black string that hung against her chest between her fingers.

"You make it?" Jeff asked, deliberately pointing to the hem.

"Yeah. I didn't want to wear the same one and I already had the pattern. It was pretty easy."

"I'll let you two talk for a moment," Judy said, and stepped away toward the photo just outside the front door. Annene watched her mother straighten the stiff photo, the one with Neil as a baby conductor. Then she turned and looked toward the street, her back to Annene and Jeff.

"Cool," he replied. "I just wanted to say I'm sorry. I'm really sorry about Neil and…"

Through the beginning sting of forming tears she squinted and glared almost fiercely at him. His kindness was an aggressive act that poked holes in her.

"You're one of the pall bearers, right?" she asked, padding her voice to buffer the inflection of the varied emotions crashing inside her. She knew the answer but needed him gone.

The photograph was the one formal family portrait that the Berry's took in 1986, the year Mr. Berry both left them and died. Neil stood at his father's right with Judy beside him and Annene to her mother's left.

Unable to watch her mother's unattended visible grief and need, Annene left Jeff without a word and joined her at the entrance where she paced. White marble walls, a red carpeted floor and the statue of the Virgin Mary were in view through the open doors, perched in the enclave before the bend into the church. To their left was the chapel.

"Mom, go in and I'll meet you inside. Mr. Hinkley is in there. She spun around and pointed through the wooden double doors.

"Okay," Judy said, pensive, vulnerable and almost childlike. "You coming?"

"I'll be there in a minute. I have to go to the bathroom," she lied, and waved to Judy. She felt her heart and the chill in the air and removed the sweater she held to her side. She quickly unfastened the row of buttons then pulled her arms through the sleeves one at a time.

As Annene looked out the front doors, a woman appeared from the path that came from the church parking lot around the back of the building. She walked slowly and swayed slightly with even and purposeful grace toward Annene who noticed the navy blue blouse with puffy shirtsleeves and scoop neck. The skirt matched. Blue also, was a wide brimmed felt hat of the same color. A white silk rose brought together the two sides of the white fabric Annene guessed was silk wrapped around the base of the crown. Annene hardly recognized her but watched as Mrs. Clement took Judy's hand and led her into the church. Relieved, Annene rolled her eyes just as soon as her mother and the gym teacher disappeared.

Sensing his presence for a split second, she saw him as he appeared in her peripheral vision, Annene spoke to Jeff so softly it could have been meant for no one but herself. "Mrs. Clement actually looks like a woman today," Annene said, when the women were out of view.

Jeff agreed, "Yeah she does. I don't think I've ever seen her in anything but a sweat suit and those gym shorts."

His tone was hushed and conspiratorial. He tried hard around her.

"That's funny," Annene said. "You're right. Where's the dog?"

"I think she left it in the car," Jeff said. "She took it for a walk before. It's cute. It's a cute dog. You like dogs?"

"You come with your folks?" Annene replied, ignoring him.

"I came by myself. They'll be here later. I had to get out and they weren't leaving for a while longer."

Jeff knew the Stones would have given him a ride, but they were kind and gave him space and he knew they liked him for it.

"How?"

"Walked."

"You didn't run?"

"No. Didn't want to get the suit messed up."

He smoothed the dark blue jacket pockets and Annene thought him more reasonably dressed than her.

"Oh."

"You going to go sit down?" Jeff asked. "A few of the…" Jeff stalled, unsure as to what direction in which to proceed. Self-conscious, he combed the fingers of his right hand through the buzzed hair on his head. Each time he touched the hair on his head, a habit linked to wandering thought or some anxious or emphatic change, he regretted it. He folded his hands together to be less obvious.

"You can call them guests, Jeff. It's okay."

"I know," he said.

"No you don't. You don't know."

"I do too," he said. "They're guests."

"I know you don't know because whenever you start pretending you know what you're talking about you start running your fingers through your hair like that. My Grandpa used to do that. He does that. Grandma Estelle always called him on it. He lost all his hair."

"Isn't he bald?"

"Yeah," Annene said, annoyed though relieved to have something take her mind off the present circumstances.

"Yeah, I should stop." Jeff looked over his shoulder in response to the voices at the door.

"I should go," he said. "They should be here in a minute. You okay?"

"Yeah, I'm fine," Annene said.

"You know, Annene. I hope you don't have hard feelings. I like you a lot. I know what you're going through too."

"You don't have any idea what I'm going through."

"I don't?" Jeff asked. He tried to be calm with her but he found the need for pity difficult to digest. He could not take it. He would not. He would not be manipulated. He could not be forced to surrender to anger. She was the same confrontational Annene. Effort or not, attempts to reach her or not, he impressed himself upon her and got nothing in return. Annene was doing him a favor, so it felt. Favors were offerings of pity. He felt for her, understood her. But the back and forth, push and pull and tugging had to stop. He was tired. It was familiar but he was tired. He was used to that need for acceptance, arresting himself to be liked, his Pavlovian response to food, shelter and love. That was the magnet. He was finally feeling calm.

"No," Annene replied.

"You're right. I don't. The difference is that you've had all of these people in your life, Annene, and you know what?"

"What?"

"You act like their collateral damage. Like that's what you are. I've had no one. If I was you I'd be happy to have had them here while they were here. It's like having visitors. When they go over to your house they stay and you get this nice feeling when they're here. Then they leave and you still have that feeling but there's no one to pin it on. It lingers and you feel it. That's kind of what I had to do. I mean, the couple of times I almost got adopted. I held onto it. I held onto any good feeling I could hold onto because when the bad feeling came up and I started feeling really lonely, I had something. It wasn't much, but it was something. Anyway," he said scratching his head. "I suppose I don't know that much, but I know what happened was an accident and all you can do is just…"

Annene lowered her head to hide the tears that welled in her eyes. She wanted to run.

"I'm gonna go," Jeff said. "I'm really sorry."

Two policemen on motorcycles pulled up to the curb in front of the church followed by a black hearse and a group of men, including Ernest and Frank, gathered next to it, waiting with their hands in their pockets fidgeting change and keys, their hands clasped behind their backs, smoking, a few of them.

Jeff touched her shoulder, barely, with his hand and walked out the door as several women approached Annene who retreated into the church before they could reach out to her. She breathed deeply as she walked quickly toward the altar and sat in the front pew. There, she set down her black purse and tugged at the tissue from the box someone from the church left behind. It was a sad thing but there were small moments of things gracious and that was one of them. She was determined to stunt the few tears and calm herself. Sacrilegious or not, she began chanting in a low mumble. God was everyone's god.

When Bernie and Claire arrived moments later they spotted the back of Annene's blunt, black head of hair.

She was seated alone in the first row of pews. Automatically, Bernie reached to her right and dipped her middle finger into the vessel of holy water and blessed herself with the sign of the cross. She scanned the room; a modern church built from brick and plaster in the Sixties with a large angular crucifix that hung prominently above the altar in front of the tall stained glass window that depicted the final scene of Jesus' death and resurrection. Smaller stained glass images depicting the story of Jesus were set in sequence into the plaster walls that surrounded the interior of the circular church set high above a brick chair rail. It was not a traditional Roman Catholic Church with vaulted ceilings, but it was comfortable. Brightly colored embroidered tapestries hung on the bare walls beside the stained glass. Plain plaster pillars terminated at the tops and were decorated at the intersecting crease with a simple scroll. The beige ceiling revealed rafters where the smell of stale incense rose and collected in the pores of the church.

Bernie took Claire's hand as they walked up the aisle toward the front set of pews. Bernie thought again of her friend and was grateful that she passed without having to live through Neil's funeral. Estelle could bear almost anything, but Bernie needed confirmation that everything happened for a reason and it was the only one that made sense. The memories paced back and forth in her mind while she jumped over their ultimate crossing like a little girl who navigated hopscotch squares in shoes too big for her. Thoughts floated as she visited those images of her friend. They came to Bernie in that vacant moment of her surrendered mind. She suddenly realized that it would be Neil's death that would allow her to begin to let go of Estelle.

They took a seat four rows behind the front row where Annene sat quietly. Organ music filled the room and Claire turned to find that the pews behind her began to fill with mostly familiar faces. Bernie sensed her anxiety.

"She'll get here, Claire. She's always been late. She was late for her own wedding," Bernie whispered.

"I wasn't looking for her. I was only looking back at the choir," Claire lied. "I have to go to the bathroom."

"I'll go with you," Bernie said. "We have a few minutes. Let's get up and sneak over through the chapel. I don't want to have to deal with talking to a bunch of people right now. God bless them. I just can't do it right now."

"Me neither," Claire said, as she slipped her feet from the kneeler to the floor. She held Bernie's soft upper arm to give Bernie more leverage to stand while her grandmother held tightly onto a rosary of small white beads. When Annene turned around in response to their voices, Claire pointed to the side door and formed the word, "bathroom" with her otherwise silent mouth. Annene nodded, and shook her head at Claire's gesture to join them. Blankly, she faced front again. Mourners seated in the front pew were left alone and Annene knew that.

They walked quickly across the red-carpeted aisle and out the side door getting a quick look at the flood of people who had arrived. Jack's absence was conspicuous but Judy had decided that the ceremony would only confuse him further and that he could show his face later at the reception within familiar surroundings less likely to confuse him. Ernest and Frank stood at the front door with Judy. A loud cough came from the entrance. A man then cleared his throat. A small child gargled his words and another one shouted only to be shushed. Claire felt her own words but could not voice them.

Inside the small, white tiled bathroom were three sectioned off stalls. Two of the taupe metal doors were closed, one with a sign taped to it that read "out of order." The middle one that Claire used quickly was open. The toilet water was still settling with its high-pitched hiss. Claire ran the faucet water over her hands then lathered them with a bar of soap. As it slipped between her palms, she wondered out loud.

"Grammy, this place doesn't have dispensers in here. Do you think it's sanitary to use the bar of soap?"

A loud flush came from the stall behind Claire's right shoulder. "I think it's pretty clean," Bernie said. "I mean, what'd they do before they had the dispensers?"

Claire lifted her hand, lathered so that small bubbles stuck to her skin.

Short, impatient sighs of strained nylon adjustments came from Bernie inside the stall. Claire saw through the mirror her grandmother's skirt fall and swish back and forth just below the stall door. Despite the "out of order" sign stuck to the other stall, she saw the dark figure of a woman inside but did not stare. The walls inside the bathroom were painted white.

Claire shrugged and vigorously twisted the soap between her fingers, under the flowing water thinking to herself that she could remove the layers of urine, the germs that anyone else before her left, and make her own hands clean. Satisfied, she lifted one of her hands to her mouth and ran her tongue across the back of her hand.

Bernie laughed and Claire jumped at the sound that bounced off the white tile and plaster walls.

"What are you laughing at?" Claire asked.

"They got new toilets," Bernie replied. "It almost took me down with all of that suction."

The door latch clicked and Bernie appeared. She took a deep breath and squinted at Claire. Bubbles had formed at the corners of the girl's mouth where she scratched an itch to taste it.

"Claire, you eating that stuff?" she asked. "You know people do that? It's called 'pica.' When people have to eat things like chalk or laundry detergent. Or, soap. Things that don't have any nutritional value but can hurt you."

"No, Gram. It got on my mouth when I rubbed my face." She looked into the mirror and wiped away the soap. Her dress was plain and black but she wore a white sweater and pearl earrings. Her hair was held up and splayed like a pine swag gathered in a banana clip.

"What are you laughing at?" Claire asked.

Bernie was already on to the next thing.

"I'm just thinking about Estelle. You know, one day we were on the phone. It was just before her surgery and, God love her, she looked out the window of the hospital. You know she was in a different room before she had the surgery? She looked out the window and told me that the nurse opened the curtains, and wouldn't you know, there was a white statue of the Virgin Mary outside of her window. She started laughing and I started laughing and we remembered how when I was living in New York at the Barbizon and Hank and Frank got in that big fight, and my aunt told my mother that I should go live in a convent. Estelle said she swore her mother planned her living arrangements because right outside her window was a statue of the Virgin Mary. We shared that. Our mothers always wanted to protect us but they never thought to teach us how to live. Maggie, with all of her faults, honey. Maybe it's her way of protecting you. Or, maybe that's what she thinks."

Bernice patted her washed hands with a paper towel. Claire reached for the door just as it gave way to a woman pushing herself in, who then took a few steps back to let Bernie and Claire pass.

"You ready?" Claire asked, and threw the paper towel into the bin.

Bernie placed her hand on her granddaughter's back and followed her out the door.

Maggie watched through the crack between the stall barrier and door as they left and waited for the other woman to finish before she could leave the stall. Still shaking, she unlatched the stall door and stood in front of the mirror where she straightened her charcoal gray blouse and black, flared pants. She adjusted the black veil of the black felt pill box hat pulling down the mesh between her index finger and thumb so it covered her face more than intended. Her eyes remained fixed on her reflection. She waited for several moments to collect herself before she fitted the wrist-length black gloves over her hands and left the bathroom. Quickly, she walked outside and around the perimeter of the building. She knew Bernie and Claire would cut through the chapel. At least, that is what she thought and she hoped she was right.

Her head lowered, she entered the single door to the right of the open main double doors to the church. She went unnoticed by most but Jeff caught sight of a slight figure and the long black flared pants she wore, a conspicuous difference from the other Alpharetta women who wore blouses and suit jackets with padded, angular shoulders, and flouncy skirts and dresses.

Jeff watched the woman's back as she glided, slithered almost on tiptoe, down the aisle. The image of her silhouette was still embedded in his mind from that day at the house when he waited. He'd seen her outline behind the sheer curtains and a shadow through the Hinkley's window panes and he knew it was her. Neil's car was parked out front and Jeff must have looked like a stalker as he waited, staring at the house, wondering if Neil would appear or not. No one else was home and Neil was supposed to give him a ride that day. Instincts, which he had learned from experience to mind, told him not to knock at the door so he just watched. He waited long enough to see them leave together.

Next to Jeff, Ernest held the coffin with cupped hands so that his fingers kept it elevated. Frank and three other golfing types were also ushers that day to assist mostly with the transport of Neil's body. Ernest's eyes were lowered so he missed her. She walked quickly with practiced evenness.

Maggie bowed, genuflected, and performed the sign of the cross. When she sat, he watched her screw the crown of the hat onto her head so it dipped forward and the veil could cover more of her face. Her newly cropped short blond and wavy hair made her profile more evident. Jeff's eyes darted between the altar, Maggie and Ernest's exhausted stare. Ernest finally caught sight of Jeff's distraction, locked eyes with him and followed his gaze though Jeff tried to avert his eyes. It was too late. Jeff watched the man's face change when he recognized his estranged wife. At that same moment, everyone around her seemed to notice the same thing. While he was out of range to hear them, he saw them whisper, leaning into each other then looking toward the back of the church where Ernest stood, helpless.

Ernest's fingers began to sweat and slip away from the brass handle that held the coffin. A cool January breeze came from the door that hadn't closed properly. Father Haute's white robe flapped at the slight breeze from the broken vacuum of air as Ernest watched Maggie fluff her hair under the black pill box. It was a disingenuous effort to hide her face and she regretted the haircut and the hat.

Organ pipes blew their hollow sounds through the distraction and turned the guests' attention to the ceremony. Twin sopranos and Mrs. Rossini, the alto, sang.

Amazing grace! How sweet the sound
That saved a wretch like me.
I once was lost, but now am found,
Was blind, but now I see.

'Twas grace that taught my heart to fear,
And grace my fears relieved.
How precious did that grace appear
The hour I first believed.

Through many dangers, toils and snares

I have already come;
'Tis grace hath brought me safe thus far
And grace will lead me home.

The Lord has promised good to me
His word my hope secures;
He will my shield and portion be,
As long as life endures.

Yea, when this flesh and heart shall fail,
and mortal life shall cease,
I shall possess within the veil,
A life of joy and peace.

When we've been there ten thousand years
Bright shining as the sun,
We've no less days to sing God's praise
Than when we've first begun.

Transporting the coffin required the length of all verses.

TWENTY | Clean

Bernie thought about the song as she stood at the edge of the buffet table, humming. Her voice always cracked at "I once was lost," then flattened out. Claire entered the room behind Judy while Ernest guided Jack into the dining room like he was a blind man. Bernie had not seen Jack for days since the memorial. His eyes, though more hallow than she recalled, did not settle on any one person. His sight seemed to scatter in every direction. He asked after Estelle but was redirected to eat or drink. Ernest called for Frank who came in from the door and nodded at someone at the entrance that Bernie could not distinguish. It was blocked by the partial wall of the arch that led into the dining room. Annene stood under the arch.

She stopped her humming, the low tone she kept to herself to block out the sounds around her, an echo of the same voices delayed only weeks. Two deaths bookended Judy. Two generations on either side of her inflicted a kind of paralysis unique to her daughter who was always in motion. It was beyond anyone's belief to have it that way.

A teenage girl's voice spoke from a cluster in the corner of the den. They all wore simple black dresses from Contempo Casuals, hair layered and teased, acrylic nails painted red, pink or in a French manicure. They were the daughters of the Alpharetta women, women who stayed home with their children and did not work. They were home after school, cooking. They looked for things to talk about. Got their hair done. Their nails done. Makeup was worn whenever they stepped out of the house. These mothers were the lineage to the Alpharetta Mafia and Estelle, who could have been one of them, thought they were most aptly satirized by Dolly Parton in The Harper Valley PTA. They headed the PTA and the school controlled them.

Shrill and too loud, one voice broke away from the soft drone of conversation.

"It was like one of those hippy parents who names their kid, like Rain or Sunshine or after a season. Or like that kid, Blue, and his sister, Gray. You know, the ones that moved from LA? That girl is so weird. She tried to tell me once how to put on my makeup like I don't know how or something. It's like her name made her have to be freaky. Why would you name a kid something like that? What if your kid was named Spring? They'd be out of season, like, nine months out of the year. You know, it's like naming a kid some adjective. Like they're supposed to be like that. It's a label."

The girl giving the monologue was tall, skinny and rested one knee on the brown sectional. Her name was Jennifer. The other girls both sat around the sofa and stood, seven in all, and listened while the tall girl held court. It was like that. Her mother was the same way, used the same technique to hold hostage her cliques. Gossip bound them together by holding them up. There were three Jennifers, one Christina, one Lisa, one Julie, and one Quiet-and-Nameless-But-Learning.

Annene looked around the room and found it full of familiar yet estranged faces. She felt no genuine emotional proximity to any of them except her mother who had been worn down into a state of almost nothing. Annene suddenly understood why the living room looked the way it did. She realized that her mother had no idea what she wanted so she chose something of everything that amounted to a chaos of neutrals.

The girl talking about the names continued. She was a cheerleader who ran for Associated Student Body President earlier in the year but lost, ultimately happy with her consolation spot as Hospitality Commissioner. Her speech was rapid like tapping feet.

"You name a kid some kind of description word and the world all knows what that means. What about Hope? Maybe that's not a good one. That's not such a bad word. You think this kid is really looking toward the future. You name a kid Horace and everyone has a different Horace in their mind."

A different Frank. A different Estelle. Claire. Judy. Ernest. No one had ever heard of an Annene, she thought to herself, listening.

"But, you name a kid Gray and all you get is different hues of the same color from gun metal to charcoal. Blue. You've got sky to indigo. Summer? Just sunny all the time. Rain? Maybe big drops from little, drizzle compared to a storm."

Annene was mesmerized at the way the girl could focus so intently on one meaningless thing. She wished she could do the same. Focus on just nothing. But, no matter how hard she tried, that something larger came to the surface and no amount of anger could press it down. She had no choice. The meaning slapped her in the face once and came back to slug her in the gut. Annene, who thought herself the teller of all truths, realized that some could not be brought to the surface. If Estelle was alive, then maybe it could be set free. But, it festered as an image, one that disgusted her. Truth would always reveal itself, Estelle told her. No matter how you judged a name or stupid girls.

Hovered over the buffet table, Bernie watched as Frank and Ernest flanked Jack and held onto his other arm.

Faces turned toward the door where the two men stood, all attention focused on Jack. People filed past him. Several ladies stopped to kiss him on the cheek. Older gentlemen shook his hand, most with a regular gentleman's handshake. A deeper sincerity was implied by his better friends and their wives who also took hold of the right elbow or shoulder. Mrs. Clement stood with a small paper plate in hand that she filled with a few small hors d'oeuvres sized quiches, deviled eggs and cheese speared with toothpicks topped with frayed yellow, blue, green and red cellophane shaped into a flame. Mr. Kissel, the math teacher, and Mrs. Clement were deep in conversation. Years ago, Mr. K sent Neil to detention for cheating. He'd learned his lesson, but the man wondered whether he played a part in any of it. Moments of silence were deep valleys of guilt some confessed.

Several boys Neil's age sat around the spot typically designated for him on the opposite side of the sofa to the girls. They trained alongside Neil, throughout junior high school football and into their years at Alpharetta High. Two lost their necks to muscle between their shoulders and the others rose out of them. They were the boys who first found Neil after he fell off the roof.

Bernie played the song through her mind as she watched the room shift. Jack sat next to Frank, the only person Jack recognized apart from his daughter, Judy, given the slipping state of his mind.

Yeah, when this flesh and heart shall fail,
And mortal life shall cease,
I shall possess within the veil, A life of joy and peace.

Together, the guests rose around Jeff who sat distracted in the back row, dwarfed but trying to escape his mind thick with panic that delayed the collective automation of the clear thus cooperative mind. To sit then to stand then to sit again was the way of the church and the formality of it was unfamiliar to him. Bernie stood at the front of the room, shoulder-to-shoulder next to the priest, a man

dressed in divinity robes. A narrow vestment laid like a
bridge across his high back connected his shoulders then
hung flat, bold in a deep purple silk, from each side of his
chest against the white robe. Black tufts of hair and
sideburns appeared at the sides of his balding head. Either
the cool January air or the vigor of a God-infused life
tinged his cheeks pink. Jeff's previous foster family, the
father, had a face like that. Red-faced from alcoholism.
Too much to think about but Jeff recognized the priest as
Monsignor Boyer, the same man who greeted Bernie and
Frank after Estelle's service. His cheeks were also tinged
with the fine red lines, the raised veins. He briefly thought
it could be something different than liquor that brought it
on.

Jeff lowered the open missallette in his other hand and
held it up closer to his chest to pretend to follow along.
Beyond the many rows in front of him, beyond the pews
and clusters of people, Bernie held a few loose papers that
ruffled in her hands at the podium. Jeff shifted to the left
to get Judy in his line of sight between the bodies that
blocked his view. Maggie waited for the guests to file in
before she took her seat. Jeff slipped into a seat beside
Mr. Calvert, a subtle attempt to trail her without being
noticed, though he was unsure whether she would have
recognized him at all.

Despite the half-hearted, seemingly disingenuous
attempts to conceal herself, to stay hidden behind the dark
veil and sunglasses, Jeff watched several teachers and a few
of the Alpharetta Mafia he had learned to recognize turn
their heads in recognition. First one locked on her then
with it the wind blew whispers and glances toward the
unwelcome visitor. Jeff saw that Ernest had placed his
arm around Judy.

Bernie cleared her throat and brushed the end of her
nose with the handkerchief wadded in her right hand.

"Thank you Monsignor," she said.

Bernie began. "Many of you know a very special friend

that I spoke of the last time I was here. I've been reading this little book that a very special young woman here discovered. Like Monsignor Boyer said, the passing of a young man is very difficult to understand. But Annene, who many of you may guess is the young friend that I'm talking about, left this with her grandmother Estelle one day. I know this because Estelle was my best friend and she marked the page so she wouldn't forget it. Many of you know her so we cannot forget everything about her. Not that we would have a choice. Estelle said that one of the things that made her want to write all of those articles was that people were so different. When someone so young dies we feel less inclined to forget because it's as though he keeps on living. There's a refusal of death that the old are not given. It's allowed."

"Neil was a young man and for some reason God chose to take him. That reason none of us knows. Only God knows the reason. His time was so short that one would think it was an exercise of the imagination that was suddenly interrupted. Now it's all done."

Bernie raised her eyes and looked toward the faces that filled the church, focusing on Claire positioned in the front row with family. Ushers stood at either side of the rows exchanging apologetic glances, unable to seat the several men who stood in the back leaning against the brick portion of the interior walls. Claire, her lowered face flushed slightly, looked up through the tops of her eyes to her grandmother. Her eyes were still pink from crying. Arms crossed, she sat to the left of Ernest who kept his arm around Judy's shoulder. To her right sat Jack and to his right, Frank. Both men were dressed in dark gray suits, something neither wore in their retired years but they owned mostly to wear to funerals. It was sad to admit, but it was true. Jack yawned, bored and restless, as he attempted to raise himself from his seat while his arms shook. He asked for Monsignor Hunt, deceased some twenty years. Frank pressed down on his shoulder and

Bernie scanned the room again, eyes resting first upon Jeff then the woman directly in front of him, seated second row from the back. She wore the pillbox hat edged and stark against unnaturally blond hair. Though several of the women seated in the pews wore hats, the one she singled out came with an air of sophistication that Estelle admired. Little short blond curls bordered the hat but she could not see the face. Anyone with that type of sophisticated fashion sense had to leave Georgia. Bernie knew. She had done it herself.

Anger flooded into Bernie's' slightly rouged complexion as she recognized Maggie. It shot through her like a bolt that began in her feet terminating at the top of her head. She stammered. She tripped over her words. Her cheeks felt hot. She shook her head. Cleared her throat.

"Excuse me. Yes, there are some people you would remember without a choice and others we choose to forget," she blurted, shaken from her grief. "Like I was saying, I'd like to read something that has given me solace. It's explained many things to me these past few weeks and at this late stage in my life when I still have so much to learn." Her tone went up a notch with a sudden rush when she spoke:

I shut my eyes and all the world drops dead;
I lift my lids and all is born again.
(I think I made you up inside my head.)

The stars go waltzing out in the blue and red,
And arbitrary blackness gallops in:
I shut my eyes and all the world drops dead.

I dreamed that you bewitched me into bed
And sung me moon-struck, kissed me quite insane.
(I think I made you up inside my head.)

God topples from the sky, hell's fires face:
Exit seraphim and Satan's men:
I shut my eyes and all the world drops dead.

I fancied you'd return the way you said,
But I grow old and I forget your name.
(I think I made you up inside my head.)

I should have loved a thunderbird instead;
At least when spring comes they roar back again.
I shut my eyes and all the world drops dead.
(I think I made you up inside my head.)

Bernie read the piece and stepped out from behind the podium and down from the platform, then walked passed the front row and down the aisle, all the while watching her feet as they stopped and strode intently toward the door. The shoes were too big so they flopped off her heel with each step forward. She refused to look at the little black hat. At Maggie. Though Bernie knew she behaved like a frightened bride herself, like a child, like an odd little girl running away, she could not stop herself. It was too much. To be still was to be taken. So she chose flight and ran after Claire's mother.

Jeff caught up to her just outside the doors that closed behind him.

"Can I give you a ride, Mrs. Hinkley?" he asked.

Bernie looked down, her feet the only focal point. They were old feet, wadded up into practical black leather pumps. A bone spur on the right side of her foot made wearing narrow shoes impossible though she managed to put them on for occasions that required formality. The ritual itself was more comforting than the resulting pain. Tears flowed down her face and she made no attempt to squelch them in the brief moment of solitude on the outside of the church doors. Bowed, she was surprised that her anger triggered such sudden sadness. Then she was not so surprised because she knew there was no one to tell. No Estelle. No friend so close it was her own mind speaking what she did and did not want to hear or know.

"Not right now, Jeff," she said, and waved her hand above her head then shook it left to right. "I can't talk right now."

Jeff took her elbow, gentlemanly, as he watched her move slowly down the stairs.

"I'm fine." Her voice quivered slightly though she tried to hide it from Jeff, clearing her throat. " I really don't need it. I'm just getting some air."

"I don't mean any disrespect Mrs. Hinkley, but I don't mind driving if you have the keys. It could do you some good to get out of here. You've been through a lot. That was hard to do."

"Jeff," Bernie began. "You're a very nice young man." She entwined the handkerchief around her index finger and wiped her eyes. "But there are certain things you just don't do and, one of those is you don't follow an old woman's tears. It's considered disrespectful. People don't care for it and, in Alpharetta, you never catch up with them."

Jeff held onto Bernie despite her half convincing argument.

"There's a lot of experience in those tears," Jeff said.

His brow beaded with sweat though the temperature was in the fifties. He measured his words.

"You're a very perceptive young man, Jeff," she said, sniffling. "Were you and Neil very close? How close were you?" Bernie asked, stricken by his wisdom.

"He was my best friend in Alpharetta, Mrs. Hinkley. I didn't know him very well though. Not for very long. He only really talked about sports and we became friends more because of Claire and Annene. I actually think he felt sorry for me."

"Oh come on, Jeff," she objected, sniffling. "Why would he think that? You are a bright young man. You have the world…" Staggered, blocked nasal inhalations broke up the words.

"I'm a geek, Mrs. Hinkley, and an orphan, for lack of a better word. Everyone in my life has done things for me because they feel sorry for me. Since my parents died, I got clothes second hand, parents second hand. I don't find things directly. It's not my life. Neil just hung around me because it made him feel better. He drank a lot and I never ditched him like the rest of his friends who couldn't stand him anymore. I hate to be frank, ma'am, but that's the truth."

Bernie nodded her head and adjusted the white linen handkerchief expertly entwined between her fingers, wiped her nose one nostril at a time then used another corner of the handkerchief to swab the inside corners of her eyes where black clumps of mascara formed with her tears.

"I just realized that it might rain, Jeff. You know why I like the rain so much? I like it because it makes everything so clean. When I lived in New York City I loved it because it made the streets so clean. Everything just got so much better then, especially in the summer when it was hot and my temperament got bad. Everyone was in a foul mood."

"I could never see you in a bad temper, Mrs. Hinkley."

"Everyone gets bad tempered, Jeff. It's part of being alive. When you're so close to people, though, they don't get to be so human."

"Is that why you read that?" He pointed to the book where Bernie still held the pages with her thumb.

"I was reading that and reading it over and trying to understand it the way maybe Estelle would understand it. She'd underlined it. It's from Sylvia Plath's book. And now I think of Estelle and everyone, and it just occurred to me that I never really knew Neil. You get to know, really know, so few people in life."

"What, because you didn't know him you made him up?" Jeff cocked his head. Music came from inside the church and seeped through the walls, slow and prolonged like loneliness, he thought, without any foreseeable end though he knew it would end.

Dark clouds hung over the roof and treetops of the large firs and over the willow just beside the chapel to the main church. Bernie made out the settling gray to be melancholy.

"Because if that's what you mean, I know what that's like. I know what it's like to make things up for what you don't have. I found that after I made it up enough times it came true."

"But not with people, Jeff. They are what they are. Neil was a boy. You said he had a drinking problem, but because he's my best friend's grandson, I didn't see it. I didn't see that and I didn't see what was going on under all of our noses for that time. I didn't see it because I didn't want to."

"Didn't see what?" Jeff asked, afraid of the question that he spoke despite fear.

"How much things changed just before Maggie left," Bernice answered. I didn't see it, Jeff. Do you understand what I'm saying? I saw the car so many times and I saw the way Maggie would look at Claire like she was jealous of her own daughter. And, I saw everything that went on but it never occurred to me that people would do those kinds of things. That people could be so bad as to do that."

Bernie's face reddened and abstract fear came into her eyes as she felt the truth simmer and bubble up into panic. Fear. Her only strength came with surrender to the truth that could alternatively cause her to drown if she did not give in.

A strong stench came from the opposite side of the church, swelling in the air as it arrived with the soft breeze.

"Oh dear Lord. When is this town ever going to get a decent plumbing system? The septic tank must have overflown with all of the ladies in the bathroom."

Bernie cringed and waved the air under her nose.

"It's just awful. Of all days."

Jeff's voice lowered as a model for Bernie who spoke loud enough for the funeral attendees to hear. "Mrs. Hinkley, can we go into the chapel and talk? If you don't want to go for a ride, can we at least go to the chapel?"

They entered through the door, a smaller version of the large wood double doors in a plain design but with the same size crow bar handles. Jeff opened the door for her and they entered the dark room, lit only by the dimmed chandelier. To the right of the entrance were several rows of red glass devotional candles. Three burned as a plea for mercy to the statue of the Virgin Mary who wore a sky blue dress and held the Baby Jesus. There were also flowers. They rested at her small plaster feet.

Aside from a middle-aged man who prayed the rosary, Bernie and Jeff were alone in the chapel entirely silent once the door to the street closed behind them.

Uncomfortable, Jeff watched Bernie dip her trembling fingers into the white marble bowl of holy water and anoint herself with the sign of the cross. He followed her to the third row, center pew and sat beside her. He did not know where to put his hands. They focused their eyes to the gilded cross that hung under the gothic canopy, a carved wooden arch painted white with hints of gold leaf. Just below the cross was the tabernacle. They sat two to three feet apart and Bernie kept her eyes on the crucifix as though waiting for the actual transfiguration to take place before her eyes.

Jeff scratched the top of his head and ran his fingers through his hair. He took a few bites at a hangnail, part grooming but mostly nerves. His shirt was bloused too much, and taking hold of his tie between his thumb and index finger, he ran his fingers down the silk strip adjusting it so it lay flat against his white, crisp shirt. Mrs. Stone bought it with the suit and he was proud. It was his first.

"You believe in God, Jeff?"

"I feel a little awkward answering that question, Mrs. Hinkley."

"Why, because you're in church?"

Jeff's eyes skirted around the room. "Yes," he answered. "I guess so."

"That's why. Half the people who come in here don't believe in God. They believe in a lot of stuff. They believe if you come here every Sunday, you'll go to heaven."

"I'm sorry, Mrs. Hinkley. I'm not Catholic."

"Do you believe in something? Anything?" Bernie asked.

Jeff kept his head faced forward as he mimicked Bernie's stern expression unaware that she squinted her failing eyes only to examine and identify the type of flowers held by their stems in the vases set at each side of the cross. Satisfied, her eyes opened full and Jeff blinked hard. It was awkward. Chrysanthemums and Hydrangea were arranged in the large vase.

Jeff picked up the tie again and let it fall against the buttons that folded in waves as he relieved himself of the absurd posture required of the suit. He took a long breath and released his shoulder forward to a partial slouched posture.

"I believe that there's something bigger. Not God, but something larger than me. Like magic. It's bigger, but so tiny you have to look through it with a lens."

"What do you mean? How can it be big and small?"

"I mean, I figured out what I wanted to do with my life when I looked through a magnifying lens and saw all those little cells moving around, and then got an even closer look when I saw pictures of DNA strains. It answered a lot of questions for me. I think that's why people come to places like this."

"And, they keep coming until the question is answered..." Bernie said, her mind drifting. "I never thought of that," Bernie said, as she looked to her left at Jeff. "I'm too old to think that they all get answered."

"I don't think people find out until just before they're dead. Then, it's too late. Some, I think don't even have the time to think about it because it happens too fast. I don't think Neil did. He didn't know."

Bernie remained silent as the words barged through the backs of her front teeth from her throat like a suddenly raucous mob at the gates.

"How do you know?" Bernie asked, slightly offended.

"When you grow up having an idea of who you are and where you're from then lose all of that and the people that created you, you find answers. You either make them up or you look at things very clearly for what they are."

"I'm going to ask you something then, Jeff. I wouldn't ask you if I didn't think you were grown enough to handle it. I don't think it's something…"

"I saw Claire's mom, Mrs. Hinkley, if that's what you're talking about."

Bernice nodded. Jeff returned the gesture and continued. "I know."

"The car outside the house," Bernie said.

"Uh, huh, I know. You don't have to ask Mrs. Hinkley. I wasn't going to say anything but, that was before anything happened."

Bernie's heart swelled and she grabbed for the young man's hand, taking his long fingers in her freckled and small hands. The urgency reminded Jeff of a TV movie; whenever someone had a heart attack or gave birth they grabbed the hand of the good-natured soul standing bedside and squeezed it to the breaking point.

"Then you know. You *know*. I thought I was going crazy. You *know*? All of that. I thought I was slipping, Jeff. I thought my mind was going because you know, I've never been so good at keeping centered, but lately I just go. So, it is true then? She did leave. She left because of him."

"I don't know, Mrs. Hinkley," Jeff replied, startled at Mrs. Hinkley's embracing need and warmth. Her errant and misplaced excitement. He barely knew her. She was like an amoeba that came into contact with another and glommed onto the nucleus while the larger cell absorbed it to make it all the stronger. Only Bernie didn't disappear into Jeff. Jeff disappeared, humbled by simpatico, a survival tactic for assimilating to changing environments.

"You know, Jeff," she said, releasing her grip just slightly. "You know, I never really cared for that woman. Not at all. But, I believe that there's good in everyone. I believe that no matter what you see, a person can be cruel or mean or even a bit unkind. A bad seed that can be used for something. Anything if there's a little bit of goodness. I know, I'm no saint. But, that woman I don't understand to do that kind of thing with a boy like that. I don't understand."

"I don't understand either, Mrs. Hinkley," Jeff said, as he looked over his shoulder at the man who left his knees in prayer to stand, then managed a slow gait down the aisle. Easy in his worn brown shoes, he opened the door to exit. Light streamed into the chapel and Bernie turned her head when she saw it from the corner of her eye.

The organ blared from the main church.

"Perhaps we should go," Bernie said. "I need to be there for Claire. This is really going to be difficult for her."

Jeff opened the door for Bernice and allowed her to walk into the right side of the church, one door over from the main door they exited through fifteen minutes earlier. Bernice regarded the thick, instrumental music as a signal that the service was coming to a close, and concerned that Frank would miss her or worry, they left the chapel and her small prayers that existed in her flight of mind. Within those petitions to God were also timid confessions.

Insincere and half-believing disclosures padded details and encapsulated the truth with adult reason fit neatly like shapes into their molds. Bernie left the details to God knowing that Jeff would, in fact (as his understanding revealed) embellish that unspoken pattern like it held chromosomes that tagged the double Helix. Life came from the placement of those pieces. Neither Jeff nor Bernice were certain it was time for that.

They resolved themselves to silent understanding.

Bernie collided with that chic, black, self-conscious veil, face to face with Maggie Hinkley, despite the pale attempt to disguise herself. Behind her, the priest followed spraying holy water across the fresh looking-up faces, some already wet with grief. That wand promised forgiveness as the holy waters sprayed from the bulb. It was pierced with many holes to release the God-graced water through the gold sieve. As the drops found skin, whatever was exposed to it, the faithful performed the sign of the cross finding brow, then heart, then each shoulder.

Just as the kneeling funeral attendees seated themselves against the hard-backed benches, Maggie squeezed between the funeral attendees negotiating four pairs of feet and one unnaturally long pair of well-pressed pant legs. Her head bowed, Maggie sat through the ceremony distracted by the whispers and swiveling necks of birdlike women aware that her presence was the cause. Their whispers brushed against her back like beating pigeon wings even though she bowed.

Dismissing her suspicions first as paranoia, Maggie averted her eyes and navigated toward the aisle past an older man and woman, strangers thankfully, who despite their sidelong glances she did not have to acknowledge. There was no refuge and as she stepped on the tip of her toes all grace left her. Those inquiring eyes shook her off balance so that her pointed, black heal dug sidelong into the tired man's shoe. When she met his eyes, she felt all others upon her. She whispered, "I'm sorry," her head down, and quickened her pace across the red carpet and out the door where she met Jeff, yet another stranger to her, as he pulled open the large wooden door.

Maggie righted herself in moments that brought her face to face with Bernice Hinkley who still stood in the vestibule. Maggie forgot already. She left but she stayed. What had she wrongly assumed?

Maggie looked over Bernie's head to Jeff who cleared his throat.

"Hi, Mrs. Hinkley," he said.

Maggie pushed the hat that was ridiculously pitched forward back to the crown of her head. At the same time she stepped around Bernice. Jeff eased the door back and allowed it to shut though it was too late to disrupt the service. She rubbed under her nose with the gloved hand to scratch an itch.

"Hi," she replied.

Bernie squinted slightly and tilted her head up at Maggie who stood nine inches taller with three inch heals. She lifted the corners of her mouth in a smile that was not pleased but a release from her stiff resolve. The putty of her face softened. Jeff shifted his weight to the right and left and ran his fingers through his hair using both hands before he stuffed them into his pockets where he felt for the Walkman.

"Mrs. Hinkley?" Bernie questioned, looking at Jeff. "Mrs. Brooks, I believe it is now, Jeff. There's only one Hinkley in this family who's a misses."

"Yes, ma'am," Jeff said.

"You have no business being here, Maggie. What business do you think you have here? No one wants to see you. Why don't you leave before you hurt your daughter any more. You make me sick. You don't belong here."

Shifting uncomfortably, Maggie dodged the old woman's words. Bernie's face reddened.

"Before she comes out. Just leave. Get out of here."

"I have every right to be here, Bernice. I knew Neil.

He did housework for me."

"He did housework for you? He was your daughter's boyfriend. The boy died because of what you did to him and all you chalk him up to be is a houseboy? That was a young man, Maggie, and you don't even have the dignity, the respect, to stay away from this place long enough for your daughter and everyone in there to grieve? For any of us. What kind of woman are you, anyway? What kind of woman does that to her child? You have no idea, do you? You have no idea at all."

The door opened and Monsignor Boyer appeared first with his procession of altar boys, Deacon Brown and another priest, who walked past. She stepped back once, then again, shuffling like a trapped animal. She looked behind her and ran into the street door exit. Several people were unexpectedly gathered outside then behind came an exodus. Maggie felt as though she was being stampeded as several men walked past her and blocked her path. Against the cement wall she sought refuge. Bernice's words carried her away and the distance engulfed her. A deep loneliness of detachment and hate separated Maggie from herself and she knew that. She was so intact and aligned and perfect when she came to mourn a boy she'd once, without a thought, made her lover. She had shown up. She tried. She told herself.

"Mom... Mom."

Claire's voice came to her, found her ears and heart that opened up to it slowly. She wondered at first if it was one of those moments she remembered from the days when Claire was young and any mother would raise her eyes to the child who spoke them. Mom was a word that any mother heard like it came from her own blood. Like it was a chord in a song that strung them all together. Maggie was there in Alpharetta, though, and Claire was close. She looked up from the pocket book she was rifling through to get the keys to the rental car and looked over her shoulder. Claire was already at her side. They both stopped and looked hard at each other. What Maggie saw was a thin, pale girl with the pink face of a fresh cry. She wore no makeup. Maggie rubbed at her jawline to try to mask the complexion change from her face to her neck. Though she told herself she was trying to put Claire at ease, Maggie's head was still rolling on the waves of the Xanax she took before she walked into the church. Claire's words oddly still echoed in the cloud of that fog like raindrops gathering there.

"Why are you leaving?" Claire asked.

Her face was so bare and honest, her eyes wide, that Maggie had to look down at the tips of her pointed black shoes.

"I'm not wanted here, Claire. I don't want to interrupt things. I came because it seemed like it was the right thing to do."

"Like it was the right thing to do? For who? It would have been the right thing to stay. You just come here and show up without anything. I told Grandma. I told her you would come. I knew it. I knew you'd be there. Here." She shook her head. "Then you just skip out like it's nothing."

"Claire. I tried."

"You tried?" Claire said. Cocking her head back, she raised her eyebrows. "I'm not sure what you tried for. What... What did you try for? I'm not clear."

People from the church had started to gather behind them at a distance: Jeff, Bernice, then Ernest. Others kept back listening, but most were still inside to mourn.

"Claire." Her father's voice, even and uncomplicated, joined her seconds before he was at her side. "It's not the time for this. You can..."

Claire interrupted Ernest. "What do you mean? She's here and she hasn't been here for over a year and now she's here? Then, she leaves because she can't deal with the Alpharetta mafia. What?"

Ernest rubbed the palm of his hand over his forehead

and face and nose, breathing through his teeth and lips to an audible wind.

"You hate me, don't you? You just couldn't deal? What was it?" She stammered. "You can't leave and not tell me why you left." Claire inhaled deeply through her mouth then nose, and shook her head at Maggie who stood composed. Like a mannequin.

"Claire. Stop. Please. She's just here paying her respects."

Bernice let out a sigh or a gasp. Just air released so she would not explode.

"You're paying your respects?" The sarcasm was thick.

"Mom, please." Ernest placed his hand on Bernice's shoulder. "Claire, let's just go back to the church. It's not the time or place."

"Oh, God, Dad," Claire yelled. "It's not the time or place for anything. Can you just stop and let me deal with this? I'm suffocating. I can deal with it. I can deal with it a hell of a lot better than you have."

Ernest stopped, took a step back and said nothing. He knew it was coming.

"Claire, I tried to call. I called a couple of times. I wrote a letter. But, the longer I stayed away the more difficult it was to reach you."

"What do you mean, you called?"

"I called. I talked to him," Maggie said, flat. Her head was still lowered. Hung low. "He just said you were busy. I knew you weren't but I was the one who left. What could I do?"

"What letter?" Claire asked. Her eyes were wide and pulled at Ernest who stood motionless. When her father did not respond she raised her voice, stronger.

"What the hell is it with you all? I'm not a little girl. I'm not someone you have to protect. Just tell me what the hell is going on."

A long silence persisted as Claire looked from face to face, all bowed. They looked like badly behaved dogs looking at the ground.

"Yeah, I didn't tell you. There's just a lot that's gone on, honey. A lot of hurt. I didn't want to tell you because I didn't want," he stopped then continued. "I didn't want you to hurt."

"A lot of good that's done," Maggie said, and gestured up and down toward Claire.

"Don't talk to her like that," Ernest said. "You screwed up, Maggie. You totally fucked this one up. Don't put it on me."

"This one's all yours," Bernie said. She and Claire reared back at Ernest's outburst. Unflappable, quiet Ernest was getting pissed.

"Just leave her alone. I didn't tell her because you just couldn't leave the girl alone. She's your own daughter. Forget what you did to me screwing that kid, but what the hell?" Turning, Ernest pointed to the church.

"What kid?" Claire asked.

"Oh, shit," Jeff muttered low and stepped back.

Annene had joined the cluster but kept her distance from him.

"That kid in there. The one who died because Maggie just had to have everything she wanted and nothing of what she had. You had me. You had Claire. You had what I thought was a happy life for you and you did that. Then, you left. I don't know what you did to that kid."

Claire started to cry. "I don't know what you're talking about." Her body felt limp and helpless but her mind caught her just before she began to close into herself and collapse like a marionette let go by its puppeteer. Those strings did not hold her up or let her slump or fall. They let her go, but she did not fall or crumble or die inside. The tears did not reveal her weakness but oddly gave her strength with the room it left for words to explain what she already knew but touched only for the first time.

Ernest took hold of her shoulders in his hands with a firm grip. "It's not you," he said, then paused and repeated again. "It's not you." He held her and tried to brace her frail body against the burden of secrets that he could not explain. She was his little girl who he still felt unfit for the pain Maggie had already caused them.

Claire closed hers as the truth settled slowly. It was what she knew but did not want to understand. She wavered between the truth and the lies before she quietly looked at her mother and let her eyes settle on her. Maggie's gaze could only be held for as long as it took Claire to blink. Maggie muttered an apology.

"I'm sorry," she said only as she zipped the thin black pocketbook and started walking toward the car again to leave.

They let her. Even Claire, who had to will herself still and stiff not to beg her mother back to love her. To hold her. To want her.

From the church steps, Claire watched her mother disappear around the corner then turned her eyes to the six men carrying Neil's coffin as they slid it into the back of the hearse. She joined her father, Judy and Annene, as they watched the black car retreat from the side of the road. Claire kept her eyes on what she identified as her mother's rental car with Georgia rental plates that jerked to a stop beside the black hearse. Jeff escorted Bernie, deeply calm and satisfied but still furious.

They carried on to the cemetery and kept quiet, except when asked to speak. No wailing. Just a quiet sea of black. They paid their respects to the dead.

She proceeded with the day, following Bernie into the Berry's home where Judy, with the help of the Alpharetta Mafia, laid out a buffet for the guests: cold cuts and ham, cream cheese and flour tortilla swirls, deviled eggs, cheese cubes speared with toothpicks, and chicken fingers. Potato salad. Decency was conveyed by the generous portions. She rented the same two tables ordered for her mother's funeral.

Judy, still fragile, raw and aware even of the air against her skin, stood by the door while her mind flashed back to the night of Jeff's party. Only three days prior, she stood dead center in the crowd behind the ambulance as she watched the gurney collapse and her son, beneath the white sheet, lay motionless as the cacophony of voices gradually faded away. Paralyzed, her hands refused the urge to draw back the stiff coarse sheet that lay against Neil's face. The lights swirled and induced funhouse vertigo in the very grounded, pragmatic Judy, dressed always in hospital scrubs and professional white clogs. Reality flooded in without respect and collapsed her thoughts as though she lingered between wake and sleep or that depth of slumber that trusts completely because, in that state of a midday nap or near sunrise, restraint is stripped and the dream beams bright and full of color. There is a brief glimpse of imagined yet lucid occurrences. Short-lived abandon broke into her mind and awakened her need for life. Much like the vacuous lust of an affair could reawaken a need for love and for life. Her late husband left for that. Died for that.

Death was so poorly timed among the living.

Loss severed her lifeline as it removed one niche then the other in carefully arranged links. It settled into her life as the moments passed between both her mother's funeral and Neil's. Hallow and extra and misplaced she felt like an air bubble that eased itself to the surface. She could barely say a word. It was the terrible absence that left her speechless. A barrage of unattached memories came to her out of sequence.

Bernie left Frank in charge of Jack who blurted weather reports mixed with sports statistics and profanity. With each outburst he was quieted by Frank's clicking through channels on the television set. Twenty years old, the set was encased in wood panels. A hinged top opened to a turntable. On each side of the set was a speaker partly covered with wood crosshatch lattice work.

Seated across from Jack and Frank, Claire flipped through a magazine then caught Jeff's eyes as they both watched Bernie make her way across the room. Bernie's fingers touched the surface of the buffet table to steady herself as she took short, strained steps. She whispered in Judy's ear then stood next to her near the door where she had not moved since people began to arrive.

Jeff stood by her and averted his eyes when he saw Bernie's approach. He fumbled a bit as he removed the Walkman out of his pocket. One of the tapes inside fell to the floor. He leaned over quickly and picked it up. The headphones dangled from his suit jacket pocket at his side. Bernie stood next to him and pulled the headphones by the wire out of the pocket. She handed them to Jeff.

"Thank you, Mrs. Hinkley."

"I'm sorry, Jeff, for being so curt with you. At the church. I just don't understand that woman. Not in the least. You know how I feel? I don't like it at all. Not at all." Then, scanning the room she added, "You haven't seen her, have you? She hasn't shown her face around here has she? I don't imagine she will."

"I think you scared her," Jeff said, as he twitched his mouth to the side, his lips pierced. He felt the sudden, inappropriate, raw need to laugh. "I think Claire did too."

Bernie smiled. "It's okay, Jeff. She's not a person that I would respect. She's not decent people. The people in this town... I know what they call us. You know... The Alpharetta Mafia? I don't care though. Estelle and I used to have a good laugh over that. We'd sit and laugh because we were the two that came up with the name. When Claire's mother and Judy, when all of those women had their own children, they took over then got out of it when those women turned it into the vigilante PTA. No one could get it going the way Estelle did. She was a unique lady. There were some women in this town that hated her, but she only spoke the truth. She knew everything about everyone. It wasn't mean, though. Not cruel. Estelle wasn't a cruel person. She loved people but she loved them enough to see them as they were. That makes people angry. She was the only person. The only person, except Claire, that is, that made me laugh at myself. It wasn't cruel. You know the difference, right, honey? You don't mind if I call you honey? You're probably used to it now that you've been living in the south for a while."

"I don't mind, Mrs. Hinkley," he said, relief in his voice. You're a nice person."

"Thank you, Jeff. I guess I'm from here now. I'm a Southerner. You will be, too," she said, and patted him on the shoulder. "If Estelle can be a Catholic Jew in Georgia, you can adapt too."

Jeff listened and blinked his eyes more than usual to swallow the experience. He rarely cried but witnessed life like an amoeba that attached and separated, split then became whole again. Symbiosis.

"That's very Darwinian of you, Mrs. Hinkley, but it still doesn't explain the absence of Estelle's Shiva."

"She didn't much like mourning."

Jeff turned up the corner of his mouth in a partial smile and watched Claire who sat in a wing chair in the corner of the living room. Her thin legs were crossed like noodles. She tapped at the air with her foot then hooked one foot around the back of the ankle anchored by her feet covered in ballet flats. She turned the pages of a book that he could not identify. The cover was hidden in the folds of Estelle's knitting bag that rested on Claire's lap. The black scarf peeked out from it.

"You like her, don't you?" Bernice asked, her voice low.

"Hmmm?" Jeff asked, too slow.

"You like her. At least I believe you do. But, you don't need to worry, Jeff. Claire is a beautiful girl. I love her more than anything in the world and I don't want her to be hurt anymore."

"She knows," Jeff said. "She already knew. She just needed you all to know too and to talk."

"But how could she possibly know?"

"She's a lot smarter than you all make her out to be. She's a smart, strong girl."

Bernie slightly jerked her head back.

"Just because people don't come out and say things doesn't mean they don't know. She'll come around to talk. She'll talk to you."

"And, how do you know that?"

"Because she loves you. I don't know. I just think it'll all come around. It all comes around."

"She's a good girl. I am so lucky with her. Ernest is a wonderful man. He's a good man, a decent man. When I look at my life I see him as my accomplishment. He's my degree and Claire is my angel. She's like her father. She's a good girl. I'm just glad her mother isn't in her."

"You're in her, Mrs. Hinkley. If you don't mind me saying."

"Just covered up by a lot of sadness. Dammit, I tried to see the good in that woman," Bernie said. She clenched her jaw and fists but still spoke in a loud whisper. "I tried to see it in her. But, some people are bad seeds, Jeff. It's like it's in their bones or something. You can't shake it out or mold them or make them into something else. They're just that way. They can't help it. It's like there's some missing link. Like dropping a stitch or something. A knitting term. You skip it. It's like God dropped a stitch with that one," she said.

Jeff nodded. *The double helix*, he thought.

Jack's voice boomed from across the room where he sat at the small breakfast table between the kitchen and den.

"Forty-nine degrees. Forty-nine degrees and snowing. It's snowing," Jack shouted as he watched the television set, pointing to summon the guests to do the same. His gray hair stood up on end as he tried to get a look out the sliding glass doors.

A cup of coffee held in his hand, Frank sat next to Jack but got to his feet to gently ease him back down onto the seat. He spoke to Jack calmly and quietly so no one could hear. Only his mouth moved.

"We're all going, Jeff. I tell you. We're all going. There was a point that I thought my life would go on forever. I thought that every moment was mine, whatever it was. Joy. Sadness. Wherever I was I thought I'd forever be there. For a while I thought what was happening to him was happening to me." She pointed at Jack who was still ranting.

"Fort-y nine degrees. Shit. Snow in Georgia! By golly," Jack yelled.

Frank stood above Jack to rest his hands on his shoulders. To quiet him.

"I'm just so relieved he's not cursing," Bernie said, then nodded to Mrs. Clement as she passed by and strained a dutiful smile. Bernie looked past Jeff's bony yet broad shoulders to the four impeccably dressed women who sipped tea and stood at the fireplace mantle in the living room.

"It doesn't matter what he says though, Jeff. He doesn't know better. Like me, he's daydreaming. My mind slips. Any day now I may be stuck there forever."

Jeff sniffled and rubbed his nose. The first sign of a cold coming on.

"Oh, you poor boy. I'm talking your ear off and all you want to do is talk to my lovely granddaughter."

Jeff cleared his throat. "Mrs. Hinkley, that's not true. I like talking to you."

Bernie cocked her head, slightly. "You're a good boy, Jeff. They don't make them like you anymore." Her tone was harmless and light until she returned her eyes to the four women. Voices hummed above the Alpharetta Mafia, drowning out the truth with lies.

"My Lord, they are awful," Bernie said, then continued, agreeing with herself. "They are. They are just terrible. That kind of person is the type that gets a person like Claire scared of her own shadow. It frightens her to be truthful because it makes *them* afraid. It gets her scared of her own shadow, and at seventy years of age, it gets an old woman like me plotting her escape over vats of lye when she should have just left long ago. I love this place, but sometimes I just hate it. I hate that woman for doing what I sometimes wanted to do myself but never did because I loved my family too much. I would never do that. I could never. We're attached, me and Claire. Me and Ernest and me and Frank."

"You're right. You wouldn't," Jeff said. "You wouldn't do that."

"It helps that I didn't." Bernie slapped him lightly with the back of her hand. "That's empirical evidence, isn't it?"

Jeff laughed. "Yes."

Mrs. Clement appeared. She held the poodle under her arm and approached Bernie. Before the woman could speak, Bernie held up her hand and excused herself. She walked out the front door and turned to the right where the swing was set. It had a white and green stripe awning overhead and matching padded cushions. The springs squeaked when she lowered herself into the cushion. She sat there half listening to the voices, her arms crossed over her chest. Her eyes looked forward across the lawns connected by driveways. Those little ranch style houses were all the same but there was no matter to it. Everything inside was so different. She changed focus to the sharp little flecks of light that hung half in the shadows in front of the closed door. Particles of dust reflected the light, floating, glinted, like tiny fireflies in January. Pretty things they were, dust or not, Bernie thought.

They would sit and watch the fireflies the following Spring into Summer and life would continue for the Hinkleys and for everyone else. It would move forward, changed. It was empty but full again, dark with little flecks that gleamed despite all things. It settled.

Jeff could find Claire. She knew that. He was a good boy.

REFERENCES

Nerius, Maria. *Soapmaking for Fun & Profit*. Rocklin, CA: Prima House, 1999. Print.

Newton, James. *Amazing Grace*. Library of Congress, 1779.

Plath, Sylvia. *The Bell Jar*. New York: HarperCollins, 1996. Print.

ABOUT THE AUTHOR

Kathryn Merrifield is an author and writer.

THE GOOD ONE is her first published novel. She has written short stories, essays, novels, poetry, and picturebooks.

She lives in New York where her family and friends tolerate and politely ignore her mutterings… most of the time.

Made in the USA
Columbia, SC
11 November 2018